THE WOODSMAN

JAMIE + VIOLET

DR. REBECCA SHARP

THE
Kinkades

The Woodsman (The Kinkades)
Published by Dr. Rebecca Sharp
Copyright © 2019 Dr. Rebecca Sharp

Cover Design:

Sarah Hansen, Okay Creations

Editing:

Ellie McLove, My Brother's Editor

Printed in the United States of America.

Visit www.drrebeccasharp.com

CHAPTER ONE
VIOLET

"Umm... Miss... We're here."

I looked up from my iPad in my lap where I'd been utterly lost in one more emotional outcry to my father that resembled an epic rather than an email—regardless, it was something I was never going to send. The last time I'd looked up—an hour ago when I started the email—we'd been on the highway.

I knew I wasn't supposed to. I knew I was supposed to leave all thoughts of work, betraying fiancés, and judgmental families behind for two weeks. But I couldn't help myself.

"No, we're not," I blurted, looking out the back window of the freaking Prius I'd been crammed in for the last three hours on the drive up to Maine from Boston since my flight to Bangor—and the black car waiting there for me—had been rerouted due to the snowstorm.

I flipped the case on my iPad closed. Leslie, my executive assistant and best friend, would kill me if she knew I'd smuggled the thing into my carry-on in an empty bag of Pirate's Booty so she wouldn't see it. *Desperate times called for desperate measures.*

"Vi, do you even remember the last time you took time off from work?"

"I just took a week and a half off," came my grumbled reply.

"A week and a half in the hospital doesn't count!" she'd cried as she took my laptop hostage. "You need to take a step back from all of this—especially from dealing with Richard."

Dick.

I shuddered at the thought of my ex-fiancé and refocused on the problem at hand.

"Well, the GPS says we're here." The young Uber driver tapped on the screen as though it would magically make the cabin I was supposed to be arriving at appear.

I craned my neck, peering out in every direction.

There was nothing around us.

Literally. Nothing.

We were sitting in the middle of a snow-covered dirt road, judging by the tracks the Prius had left, surrounded by steep evergreens which looked like they'd just received a fresh blanket of snow.

Stranded in a snowstorm with a disappearing destination.

In a fucking Prius.

My chest swelled like water was being injected into my lungs. The already small car felt like it was closing in around me...

Montgomery, Alabama. Juneau, Alaska.

I heaved another breath.

Phoenix, Arizona...

My doctor suggested counting back from ten with corresponding deep breaths when I felt anxiety begin to creep in. Counting backward seemed pointless; I needed some *other* method of reining in the panic.

After some back-and-forth, I'd decided on states and capitals in alphabetical order. Boring but not pointless.

I'd made it to Alaska when the pilot announced the flight was rerouted. Arizona when the only car willing to drive me from Massachusetts to Maine—*in a snowstorm*—was a Prius. And now, when I was supposed to be arriving at my *Winter Wonderland Cabin Retreat* (as it was called on the listing) and instead found myself stopped in the middle of nowhere, I breathed right through to Arkansas.

"Let me check the address again," I offered through clenched teeth, tapping back through my emails to the confirmation Leslie had sent a few days ago.

Flicking my eyes back and forth between the iPhone attached to his dash and the address in the email, I groaned and realized they matched.

"Nope, this is right." I turned and looked out the back window, once again greeted with road and trees and snow. *But no cabin.*

"Maybe I should take you back into town?" the young kid, who I was pretty sure had been smoking a joint in the car as he pulled up to get me, asked.

I grimaced. "How far back is it?" I didn't even remember passing through Friendship, let alone how long ago.

His head tipped to the side and for a second, I thought he might ask Siri, judging by the blank stare on his face. *Millennials.* "Dunno. Maybe like fifteen minutes."

Breathe, Violet. It's fine. You're fine.

"No. Let me just look around for a driveway or something. Give me one minute." Shoving my iPad back into my bag, I pulled on my winter jacket and opened up the door.

"*Jesus Christmas,*" I swore as the cold ate right through my jacket and scarf.

I hadn't prepared for a snowstorm. Of course, I was going to Maine in the dead of winter. I knew there would be snow. But the six inches my feet sank into with flurries still falling was *not* what I'd signed up for.

Then again, I hadn't really signed up for any of this.

I scanned down the road on the driver's side of the car. *Just more trees.*

"This is ridiculous." I jammed my fingers against my phone to call Leslie; the hundred-dollar gloves my mother bought me with the touchpad fingertips didn't quite work as advertised.

After seconds of silence, I pulled my phone from my face to see why nothing was happening.

Of course.

At this point, there was nothing left to do but laugh as I stared down at the minuscule text in the upper left corner informing me that in addition to no flight, no car, and no cabin, *I also had No Service.*

Little Rock, Arkansas.

With slow, sinking footsteps, I made my way around to the other side of the car and *finally* met with success.

Up the road about another twenty feet or so, sat a small, wooden mailbox. I couldn't make out the name on it but it was the only one in sight.

Whatever. Even if it's not my cabin, they should know where I can find it.

"I think it's right there," I said as the scrawny, beanie-wearing kid rolled down the passenger window. "There's a mailbox there, so I'm assuming that's the driveway."

"Oh," he stuttered and rubbed his nose twice with the back of his sleeve. "Well, I can't take you up on that."

I gaped.

He went on, "I'm lucky I made it down this road with the snow. I can't get stuck up here. My mom needs her car for work in the morning. What if I slide into a drift? Into a tree?"

I slow-blinked at him and then let my head drop for a split second.

Drift into a tree... in a Prius.

For a sadly humorous split second, I wondered if that kind of accident would be called an *electric slide.* A small puff of warm breath burst from my lips, fogging the frozen air in front of me.

"Of course. Wouldn't want that..." I trailed off softly as I opened the back door and grabbed my purse and tote bag. "I'll just get my stuff and walk from here then."

Perfect.

Making a mental note to seriously threaten to fire Leslie as soon as I had the service to do so, I pulled my suitcase from the trunk, snow spraying up in my face as I set it on the ground.

"Thank you." Because it doesn't matter what situation you find yourself in, there is never an excuse to not be polite.

My mother's words rang out in my head, though I doubted Carmella Royale had ever been stranded on a dead-end road in the middle of nowhere, Maine, in the middle of a snowstorm with no cell service.

Holding my head high, I wheeled-slash-dragged my suitcase down the road, purse on one shoulder and tote bag on the other. I knew I looked a sight. Dark designer jeans. Fur-lined snow boots that were functional *and* fashionable, and a bright-white puffer coat that probably cost more than the Prius.

'Even if you don't feel good, Violet, that's absolutely no excuse for not looking good.'

My phone might not have any service, but my mother's voice was coming in loud and clear.

I just needed to get to this cabin. I needed to curl up in front of a warm fire, relax, and shut the world out.

Maybe the "no service" would eventually be a good thing.

Retreating from the stress of my life was the whole reason I was up here. Correction: Not ending up back in the hospital was the whole reason I was up here.

Stopping at the mailbox, I used the back of my glove to brush off the carved wooden slab above it.

Kinkade.

I hummed, hoping it would say "Cottage." But apparently, that would've just been *too* much good luck for the day.

The snowy drive disappeared into the thick of the trees. I looked over my shoulder. The Prius was gone. *No turning back now.*

It wasn't until I'd walked a good few minutes that I realized the driveway was on a slight incline.

Uphill. In the woods. In the snow.

"This is the kind of thing horror movies are made of," I grumbled, tugging my suitcase that had ceased to even pretend to roll a long time ago, now sliding and forcing me to pull not only the weight of my clothes but what I estimated to be thirty snow cones worth of snow along with it.

Another ten minutes, and I was cursing the Mother Goose that donated to my coat which was melting me from the inside out.

Cresting the top of the drive, I let my bag drop from my hand and heaved an exhale. My gaze tumbled down the short remainder of the drive until it ended at a stone path that led to the most picture-perfect cottage I'd ever seen.

Thank God.

The brutal winter gods of Maine had *finally* shown me some mercy.

My exhale of relief quickly transitioned to a deep breath of awe as I stared at the cottage. Nestled in a clearing in the evergreens, the rough-hewn cottage was made of round, gray stones trimmed with earthy red shutters. The round little humps of the roof were completely covered in undisturbed white snow, and jutting out from it were two distinct chimneys—*with smoke rising from each.*

From the paneled windows, the warmest yellow-orange light emanated, gently reflecting off the surrounding carpet of snow.

Small, rich-green bushes, their branches laced with white, rimmed the perimeter of the cottage, and there was a single lamppost a few feet from the front door, eagerly lit and expecting a visitor: *me.*

As I took in the storybook surroundings, I half expected to hear the classic "Heigh-Ho" whistle of the Seven Dwarfs as they returned home for the night.

Now I knew the stress of the day was really getting to me.

Even though I was the most uncomfortable mix of frigid from the weather and hot from the exertion, my arms and legs burning from the trek, I found myself lingering at the spot, thinking that every other disaster which had occurred so far on this little trip was entirely worth it—*worth it for the feeling of hope radiating from the cottage's light.*

The inside was even more quaint than the exterior, although a bit sparse for what I expected from a private vacation rental.

Dr. Silvaggio told me I needed to take some time off after what happened to go to a resort and spa and "just chill." The problem was my family owned those kinds of hoity-toity resorts, and for the last five years, I'd been one of the few responsible for not only managing them all, but expanding our brand. I'd been responsible and now, at thirty-two years old, I was going to have nothing to show for it.

How was I going to escape work by going to one of my prior workplaces? And going to a competitor? Out of the question.

Leslie had been the one to stop and ask, *If I could go anywhere, where would it be?*

Maybe it was the hospital stay—the cold, white sterility of the place, but I told her I wanted to go somewhere cold but be warm and cozy. I told her I didn't want to be surrounded by people for once. I wanted my own space.

And that was how she ended up on VRBO looking at cottages in Maine.

Propping my shoulder against the doorframe between the main living space and the bedroom, I sighed and listened to the snap and crackle of the fire that warmed it. I wrapped the soft plaid shirt tighter around me; I'd found it laid out on the bed like a hotel robe and thought the substitution of white terry cloth for oversized red flannel was an adorable touch. *Along with the warm wool socks next to it.*

It was thick enough to hold in the heat and just big enough to cover everything, which was perfect because none of my clothes had made it to the cottage dry.

It turned out that the woven cloth of my suitcase wasn't

exactly waterproof. And all that snow I'd dragged along with me from the road? It had soaked right through.

And then froze.

Sacramento, California. Denver, Colorado...

I stared at the contents of my suitcase draped over the brown leather sofa and ottoman in front of the stone hearth, which popped and fizzed with a real wood fire. My brightly colored thongs speckled like neon stars against the dark surface.

I laid them all out before my shower, but there had yet to be a pair dry enough to put on. So, shirt, socks, and no skivvies it was.

All of the cottage windows had steamed up from both the living room and bedroom fires, making it feel like I was housed inside a toasty cloud perched on snow.

Trailing my eyes to the dining space to my left, there was a small carved table with two matching chairs. The workmanship was very fine. I made a mental note to have Leslie contact the owner of the property and ask where she'd purchased them; I had a resort in the Adirondacks they'd be perfect for.

Had.

Past tense.

And you didn't have it, Vi; Royale Hotels did.

I pressed my fingers into the sides of my temples and forced my gaze to continue its sweep of the space.

Next to the table was a bare-bones kitchen. The retro, white refrigerator purred on the wall next to me. Along the counter came a sink and then tucked against the side wall sat a wrought iron wood-burning stove.

I turned back to the bedroom, the firelight glimmering off the rich-navy bedspread, a handmade quilt draping across the bottom of it, and headed into the bathroom.

My toiletries littered the small counter around the sink and filled the shelf in the shower. Taking my hair down, I ran my fingers through it and hung my towel. If I were in New York, I'd be cycling through a hair regime and drying it straight because at no point could I look undone. I laughed softly, thinking of my mother's face if she knew I hadn't even brought my hair dryer with me.

Returning to the bedroom, a gust of wind rattled the window, so I climbed over the mattress like a little kid. Using the end of my sleeve to rub a circle in the steamed-up window, I looked out into the storm.

My brows rose. *Wow.* A few more inches at least had fallen since I'd made it inside the cabin's respite. The wind picked up the soft flurries and twirled them in dancing gusts.

It was so... *magical.*

But from the inside. Outside, I was sure it was brutal.

I felt my muscles—especially the ones in my shoulders and lower back—relax a little more.

Maybe Leslie was right. Maybe this was what I needed.

Of course, I'd never tell her that. Nosy woman already thought she knew everything. But, as soon as I made it into town in the next day or so and found an establishment that had *some* sort of internet or service, I would concede that she'd picked a perfect place.

Maybe here I could find some clarity about my life—a life that had always been brimming with work but had spiraled out of control in the last six months after I caught my fiancé, Richard —*Dick*, with the manager of the hotel we'd lived at.

That's right. My family was paying the woman who my fiancé cheated with.

I groaned. If I had any desire to know, I'd bet she was on the clock while they were doing it, too.

I don't know how long I sat there, staring at the falling snow with the gentle heat from the fire rolling over me in waves. There was just something magical about this place, drawing me in, wrapping me in its quaint and comforting arms, and making me feel that everything was going to be okay.

Right then, I felt more than okay. My eyes drifted shut, and I sighed, savoring the way the warmth bubbled around me... until a gust of cold tore through the hot bubble.

My head whipped to the bedroom door.

The frigid draft came first, but it was the sound that followed that sent my heart cartwheeling and catapulting against my chest.

The sound of the front door closing.

I hadn't locked it.

Had there even been a lock?

It wasn't locked when I arrived.

I scrambled off the end of the bed, *definitely* hearing the sound of boots being wiped on the entry mat.

I looked around. I had no weapon. I had no nothing.

I didn't even have fucking underwear.

I spotted a small poker hanging on the side of the fireplace. Grabbing it, I raised it like a sword and crept toward the doorway to the front room of the cabin.

"What the..." A low string of curses leaked from the living room, and I leaped into the doorway, brandishing the poker in front of me.

"Stop!" I called, leveling my weapon at the intruder. "Who are you?"

Twin hot-chocolate eyes dragged slowly to me, and it was a good thing my words were already en route from my mouth because if they hadn't been, there would've been a three-word pileup at the exit of my lips.

The first thought that came to my mind—after, *Who the hell is breaking into my cottage?*—was how big he was for the tiny space. Too tall. Too broad. Too strong.

Heavy snow boots. Worn jeans. Thick cabled gray sweater. His black scarf came off with the navy jacket, and his hand that had been in the process of removing his hat finished tugging off the black knit cap to reveal a messed mop of rich-red waves.

My lips parted. The man looked like a transplanted James Fraser—Scotsman turned woodsman—and the lower parts of me squeezed in appreciation.

Was I turned on by the removal of a hat?

Was I really in that desperate of a need to get laid?

Well, I was ogling the gorgeous woodsman who was probably an axe murderer. Because that was the only kind of crazy who'd be out breaking into houses in a storm like this.

"Who are you, and what do you want?" I repeated.

His eyes narrowed too speculatively on my scantily clad body, raking down from the poker to my chest and then to my bare legs. I squirmed under the heat of it. He stepped closer, his arms crossing over his broad chest, highlighting the muscles that bulged against his sweater.

"Jamie Kinkade." *Oh, of course. Jamie. Might as well just orgasm now and get it over with.* "And I want to know who the hell you are, and why are you in my cottage?"

His cottage? My chest constricted.

Hartford, Connecticut. Dover, Delaware. Tallahassee—

"And why are you wearing my shirt?"

—Fuck.

Chapter Two
Jamie

"Y-Your cottage?" she stammered, the damp blonde strands of her hair swaying over her shoulders with each shake of her head. "I'm sorry. I think you're mistaken."

Surprisingly, a small laugh rumbled up from my chest as I glanced around the room. "Mistaken? About knowing my own home?"

Her mossy eyes narrowed. "Well, no. I mean, *if* it's your home, obviously you wouldn't be mistaken about that." Her chin rose a notch. "But I rented this place, so I have every right to be here."

"You rented... my cottage?" I gaped at her. *Rented.* How the hell would someone rent my cottage without—"Dammit," I expelled the curse with a hiss.

There was only one possible explanation for the blonde nymph standing in my cottage, her curves half clothed and half-concealed in my shirt.

Goddammit, Frankie.

"Yes, I rented your cottage. I have the email confirmation to prove it." The poker waved in my direction like a teacher scolding a bad student. "You can't... You can't just show up unannounced when someone has rented your place. That's against the rules."

My nostrils flared. I was going to wring my little sister's neck.

"That won't be necessary," I said in a rough voice, tearing my eyes from hers. A mistake, I realized too late.

It was increasingly difficult to focus solely on the situation at hand when she lacked so much clothing. But when the first thing my eyes landed on was the array of lacy, neon thongs strung across my very manly brown couch, my attention jerked back to her as my cock jolted in my jeans.

Was she wearing anything underneath my shirt?

Instead, I heard myself ask, "Who are you?"

She hesitated for a moment before replying, "Violet. Violet Royale."

Violet.

Her name made sense. Her stature relatively small and unassuming, like her namesake flower, yet her personality packed a punch—*or pointed a poker.*

"Violet." Her name tasted sweet on my tongue. "So, you rented this cottage... and are wearing my shirt..."

Christ.

Her eyes sank down to look at the half-buttoned flannel as though it were dyed with a scarlet letter rather than the red-and-navy plaid.

"Oh. My. God."

I flinched as the poker she'd been aiming at me clanked and clattered to the floor, one hand cinching the gap in the top of the shirt closed over her chest while the other tugged the bottom edges down farther over her thighs.

I cleared my throat and averted my eyes a second time. *The second time was much harder.* And for a split second, I swore I heard the names of some states escape her lips.

"I think there's been a misunderstanding... Violet," I said, unable to stop the low rumble in my voice. "Ahh... maybe you want to put some of your clothes on—"

"Ohmygod."

I caught her whimper just before her small form dashed into

my sight—*again*—and began to scoop up all her clothes and underwear from where they were scattered over my furniture, giving me far too many almost glimpses of her nakedness underneath.

I was going to kill my sister.

A low rumble escaped my lips as I turned toward the opposite wall, gripping the back of the dining chair I'd just dumped my jacket on, and forced myself to stare blankly at the stove while I heard her scurry about.

I cleared my throat and began again, "Maybe if you want to put some of your clothes on—"

"I can't," came her firm but defeated voice.

"You ca—"

"They're still soaking wet."

I bit into my cheek with the restraint it took *not* to turn and face her.

"I had to drag my suitcase here from the road, and the snow soaked through the fabric, but I didn't realize, so I laid them in front of the fire, but they haven't dried yet."

The way she rambled off facts with a forcefulness that *almost* completely hid her anxiety was more endearing than I wanted to admit.

My head dropped and hung between my shoulder blades. "I have a pair of sweatpants in the top drawer of the dresser in the bedroom," I offered gruffly. "Then we can sit and talk."

There was another second of hesitation before I heard her feet —*covered with my socks*—shuffle back into the bedroom, and my shoulders sagged with relief.

"Dammit, Frankie," I muttered as I glanced over my shoulder, confirming Violet had gone into the other room before yanking off my boots and groaning with relief.

Seeing the couch clear of undergarments, I dropped onto the well-worn leather in the spot directly in front of the fire, lifting my feet up onto the ottoman so the flames could start to bring feeling back into my toes.

The weather had predicted snow. But they hadn't been calling for the kind of storm that continued to rage outside, that was for damn sure.

After living my entire life in Maine, I knew to expect the unexpected when it came to these wintery blizzards and just how drastically they could veer from what was predicted.

One to three inches.

I estimated we were working on close to a foot.

"Thank you."

My head snapped up, hearing her voice, and I rose. After a minute to process, I realized how warm and rich her voice was. Like salted caramel. So sweet the way it stuck to my skin.

I swallowed hard and nodded.

Fuck if I couldn't stop myself from imprinting the image of her in my clothes—naked underneath—for a future fantasy.

"Please, sit," I motioned to the chair. "Looks like we might be here a while."

I didn't hear it, but I saw the way her chest hiccuped against my shirt. And with the way her arms were wrapped in front of her stomach, it pushed the swells of her breasts against the flannel to where I could say with certainty they'd fit perfectly in my palms.

Dammit, Jamie. You can't have her.

She's your guest, whether you invited her or not...

She pulled her lower lip between her teeth before deciding firmly, "I think I'll stand, thank you."

"Suit yourself," I grumbled. Propping my elbows onto my knees, I ran a hand through my hair. "So, Miss Royale... You *rented* my cottage?"

"Yes—well, my assistant did. On VRBO." The pink tip of her tongue darted out over her lips, and I wondered if it tasted as sweet as her voice. "But this was the one in the photograph in the confirmation email. Minus all the snow."

A half laugh, half groan rumbled from my chest as I dragged my eyes to the crackling fire and shook my head at the flames that seemed to dance and laugh at my predicament.

"I take it... you weren't the one who listed it?" she asked.

I looked over at her, fascinated by her personality.

She was clearly anxious, and yet, she was so composed. It was like those summer showers where the sun was out, hardly a cloud in sight, and yet it was raining. Or those rare spring skiing days when it was in the high sixties, and yet there was snow on the ground.

It was possible to be those two opposing things at once, just uncommon.

"No, I didn't."

Her head began to move like one of those bobblehead dolls sitting on a dash. Up and down. As though she had no say in the matter.

My gut clenched when I saw her eyes blink in rapid bursts, and after raising two younger sisters, I knew the look of impending tears when I saw it.

"It's alright," I began thickly and tried to tamp down the insane notion of wanting to hold her close as I said it.

"Alright?" Her face flashed with a smile that, without the bitter laugh, would surpass the brightness of the sun reflecting on untouched snow. "*Alright?*"

Her head shook in the opposite direction.

"My flight was rerouted to a different airport, *hours* away. The only car that could bring me here was a Prius—oh, no." She stopped herself and waved a finger in my direction. "The only car that could bring me to the *mailbox* was a Prius. I had to hike to this place in a foot of snow with my bags."

She began to pace a few steps in either direction, I was sure the level of her anxiety was the only thing that kept her from breaking down and bawling then and there.

My hands tingled.

I wouldn't be able to stay away from her if she cried.

"All of my clothes are completely soaked," she went on, her voice rising in pitch. "And now, come to find out, I haven't *reserved* anything for the next two weeks. Come to find out, I've broken into—*I've trespassed into a stranger's home.*"

"Miss Royale—"

Her hand rose to her chest as though she were trying to physically hold down the racing of her heart. But all it really did was pull her gaze down to her person—*and my plaid.*

"And I'm wearing his clothes!"

Gripping both hands on the back of the leather chair next to her, she bent forward and began to suck in air and exhale... *state capitals?*

I started to rise but was quickly put back in my place when I realized my large shirt draped forward to give me a clear view down to the full swells of her tits.

Fuck.

I whipped my head to the fire, trying to burn the sight from my mind before my dick really started to have a problem.

"Look, Miss Royale, I was the one who told you to use some of my clothes," I said, gritting my teeth. "And you're not trespassing. You... rented the cottage. The fact it wasn't meant to be listed isn't your fault nor your problem to handle."

I glanced at her from the corner of my eye. The uneven rise and fall of her back started to slow and steady. But only when she rose up straight a few seconds later did I allow myself to look in her direction again.

"I'm sorry, Mr. Kinkade—"

"Jamie," I cut her off, realizing too late how harsh the word had sounded. Clearing my throat, I tried again more softly, "You're in my home and wearing my clothes. I think we're beyond formalities." My lips quirked in a grin. "Call me Jamie, please."

Her teeth sank into her lower lip as she nodded in agreement.

"Thank you... Jamie."

Well, if the sound of my name didn't just spiral right down to my cock... Fuck.

"So..." Her forehead scrunched. "Who would list someone else's house on—"

"My younger sister," I didn't hesitate to answer. "Frankie." A low growl rumbled in my chest. "It's possible Elouise—her twin —was involved, too, but she usually tries to stay out of Frankie's schemes even though Frankie doesn't usually let her."

I was mostly sure it was Frankie—only she would have the nerve to do something so outrageous.

"So... this was a prank?" Violet squeaked, her eyes bulging. "Someone—*your sister* listed your house on a vacation site as a joke? *I'm stranded in a stranger's house in the middle of a snowstorm with said stranger because of a prank?*"

My jaw ticced. I knew it was more than a joke; I'd survived Frankie's jokes before. This was something more. But the last thing I was going to do right now was get into the inner workings of my family with a complete stranger—*no matter how close I'd come to seeing her naked.*

"Something like that." As though there was a downhill slope between us, my eyes kept sliding to her no matter how many times I dragged them back to the fire.

She dragged in a breath. "You could be an axe murderer living in the woods."

"I'm not an axe murderer." Though I worked with axes, I'd only ever struck them on wood. Though my younger sister was sorely tempting me to expand my horizons.

"I mean... that's not what I meant. I don't think you're an axe murderer. But you get my point."

"Thank you... I think..." I said, too entertained by her to even think about being insulted.

This woman was something else.

"How long did you rent it for?" I asked again; she'd mentioned it earlier but the whole seeing boobs moment made it slip my mind.

She gulped. "Two weeks."

Wait... two weeks...

"You're staying through Christmas?" I couldn't stop myself

from asking, wondering why a woman as captivating... and beautiful... as she was wanted to spend the holiday alone.

Her spine stiffened defensively.

We stared at each other for an inappropriately long second before she wet her lips and spoke again, "Of course, I won't actually stay here now. I'll call around in the morning, maybe go into town and see what hotels there are and what's available..."

She trailed off as I began to laugh and shake my head.

"What's so funny?" she demanded, the faintest hint of pink staining her cheeks.

I sighed. "Have you looked outside?"

"Yeah..."

I groaned. I shouldn't find it adorable the way her face scrunched.

"I was looking outside before you broke in—" She clapped a hand over her mouth. "I mean, well, you know what I mean."

I chuckled and nodded. "Hate to break it to you, but there's no way either of us is going anywhere in this storm."

"Well, I didn't say right now," she retorted. "But I'm sure by the morning it will let up and then—"

"Have you been to Maine before?" I cut her off. "In winter?"

"No, but I live in the Northeast—"

I held up a hand. "I've lived here all my life, so you are welcome to hope all you like, but when Friendship gets a storm like this, it'll be a few days before the snow lets up and another before you should even think about venturing out in it," I said firmly.

She just stared at me like a deer in headlights before pulling a hand through her damp hair. Her lips moved in quick little motions, and I swore I heard the faint whisper of state names once again.

"I almost didn't make it back here. My snowmobile got stuck about a half mile out in a drift."

Thankfully, I'd brought the cover for it in the seat compartment so at least it'd be easier to clean when I had to go back out and get it. With Maine winters how they were, the snowmobile was a necessity in order to get around.

Of course, I also had a truck that could handle a lot, but I'd left it at my shop knowing there were a handful of holiday orders that I had to get out. I had a feeling this storm was going to throw a wrench into everything, and I didn't want to risk the snow delaying their arrival.

I cleared my throat and tried to pull back from the worst-case scenario I'd presented her with. "Look, they weren't expecting this storm, so maybe it won't be as bad," I said gently, fighting back the sudden urge to walk over and wrap her in my arms to soothe her. "I'm sure it won't be..."

She nodded too quickly for me to think she believed me, especially when she'd stared off into the fire as though she wanted the flames to leap right out of the hearth and consume her.

"Violet..." I took a risk using her first name. I took a risk with the familiarity. I took a risk with her panic. And it felt like I took a risk with a whole slew of other things I wasn't aware of yet—*and wouldn't be until I'd lost them.*

Her trance broke and her hazel eyes, that seemed to absorb some of the gold from the fire, returned to mine.

"We're stuck here for tonight," I began slowly. "There's no avoiding that."

"Yeah," she said thickly and nodded before sliding her eyes toward the single bed in my bedroom.

The firelight caught the faintest quiver of her chin, and it cracked right along with her resolve.

"You'll take the bed," I declared; she was a guest even if she wasn't technically mine. "I'll sleep out here, and we'll see what the morning brings."

"I can't... you don't have to do that. I'll take the couch. This is your house—your bed. I'm the one who doesn't belong," she insisted fervently. "Please. I don't want to sleep in your bed and make you—"

"I'm already on the couch." To emphasize my point, I relaxed back and lifted one leg and then the other to stretch along it, my legs hanging over the end near her. "I've had a long day, too, so I'm really not planning on moving for the rest of the night."

I shrugged my shoulders and leveled my eyes on hers. This was the kind of woman who weathered bad luck and unfortunate circumstances alone. *I could see her armor in her eyes.* And I could see its heaviness and the way it lifted as I offered her my bed.

She wasn't used to being taken care of. *And she wasn't sure what to do about it.*

Her gaze traveled warmly down the length of my body, leaving behind it a trail of stone. She might not be sure what to do about it, but the raw flecks of desire in her eyes spoke loud and clear.

Fuck. The couch was going to be more uncomfortable than I anticipated.

Composing herself, she pressed, "Are you su—"

"Violet..." I let out her name on a low growl, regretting how it startled her. "Unless you feel more comfortable sleeping on me rather than on my bed, I suggest you go into the other room and get some rest because I'm not moving."

Her eyes widened and her mouth parted into an *O* that would definitely haunt me tonight.

"I... umm... okay." She nodded twice and spun on her heel to the bedroom, pausing just as she was about to close the door, peering at me against its edge, and murmured, "Good night."

And though I had to admit her bad day had taken an unexpected turn for the worse, there was a hint of *good* in her good night.

Chapter Three
Violet

I snuggled farther into the warm cocoon of the covers, feeling the way the air iced into my lungs as I took a deep breath. There was no way I was getting out of bed anytime soon, I didn't care how late I was to the office or how many times Leslie called, I wasn't getting—

I gasped and jolted awake—*remembering everything.*

The cottage. The flannel. The handsome woodsman who'd offered me his clothes and his bed. *And who was probably freezing out on the couch right now.*

Jamie.

Steeling myself against the cold, I sat up and saw the fire had gone out some time ago.

My gaze snagged on the stream of sunlight stretching over the bed, following its fingers to the window. I could see perfectly through the glass, and my jaw fell.

It was still snowing, and it looked like it hadn't stopped.

My stomach dropped like a stone.

Another day here. With Jamie. *Alone.*

The thought brought my anxiety to the fringes of my awareness, yet the memory of him—gorgeous, flannel-wrapped eye candy—brought a rush of warmth that kept my worries at bay.

Of course, there was still a chance he was an axe murderer. But he'd have to be a pretty bad one to not have walked through the unlocked bedroom door overnight and killed me in my sleep.

Or at least, a very lazy one.

My hands felt for the clothes I'd laid on the other side of the bed, surprised to find them exactly where I'd left them. I normally tossed and turned overnight, too plagued with work and stress to relax even in my sleep.

Grabbing my navy thong, the comfiest pair of light-gray sweatpants, and my Columbia University T-shirt, I quickly changed out of Jamie's clothes. My stuff wasn't nearly as warm as his, nor did it have his sandalwood musk to it.

God, Vi, get a grip. Stop ogling after a man you just met while trespassing in his house.

Heading into the bathroom, I shuddered when I saw myself in the mirror. *Great.* Tossing my hair up in a messy bun, I quickly washed my face and brushed my teeth. Sandalwood soaked my nostrils when I pressed one of Jamie's towels to my face.

My head tipped, hearing clanking and thuds coming from the other side.

From Jamie's side.

I shivered, and without giving it too much thought, I went back to the bedroom and reached for his flannel shirt, tugging it over my shoulders.

I pulled open the door and rocked back on my heels, hit with the mouthwatering aroma of eggs and bacon. Almost immediately, my stomach growled. *And my brain recalled that, aside from the protein bar I'd eaten in the Prius, I hadn't had anything since.*

In the light of a new day, the cottage felt just as warm and cozy as it had last night—even with the unexpected addition of its owner. *The woodsman's cottage.*

The fire in the main room was still lit. I started to wonder if he'd managed to keep it burning all night when my gaze caught on the small red afghan strewn along the couch.

Blankets. Guilt washed over me.

I winced. I'd come across an entire drawer of extra blankets in the bedroom but I hadn't even given them a second thought after everything else that happened.

Way to go, Vi. Some hospitality mogul you are.

Jamie's imposing form caught the corner of my eye. He was so big it was practically impossible not to see him from almost any point in the cottage.

And it seemed pretty impossible not to stare in appreciation at the sight of him in front of the wood-burning stove—*his naked back to me.*

Wide shoulders tapered to a narrow waist. His muscles moved in concert, hard and hewn as they worked over the stove. Two small dips centered into his lower back like they were begging for hands to grip them as he—

I sucked in a breath so fast, my lungs revolted with a coughing fit.

Sweet South Carolina, Vi. Stop fantasizing about your host before you ruin that pair of underwear that just finished drying.

Startled, Jamie turned over his shoulder and something flashed in his gaze as it skated over me.

"Morning." He cleared his throat and the look from his eyes.

Setting the spatula aside, he grabbed a glass from the cupboard, filled it at the sink, and handed it to me.

"Drink," he instructed gruffly, careful not to touch his fingers to mine.

"Thank you." I pulled the glass to my mouth and chugged, hoping it would hide the way my eyes bulged at his naked chest. I wasn't sure I'd ever seen such perfectly formed pecs.

He quickly grabbed the white tee draped over one of the dining chairs and tugged it on.

"Not sure what you like"—he pulled two plates from the cupboard—"but I've only got eggs and bacon."

"That's perfect, thank you," I said with a nod, my stomach practically clawing for a piece of crispy bacon.

Ever since I'd started dating Richa—*Dick,* it was only vegan, gluten-free, smoothie acai bowl concoctions—or whatever diet fad he'd been on at the moment. I'd never been overly concerned about my weight—stress and genetics kept a tight rein on my calories—but *Dick* always made me feel like I should've been.

Truth be told, since around the time when I called off our engagement until now, I'd been steadily—*and unhealthily*—losing weight. *And the week and a half of hospital food hadn't helped.*

"Can I help make some coffee—" I stopped when I noticed there wasn't a coffee machine in sight.

Hell would freeze over before I was able to survive without coffee. *Then again, with this storm, it very well might.*

My throat constricted.

Atlanta, Georgia. Honolulu, Hawaii...

A teakettle whistled and my eyes popped back open just in time to see Jamie turn and thrust the steaming pot at me.

"Here." My mouth dropped open, catching his nod to the counter. "There's coffee in that pour-over funnel."

I carefully took hold of the kettle's handle and examined the primitive contraption. Ground coffee piled into a filter-lined funnel.

Two mugs were already waiting, one from *"The Maine Squeeze"* and the other *"The Candle Cabin."* Like magic, I poured the piping hot water onto the grounds and watched the familiar, dark aromatic liquid begin to drip into the mug.

Sneaking glances over to my mysterious host as he doled out a full plate of food for each of us, I found myself filling with questions that had nothing to do with my current, borderline-unbelievable situation and everything to do with the man I was trapped with.

I let out a squeak when I almost overflowed one of the mugs.

"Looks like you were right," I said, covering up my distraction with conversation. Outside, the fine white confetti continued to litter over an already frosted landscape. "That the storm wouldn't let up, I mean."

With a sigh, I carefully took a sip of the fresh, semisweet coffee, letting the energizing and smooth tartness begin to feed life back into my cells.

And it was damn good coffee for coming out of a funnel.

His throat rumbled, and I caught him looking at me through thick lashes, his murky green eyes questioning mine. I realized, with a flush, I must've let out a small moan as I drank.

With an expression of displeasure, he looked away from me and turned the stove off. "It will eventually."

I felt a twinge of jealousy, wondering how he could be so calm at the idea. Granted, he'd grown up here and was probably used to being trapped by Mother Nature, but still, I envied his calm in the face of trials.

Even last night, when I stood pointing a poker at him—*alright, probably not the most frightening threat in the world*—he'd been calm. Confused, but calm.

He'd been calm about my presence. He'd been collected when thinking of the storm. And while I'd found myself leapfrogging through states and capitals numerous times in that tumultuous hour, he'd been steady.

Maybe that was why I'd been half tempted to take up his offer to sleep on him—the desire to lie back and bask in that steadiness.

Or maybe it was the desire for something else...

"Sit," he instructed, and I complied.

As soon as my butt hit the chair, a thick sinewed arm reached in front of me. The ridges of each muscle were wrapped with distinct veins that made my mouth water as much as the plate of food Jamie set in front of me.

I scooped my first bite and almost melted onto the floor when the rich, salty and satisfying flavors of crisp bacon and fluffy eggs hit my tongue.

I probably should've waited but I couldn't stop myself from blurting, "This is delicious."

Jamie hummed low in response and dug into his own plate.

The minutes that followed in silence were on par for two

strangers who'd been stranded together in the middle of a blizzard. Our eyes kept catching each other's, trying to discreetly assess the other person but inevitably getting caught.

"So, what do we do?" I finally asked quietly, licking my lips clean.

He cleared the last bite from his plate and answered, "Only thing we can do. Wait the storm out and go from there." He looked out the window again. "The snow is pretty light. Once it stops falling, it should pack down pretty quickly under the sun, even with the cold, and I'll be able to go out and get my snowmobile."

I put both hands around my mug, letting its warmth seep into my fingers.

"I meant what I said, I'll find a place in town as soon as... as soon as I can get to town."

He stared at me, assessing for a long second.

"We'll cross that bridge when we come to it." And then, with a quick but absolutely devastating small smile, added ruefully, "Once the bridge is clear of snow."

My lips peeled apart, watching that soft smile disappear over the lip of the mug. The way his eyes drifted slightly shut, the way his auburn hair fell in tousled waves over his forehead as though someone had disturbed a sunrise drew all moisture from my mouth and sent pools of it down much lower in my body.

Oh my.

My core clenched, wholly unprepared for the wave of desire through me.

I hadn't *wanted* like this in a long time. The feeling opened up a pit of shame in my stomach. *Maybe that was why Rich—Dick had cheated.*

'There is no reason good enough to excuse what he did, Vi.' Leslie's words rang in my mind. Ironically, they were the same ones she'd said as I broke down in the hospital bed, only this time, they'd been about my father for cutting me out so carelessly after everything I'd done for Royale Hotels.

I chewed on my lip for a moment before asking the question that had been gnawing at me all night.

"So... why would your sister list your house on VRBO without you knowing?"

He sighed and ran his hand through his hair, yet remained so calm and reserved. When his gaze met mine, the color reminded me of the plaid fabric I'd picked out for the furniture upholstery in one of my Scottish hotels. Made from the same cloth as clan tartans, the material was both soft yet coarse at the same time.

"Frankie... has her own way of solving problems," he said slowly, carefully choosing each word. "But I can't even pretend to tell you what she thought the problem was that this would solve. Either that or she was—*is* very mad at me. Could go either way."

I gave a small smile, the desire to meet this sister far outweighing the desire to throttle her for our current situation.

"I don't have a sister," I offered. "But once, I forgot my best friend's birthday—I mean, I didn't *forget* forget, I just got caught up at the office and was running late to her birthday dinner... very late..." I winced. "After giving me a piece of her mind on the phone that night for missing it, I went into my office the next day to find the entire thing wrapped in birthday wrapping paper."

His eyebrows rose and a smile tugged at the corners of his serious lips once more.

"And I mean everything..." I wasn't sure why I was sharing this story—*or why I was sharing it with him*—but, as my thumbs rubbed over the decal on the mug, I continued, "Not only my chair and my desk. But papers. My printer. The paper in the printer." I felt my smile growing along with the urge to laugh. "She pulled the tissues out of my tissue box, wrapped them, put them back, and then wrapped the box."

The first chuckle broke free, and I caught the bright glint of white teeth from beneath his lips.

"She wrapped everything and then filled the room with balloons." We were both laughing now. "Only to firmly tell me that this time was just a warning. Needless to say, I know what it's like to have someone who makes a point when they 'solve' problems, and I haven't missed a birthday since."

We sat like that, holding our mugs at the table, warm from the fire in the hearth and from the just-lit stove, smiling and laughing at my friend's ridiculous nature, and it wasn't until my eyes glanced toward the window that I wondered if anyone standing outside, looking in at that exact moment, would've thought we were strangers, only introduced less than a day ago.

"Sounds like someone Frankie would get along with," he mused as his laughter died down. "I'd appreciate it if you didn't introduce them. My sister doesn't need any more ideas..."

I grinned again. "It doesn't sound like it."

Clearing his throat, I watched the humor melt from his face as he reached over and grabbed my empty plate, taking both of them to the sink.

"I can do that," I said as I stood.

He shifted his stance, the width of his back completely blocking me from the area as he glared at me over his shoulder.

"You're my guest, Violet. Expected or not, you're not doing the dishes."

His low warning growl had me swallowing my protest and shuffling my feet from the kitchen to the fireplace. The wood floor was cold on my toes, and I wished I would've put his socks on along with his shirt, but the roaring fire was a quick fix for that.

"Is Frankie your only sister?" I asked over the low crackle and the cooing of the wind outside.

There was a pause, and I wondered if he'd heard me over the water—or if he pretended not to hear me on purpose.

"No." The lone syllable rang out as he shut off the faucet and turned toward me, drying his hands as he offered up, "I have two and a brother. But Frankie and Elouise are twins. Like trouble and temperance. I swear, Lou was born as calm as Frankie was born wild." He shook his head. "They were a handful to raise, and now that they're adults, I can't really ground Frankie for listing my house for rent on the internet."

His lips quirked wryly as he turned toward me but then froze.

A handful to raise... *Had he raised them?*

"How old are they?"

"Twenty-six on April second," he said without missing a beat, and I couldn't help but remember how *Dick* scolded me when I'd asked him about his older sister's birthday, embarrassed that he couldn't remember the actual date.

And that was aside from all the times he'd confused my birthday and forgotten our anniversary.

"It's not like it's our wedding anniversary, Violet. Stop being so dramatic."

I shuddered.

Les told me that it wasn't a good sign, but like an idiot, I'd argued this was common to all men and not to read into it.

And now I sat in front of a man who remembered without thought—without so much as a blink—his sisters' birthday, and there was no doubt in my mind he would've remembered our anniversary.

I ducked my head before he could catch my embarrassment.

Our anniversary.

Stop being crazy, Vi.

"They were due on April first but arrived a day late," he continued as though lost in the memory. "I've always said it was because, even from the very start, they were out to make fools of us all."

And it was that moment, right there, when I knew without having met the twins, without having seen Jamie with them, without even really knowing that much about him, that this man loved his sisters and would do anything for them.

And combined with everything else, a question meant to lead nowhere, instead presented me with more forks in the road.

He pulled a hand through his hair. "If it's alright, I'm going to take a shower."

I blinked, his words taking a second to register.

"Of course." I nodded enthusiastically, tempted to insist he didn't need to ask to take a shower in his own home, but I knew why he did it—*and why it made my heart flutter.* "Let me just grab my bag from the room."

In my haste, my steps weren't precise, and my arm brushed against his chest as I walked by him. Fire sparked at the contact and my breath caught, my gaze smacking into his for a split second.

There was nothing calm in his eyes now. Though his body remained still, the same turbulence in his stare made me shudder.

Boise, Idaho...

Boy-see, I-da-ho. I groaned pitifully.

If I wasn't careful, being an unwanted guest in Jamie's cottage would be the least of my concerns if I couldn't better conceal how attracted I was to him.

Chapter Four
Jamie

"Sorry about the food." I glanced at Violet as I scrubbed down our plates from the pasta and meat sauce I'd made for dinner. "Usually just cook for myself out here."

Wide, warm eyes stared at me in surprise.

"I thought it was delicious," she replied immediately, which only marginally assuaged my worry.

She might've been wearing my clothes when I met her, but it didn't take a genius to figure out the world she came from.

From her fur-lined snow boots with the little lift in the heel that were parked on the mat by the front door to the expensive jacket slung over the back of one of the chairs to every coordinated piece of clothing I'd seen draped across my living room, and the fancy striped bag she'd hauled from the bedroom earlier along with the suitcase covered in initials...

Not to mention the lace underwear I'd caught too much of an eyeful of... I was familiar with the lingerie racket: the less the fabric covered was inversely proportional to how much it cost.

And there wasn't a whole lot to those panties.

Violet Royale came from money, but she wore it like a uniform: because it was required, not because it was something she'd chosen.

No, what she'd chosen was to stay in a cottage in the woods for two weeks instead of some luxury resort in the Mediterranean.

"I can't remember the last time someone cooked for me." Her sad smile obliterated all other thoughts of myself. "My fiancé—*ex-fiancé* always wanted to eat out."

I tensed at the mention of the *F* word. And the pain that flashed in her eyes when she said "ex."

We'd existed in an ebb and flow of small conversations and drawn silence throughout most of the day. Conversations about the weather. About winter in New York City, where she was from. Conversations about the cottage and surviving snowstorms.

Talk that was as small as snowflakes.

But just like them, it wouldn't be long before what seemed like meaningless little pieces of information piled into something unable to be ignored.

For most of the afternoon, she'd worked on her iPad while I sat at the table, getting some paperwork done for new shop orders and then sketching up ideas for my next batch of pieces. Both of us intently focused on our work and yet entirely aware of each other.

Or at least, I was aware of her.

Far too aware.

Both of our attention jerked to the kitchen window as the panes rattled against the glass. The wind had picked up throughout the day. And then, for the first time, the lights inside flickered.

"Do you want to sit by the fire?" I asked, seeing anxiety begin to pull the color from her face.

With a tight nod, she stood and sank back to the seat she'd occupied on the far end of the couch, pulling my flannel shirt tighter around her.

She was still wearing my shirt.

She'd worn it all day.

And I didn't want to tell her to take it off.

Violet Royale was the kind of woman made to wake up and

stroll out into the kitchen every morning wearing nothing underneath a man's shirt. It didn't matter it was several sizes too big, the way it fell over her breasts and caught on the swell of her hips... it was my shirt—*but it was made for her.*

Pulling the hot water from the stove, I poured it on top of the chocolate powder, which sat in the bottom of two mugs. Reaching up to the top shelf, I grabbed a small bottle of whiskey and looked at her.

"Would you like some?" I asked as I tipped a dash into my mug.

Whiskey and chocolate in front of the fire were how I'd spent far too many nights alone in this cottage.

She hesitated until the windows rattled again before saying, "What the hell... sure..."

Moments later, I carefully handed her *The Maine Squeeze* mug that she'd claimed as her own, watching as she pursed her lips and blew steam across the top.

"So, what do you do?" I said, turning and sitting on the other side of the couch before I fantasized too long about those lips.

We hadn't been this close all day, I realized as I saw the shadows douse her face.

"I work in the hotel business," she added, taking a cautious sip.

My brows rose. "And you chose my cottage for your vacation?" I couldn't hide my surprise.

"I read really good reviews about the home-cooked meals," she returned blithely, catching my eyes for a second before we both laughed lightly.

"And here I thought it was the luxurious accommodations that drew you in," I teased right back, knowing my cottage was sparse.

It was only ever meant to be me up here.

"Well, the complimentary flannel robe was definitely a plus." She smirked, taking another sip. "But I think it was the promise of the real fires consistently stoked by a sexy lumberja—"

The sound of her gasp was like an axe swinging through the air before it struck us both into silence.

"Anyway," she forged forward, partially hiding her flushed face with her mug as she asked, "What do you do, Jamie?"

I couldn't keep looking at her—not with the way I wanted her.

"I have my own woodworking business." My thumb rubbed across the front of my mug. "Mostly furniture now, but I'll do custom pieces on occasion—"

"You made the table and chairs, didn't you?" she interrupted, eyes widening as she indicated the set in the kitchen.

I nodded, surprised she'd noticed them.

I'd made them several years ago, so to me, they weren't incredibly impressive, but I liked how they had come out. The circular table was large enough to fit four, but in the small space of the cottage made a full table feel cozy. The pedestal base supporting the center of the table I'd carved to look like a tree trunk, thick knobby veins knotting and swirling upward from the root-like feet sprawling out on the floor.

It wasn't the cleverest idea—to carve a tree to look like a tree —but it wasn't common either.

The chairs were less ornate. I shaped the bars along the back support to look like branches, but otherwise, let the table be the focus of the set. I'd stained all of the pieces until the light maple shone a rich honeyed-amber color.

"I wondered," she mused with a small laugh, feeling a little more comfortable as she crossed her legs and settled deeper into the couch only a few inches from me.

Too few.

"I've been eyeing them since I got here. I was looking for something exactly like that for one of my—I mean, one of the hotels I manage. A few weeks ago, I would've been convincing you to make a few sets for me."

"For a hotel?" I croaked.

I knew my work was good. I took my time and gave my attention to every detail and every grain. But still... a hotel chain was a far cry from supplying the folk in Friendship and their crazier counterpart, Stonebar Ridge.

"They're really beautiful."

I shifted in my seat. I wasn't used to being complimented on my woodworking by someone I currently had a raging hard-on for.

"Thank you," I replied gruffly.

"Who taught you how to make furniture like that?"

A small smile tugged at my lips. "I got my attention to detail from my father, but as far as learning how, my uncle is a carpenter up in Stonebar Ridge. I trained with him for..." I trailed off, thinking of all the times I went up there to avoid fighting with Jason McHale. "For most of my life really."

The darker memories of my past faded against the light in her eyes. "That's wonderful," she replied wistfully. "It must be nice to have family so close."

"That's one word for it." When her face fell, I retracted slightly with a laugh. "A handful of cousins, combined with my siblings, and topped off with my mother and grandmother. If renting this cottage came with the crazy but caring, *but still crazy*, in-your-business family as an added bonus, you'd see what I mean." I shook my head. "Case in point, *my* winter cottage was rented out during the two weeks I took to relax."

I hazarded a glance to see her smiling.

I couldn't help but stare at the way her face lit up, slightly flushed from the warmth of the fire and from the alcohol in her drink.

"I don't think I would mind that addition to the rental," she said as sadness trickled into her eyes. "Not at all."

For one crazy second, I wanted to give this woman—*this stranger*—my family. Just to make her smile again.

So, I did.

"Then you'd get Frankie and her damn candles; my brother, Kit, and his broody-artist silence; Lou... well, Lou's pretty tame, but my grandmother, Gigi." I sucked in a breath and shook my head. "Her crazy hair only scratches the surface of her crazy ideas."

I went on, fueled by the way she wet her full pink lips.

"And my mother." I pursed my lips and gave a shake of my head. "Well, I'd get an earful, that's for sure, for how I've kept this place, and that'd be right before she talks your ear off and gets you to confess your life's story and deepest secrets."

Violet's eyebrows rose. She was intrigued.

"They call her CI-Ailene around these parts. There's no secret between here and the Maine border on either end that my mother doesn't know or wouldn't be able to find out if she wanted."

I chuckled, not because it was a joke but because it was the truth.

Ailene Kinkade was the boss around these parts. A matriarch through and through. *And a damn nosy one.* Her door was always open, but if you walked through it, that meant you were treated like family—which meant you had her support, her care, her protection, but it also meant there was nothing she asked that you didn't answer.

"They say there's truth serum in her blueberry jam," I mused. "More likely, she bribes anyone reluctant to share with her jam that's usually sold out."

"Jam?" Her eyes widened.

"Her blueberry jam is worth more in these parts than gold bars and bitcoin," I murmured.

A jar of Coastal Maine Blueberry Jam from Stonebar Farms was a pretty hot commodity.

"Oh, wow. I love jam. Strawberry is my favorite though." She hummed and took another long drink of her spiked hot chocolate. "So, she has her own business? Does she have a store? I'd love to check it out."

My mouth shut, halting the direction I'd been taking the conversation. I'd been too lost in the vibrant display of emotions on my beautiful guest's face to realize what I'd been sharing.

"Something like that."

It had been a long time since Eleanor was a part of my life—*or trying to be*—but some old wounds still held the reflex to draw back.

"Oh..." She trailed off and looked down at her mug.

I bit off a curse.

Violet wasn't Eleanor. *Not in the slightest.* Violet had her own wealth. And Eleanor... she'd been in love with mine, not me.

"My mom and my uncle own a store—a business together canning and preserving. It's pretty... popular... up in this neck of the woods. Mom mostly works with the recipes and the fruit itself, and my uncle handles the business end."

"I thought your uncle was a carpenter?"

I didn't know why it thrilled me so much that she remembered or that she was so interested. She had to have met far more interesting people living in New York City, yet she wanted to know about my family with an eagerness that was intoxicating.

"He was." I lifted my hand and wiggled my fingers. "A few too many accidents and the onset of arthritis made him look for a new career and slowly shift his business over to me."

Her lips formed a tiny *O* and my tongue wanted to trace around it before sinking inside the inviting opening.

Clearing my throat, I adjusted my seat again and went on about my family just so she wouldn't notice how hard she was making my cock.

"He started packaging and selling Mom's jam. My cousins help some, too, and my grandmother—she's ninety-one, so she's only responsible for labeling."

Violet jumped as the wind knocked against the windows again. It was really picking up out there. Not uncommon for a winter storm, so it was a safe bet that I was going to be treated to some more one-on-one time with my far-too-pretty guest—*and some quality hand-to-dick time in the shower.*

"Your grandmother? Is ninety-one?" Violet gaped, and I had

to laugh because it looked like she was about to topple from the couch in surprise.

The lights dimmed for a second. My jaw flexed tight. I didn't have high hopes for the power lasting through the night.

At least she didn't seem to notice when the power flickered this time. I couldn't handle seeing her scared like earlier. It made me want to pull her close—which wasn't good for a woman I'd met only twenty-four hours ago.

"And she helps?"

Well... "She tastes the jam, sticks the labels on, and... ahh... sometimes picks out names for special batches."

There was no point in telling her that Gigi used jars of jam like fortune cookies, doling out either scrawled gibberish or life fortunes on the front labels, providing unique batches of limited-edition *Premonition Preserves*.

"That's... wonderful. I can't imagine having a family like that," she broke off and turned toward the fire as though its heat could dry the sadness I saw pooling in her eyes. "My family is nothing like that."

Damn.

I watched her pull her mug to her lips like she needed that last drink, and I was about to ask when she declared, "I should probably get to bed. I haven't had this much to driiiinnn—"

The word was like a slow-motion sound effect as Violet rose too quickly and toppled toward the ottoman, sending her into a tailspin of overcorrection so she didn't fall forward.

I tossed my empty mug to the ground and tried to stabilize her in time, but she careened backward with a squeal and sent us both dropping back onto the couch—*with her in my lap.*

Jesus Christ.

I groaned as she squirmed in my lap, desperately trying to recover but only succeeded at rubbing along my cock in a way that was going to send me out, dickfirst, into the winter storm just to be able to cool off.

"*Stop,*" I growled and gripped her upper arms.

Her breath caught and she complied. With both of us frozen in place, everything came into focus. The way she smelled like lavender. The way I was touching her. My hands to her arms. My chest to her back. Her ass against my... I ground my teeth together, desire electrifying every cell, awakening them from a slumber I'd forced them into.

I hadn't felt like this in a long time.

I couldn't afford to.

I had my business to run, my family to look after.

Dammit, Jamie.

I struggled to get myself under control. She felt so soft, so warm. I just wanted to hold on for a little longer.

My fingers gripped into *my flannel* shirt on her arms, and just when they found the strength to lift her away, Violet turned her head over her shoulder. Exhales collided, hot and uncertain, as our lips hovered a literal breath apart.

Her eyes liquefied into molten golden brown, like thick maple syrup, sticky and sweet with desire. *Fuck.*

My cock thickened along her ass and her lips parted, a wordless acknowledgment of the ache in my body.

Her tongue slipped out, wetting her lips, first the top and then the lower, fuller one. An invitation. *Signed, sealed, and delivered.* She wanted me to kiss her.

My head drifted closer to hers and the world fell away. There was no snow, no storm. The fire only a distant light and the warmth in the room solely stemming from our desire.

"*Violet,*" I warned, the final thread of control popping inside me.

"Springfield, Illinois..."

My eyes popped open and met her wide, horrified ones for a beat before she popped up off my lap, catching herself on the ottoman before launching toward the kitchen—*and to safety.*

Springfield?

"I should get to bed," she offered hastily through the deep draws of air, striding to the sink and soaping out her mug. "Sorry.

I haven't had a drink in a long time. I didn't realize how tipsy I was."

"Violet—" I started, wanting to apologize. The last thing I wanted was for her to feel like I was trying to take advantage of her while she was stranded here.

"Thank you so much, Jamie," she cut me off, folding her arms across her chest, wrapping my flannel shirt tighter against where I wanted to be. "I'll see you in the morning. Good night."

And with that, she turned into the bedroom and shut the door behind her. The click of the lock into place was like a gun being cocked.

With a groan, my elbows dug into my knees and my head dropped into my hands.

What the hell was I thinking?

I was the rational one. The responsible one. I was the eldest who took care of my brother when our dad died, my sisters when their shithole father, our mother's almost second-husband, left, and who took care of my mother when my brother went off to war and came back a different man.

I didn't have room for emotions or desire to get in the way.

Especially for a woman who, though trapped in my house, definitely didn't belong in my world.

CHAPTER FIVE
VIOLET

I SAT UP WITH A START, my head whipping from side to side, looking for the source of the loud pop which I swore pulled me from my sleep.

Nothing.

My gaze swung to the window next to the bed as it rattled with the wind outside. I squinted against the glass, but it was too dark to see anything. It was hard to even tell if it was still snowing or if it was only the wind that brought sprays of snowflakes against the pane.

I swallowed, my throat tight, and looked to the door.

Springfield, Illinois.

I'd almost kissed him. A stranger. The man whose cottage I thought I'd rented.

The jaw-dropping woodsman with a family I wished I could complain about.

Jamie.

I thought it was the alcohol. I mean, it definitely was the alcohol that made me fall onto him. But really, I was intoxicated with him. The way he moved and spoke so decisively, as though everything he touched was his responsibility. *Even me.* Even though I didn't belong to him. *No matter how nice that might be.*

And the way he spoke about his family was proof.

I knew there were good families out there; I also knew that mine wasn't one of them. My family wasn't bad, and I would never complain. Not when there were kids who lived without a roof over their heads or with parents who were physically abusive.

There was just no winning with my parents.

My mother wanted the perfect spoiled princess. *Yes, that's right. She wanted me to act spoiled.* She and my father wanted me to sit still and look pretty in order to attract a suitably rich and well-connected husband—preferably in politics who came from old money. And they wanted my brother to take over our luxury hotel line.

The problem? My brother, Gerald, was the one who wanted to live like a spoiled princess.

Alcohol, drugs, women. He leapfrogged from one party to the next before the last story had even blown over.

First, it was because he was young and at college that my parents let it slide; they looked the other way as I stepped in to fill his shoes. My father groomed the both of us, wordlessly expecting me to make sure my brother didn't make any mistakes.

And he didn't. Because Gerald never worked.

After his extra year in college, the classes stopped, but the party lifestyle didn't. Our mother insisted he was simply keeping up with the family's social obligations, mingling with the rich and famous.

All the while, I worked my ass off to make a difference for Royale Hotels; I was determined to show them that being a badass businesswoman was a *better* option for me and for them.

Stop, Vi.

My chest constricted, and I put my hand up against the frigid glass of the window, physically jarring myself away from my reality. I was supposed to heal here, not rehash all the things that brought me here in the first place.

And definitely not kiss random lumberjacks, no matter how gorgeous they were.

My fingers peeled off the window, the warmth of my skin sticking to the cold.

With a groan, I turned to the other side of the bed, deciding it was better to pee now that I was awake. With the fire out, I reached for the small lamp on the bedside table, fumbling until I found the beaded string and tugged.

Click.

Nothing. No light.

I pulled once more, feeling the distinct resistance before the definitive click that should've turned the lamp on. Still, there was no light.

Frantic to believe otherwise—I yanked a few more times only to meet the same result: the power was out. That was the pop that woke me.

My heart started to pound.

It's fine. You're fine, Vi.

I was in a cabin in the middle of nowhere. No phone. No fire. No power. *No... I was not fine.*

Indianapolis, Indiana.

I sucked in long breaths, trying to put the brakes on my pulse as it continued to accelerate. My hands clambered for the edge of the bed as my legs slowly caught up.

I hated the dark. Ever since I was a child, I have been afraid of the dark. Not spiders. Not heights. *The dark.*

Which was why I hated the panic so much... because it came with its own darkness.

The air was thicker by the time my bare toes touched the floor.

What do I do?

There was a chance it was only that wall—that maybe the lights in the bathroom were working if I could make it there. Or maybe there was a better chance that Jamie still had the living room fire going if I could just make it to the door. I squinted in the direction of the bedroom door, but couldn't see any ring of light around it.

Of all nights, there was no light from outside—not even from the moon to give a glimmer of relief to my eyes. The world was in shadow. *And there was only ever one thing that brought my entire world to darkness.*

I shook my head, trying to will it away, but there was no stopping it.

My phone.

It had no service but it had a flashlight. If I could just —*Thump.*

I swore my stomach made the exact same plummeting noise as my frantic hands knocked my phone off the nightstand and it toppled and rolled on the floor.

Like a dam bursting, my skin broke out in a sweat and I gasped. Short, staccatoed breaths felt like buckets of water were being dumped into my lungs, drowning me with my own air as I forced myself to stand.

It's just the dark. Don't panic.

You're not going to panic, Violet. Not now.

Not again.

I took a step and realized I no longer felt my toes. The band around my chest grew tighter.

What if we were trapped here?

What if the storm didn't stop, and we had no power? No heat? No water?

I took another step but no longer had any sense of what direction. My world had become a sphere of darkness, no beginning, no end. My throat was an hourglass, only the tiniest grains of breath fitting through the restricted space—*letting me know my time was running out.*

"*Help...*" The voice didn't even sound like mine—it didn't even sound like someone I knew, let alone who I was.

I heard gasping and choking, all sounding far away to ears that only heard the rampant hammer of my heart. Tears spilled down my cheeks, even though I saw nothing. And with my next numb step, I went down, the hard thud of my knees against the floor masking the pounding on the bedroom door.

I was never going to get out of here.

It was always going to be dark.

And I was always going to be alone.

The world tilted and spun. I had no idea if I was sitting or if I'd completely fallen. The cinch around my throat felt like it had shut. There was nothing left of me except my panic.

Empty.

Dark.

Worthless.

I was nothing except a ball of panic, rolling, *snowballing* out of control. My heart raced furiously, like a thoroughbred going too fast to stay stable on its feet.

It doesn't matter if you get out of here.

You have no one and nothing to go back to.

Nothing.

You are nothing.

No one.

I was going to crash, and what was left of me wouldn't be worth salvaging.

No one.

You are no—

"*Violet!*" The snowball stopped with my name and disintegrated against the strength of his voice. I still had no sense of anything, but I could sense him—*feel him.*

There were loud thuds, like reality was trying to ram itself back into my brain, followed by a crash.

The noises anchored to reality when strong arms scooped up my numb limbs that hung limply from my body, paralyzed in irrational fear. *He'd broken through the door.* Warm fingers skated over my face, my cheeks, wiping away the cold wetness from underneath my eyes.

"I'm here, Violet. It's going to be okay."

I'm. Here.

Those words shouldn't make a difference, especially coming from him. But they did.

I'm here.

His words draped over me like a warm blanket lit with stars— stars that soon coalesced into the whites of his eyes as they stared worriedly down at me. "You're going to be okay."

My mouth opened, but nothing came out. My body, previously feeling like an ocean had been laid on top of it, heavy as it forced me to drown, now felt the weight begin to lift; everything about him reached out to me.

"I'm here, Violet," he murmured again, brushing my hair from where it had stuck to my face as I stayed curled in his arms.

He was so warm. So solid. So... *safe.*

The last time this happened, no one had been there. It wasn't anyone's fault really that they hadn't, but it meant I'd been gasping for air, silently sobbing and choking on my kitchen floor for almost twenty minutes before Leslie showed up and called an ambulance.

I'd been making myself some dinner when I got the call. The news that slowly sent my knives and plates clattering to the floor around me. Even though it had been an accident, and I only had a few minor cuts and scrapes, I knew the doctor was concerned about suicide. I wasn't offended. I saw how it looked.

"It's okay, Violet." His soft timbre soothed me again, and I sagged further against him.

I didn't know what it was about his voice. It was almost like his hot chocolate. Warm. Familiar. Soothing. And, if I wasn't careful, too easily intoxicating.

His heart pounded against my cheek as he sat with his back propped against the bed. With the bedroom door open, there was a faint light from the fire in the other room. It wasn't much, but it was enough for me to see I'd only made it about two feet from the bed before collapsing.

If I wasn't still trying to equilibrate, I would've laughed at how pathetic it was. My body behaved as though I'd just run a mile underwater, not taken three steps on normal ground.

And Jamie probably thought I was crazy.

Still, he held this crazy person to his chest like I was his most treasured possession.

"I've got you." An electric shiver crawled up my spine. He had me for the moment, held me because I was unwell. But his tenderness flared like a fuse attached to a stick of dynamite inside me, setting off something that couldn't be stopped.

"I'm sorry," I murmured weakly, annoyed by how threadbare and choked my voice sounded. *Annoyed that I could be rendered so weak over nothing. Over darkness.*

And over him.

And then the tears came. Gushing out of me like my apology had turned on a faucet.

"Hey, hey." His hand began to rub up and down my arm. "It's alright, Violet. It's alright."

Like the darkness, once the tears started, I couldn't seem to stop them. And suddenly, it wasn't just the panic attack or the embarrassment of the situation I was in. It was everything. The life I'd escaped up here to forget. The Uber ride. The storm. The snow. The drink. The way I shouldn't be in his house, yet wanted to be in his arms. I curled deeper against his chest and cried for it all.

And my handsome host continued to hold me, murmuring soothing endearments while I shook and bawled in his arms like I'd known him for years—like I'd known him long enough to feel comfortable in my weakness around him. I hadn't... yet I still felt safe.

Minutes later, the overwhelming urge to cry began to subside, and I felt myself calming, possibly from exhaustion alone.

"You okay?" he rasped against my hair, his arms still tight and locked around me.

My head jerked slightly as I tried to nod. "I get... panic attacks." I gulped.

The words sounded foreign on my tongue, probably because I'd never admitted them before. No one except my doctor and Leslie knew, and Leslie only because she'd been the one to go with me to the hospital.

How was it that the first person I'd ever told that fact to was a stranger? Maybe it was easier to confess to a stranger because a stranger held no preconceptions or prejudice about who I should be.

"I-I think the power went out... and I'm afraid of the dark."

God, I probably sounded like a child.

But he deserved to know what sent his guest into a sobbing, gasping fit in the middle of the night.

"I see." He paused and my breath caught, wondering if that was the only response I'd get. *He thinks you're crazy, Vi. Of course, that's all—* "And here I thought you were taking advantage of the complimentary midnight cuddling that comes with your cottage rental."

My jaw dropped. Was he—Did he just—

A watery choke escaped me. I couldn't laugh. It was too much for that thing inside my chest to handle. But I did feel the beginnings of a smile tugging at my lips. I wasn't an expert at panic attacks—no matter how much what I read on the internet liked to let me believe. But I was pretty sure that smiling wasn't part of them and yet, here I was, toeing the line of a heartfelt smile.

I shifted in his lap, freezing when he grunted in pain. My gaze stuck in his as I felt the length of his arousal, as hard as it had been earlier, pinned right where the side of my ass met my hip. Suddenly, my body was flooded with a whole new sensation. The same one I literally ran from earlier, only this time, I didn't want to run.

With a strained sense of propriety, he drew his eyes up and away from mine and asked, "Would it be okay if I carried you back to the bed?"

I stared up at him, willing him to meet my gaze, but when he didn't, I finally responded, "Yes," and nodded.

Like I weighed little more than a snowflake, he rose with me held tightly to his chest and my arms instinctively reached up and locked around his neck. The bed felt cool as he tucked me back under the covers and vaguely, I wondered how and why this motion could seem so familiar to him. It was a thought that was lost as I felt his heat begin to pull away.

Fight for what you want, Vi.

One hand sprung out and clamped onto the thick muscle of his shoulder as he rose. I met his widening eyes and pleaded softly, "Don't go." I licked my lips. "Please."

He looked down at me questioningly.

"I just... I don't want to be alone right now." My voice was even softer than before.

I wasn't asking him to stay for sex. I was begging him to stay because as the world continued to crumble around me, it seemed as though nothing would ever shake the solid roots of this man. I felt safe and calm in his arms—something it had taken hours and heaping loads of drugs to achieve in the hospital after the first attack.

He hesitated.

"Please, Jamie," I repeated, shrinking my hand back, savoring every taut ridge and valley along the corded muscles of his arms. There was something about feeling them when I wasn't able to see them, something that made them stand out more.

He grunted and pulled away, and I curled into myself with my eyes clamped shut, not wanting to see the back of him as he walked away.

And then I felt the covers shift and the mattress sag as Jamie climbed in next to me.

He was still fully clothed, and I noticed belatedly how he'd made sure to lie on top of the blankets while I huddled underneath. His warmth cocooned me, and when his arm came up, my head lifted to rest on top of it, reclaiming my place curled against his chest like it was the most natural thing in the world.

"Good night." His low grumble rolled over me. I heard every

grating syllable with his mouth just above my head as the wind outside finally died down.

No. Not a good night.

I tipped my head up. His eyes locked with mine, concern bleeding into their rich warmth.

"Vi—"

My hands, which were curled against his chest, clung tight and brought me up the inch or so needed for me to press my lips to his, cutting him off and taking him completely by surprise.

It was probably the wrong thing to do—kissing him. Especially when I wasn't looking for it to lead to anything.

It just felt... essential... to kiss him at that moment.

Like putting a period at the end of a sentence or a question mark at the end of a question. All of our encounters today kept ending in ellipses, and I needed his kiss to finish the thought. I needed to know if his kiss was as warm and welcoming, as strong and sexy as the rest of him.

And the moment my lips touched the heat of his, I knew it was.

Now, with my eyes closed, I saw nothing but light. I felt nothing but bright hot heat, pervasive as it flooded my body and pooled much lower.

His low growl vibrated against my aching breasts and pushed through his lips to escape. The warm concrete of his body tensed, and his hold on me tightened.

In his arms, I felt no panic, and I just wanted one kiss to remind me that the feeling was possible, though almost impossible to find.

I clamped my teeth shut to stop my curious tongue from darting out to taste him.

Enough, Violet.

I drew back with a ragged inhale, but kept my eyes lowered, afraid of what I'd find in his stare if I looked: *desire or disapproval?*

"Thank you."

I wouldn't apologize for the kiss.

"Get some sleep, Violet," he said with a low, strained voice as though he were holding on by a thread. "I've got you."

Jamie had me.

And the dynamite lit inside my brain exploded as the sensation felt so... *right*. As my breathing began to calm and sleep overtook me once more, I no longer saw the darkness—the panic and anxiety that plagued me. There was only him.

Stranded in a snowstorm, in the fire-lit woodman's cottage, I could pretend I wasn't who I was, and the man holding me was mine forever rather than only for tonight.

CHAPTER SIX
JAMIE

I SHOULDN'T HAVE STAYED.

But as I lay there, watching the soft tendrils of Violet's blonde hair as they fluttered with the steady, measured breaths of her deep sleep, I couldn't regret the choice I'd made—*especially after seeing her like that.*

I'd learned to be a light sleeper, though it wasn't a skill I'd had to use in the recent past, but when the twins were younger, someone had to catch them trying to sneak out of the house in the middle of the night.

With Violet here, my senses were on high alert—*for many reasons*—and sleeping on a couch that wouldn't be comfortable for a man half my height helped keep me teetering on the verge of being awake.

The pop of the power going out jarred me. I was surprised it lasted as long as it had with the way the wind had been howling. Settling back into the couch, my eyes had just drifted shut once more, knowing there wasn't much I could do about it now. I had a small generator out in the snowmobile shed in case of an emergency but I'd never had to use it out here yet.

And that was when I heard the first rustle. So soft I reasoned it came from the fireplace. But then there was a thud and tumble on the floor that had me sitting up and throwing the blanket off me, craning toward the door. It sounded like a phone. Definitely too light to be Violet. But it was the sound I heard only a few seconds later that slung my heart against my rib cage, pounding violently with adrenaline.

The soft whimpers and cries. Shuffled steps.

The second thud of her knees crashing into the floor.

Her cry for help.

A chill washed over my body at the sickening memory, and I glanced down to make sure I hadn't woken her.

I was familiar with panic attacks and how debilitating they could be.

Kit suffered them frequently after returning from his last tour in Iraq. Combined with the nightmares, it had broken our mother's heart. Finally, he'd moved out even though she begged him not to; and he didn't just move out—he moved the farthest out you could go in Friendship without living underwater: he moved into the town's lighthouse.

The sun peeked through the window that was frosted around the edges. The storm had finally stopped. Based on past experience, the cottage probably wouldn't get power until later in the day, which normally I would stick out, but with Violet here, I needed to get the generator going.

I settled one last look at her, curled against my chest. She hadn't moved all night, as though I might disappear if she did.

Christ.

I couldn't remember a time—even when the twins were younger when I'd been so damn afraid. Maybe it was because I didn't know much about Violet, and I didn't know where the attacks came from. Or maybe it was the hollowness in her eyes—bottomless orbs dilated into pitch-black fear.

Or, hell, maybe what really scared the shit out of me was my suspicion that I was the only person who'd ever come for her—ever comforted her.

My jaw tensed as protectiveness surged inside me again.

I trailed a finger along her jawline until it caught on the piece of hair resting on her cheek. Careful not to wake her, I pushed the fine silk strands back behind her ear and then let my gaze drift down to her lips.

Shit.

I needed to get out of this bed before I did something I shouldn't *but wouldn't* regret.

Gingerly, I slid my arm out from underneath her neck. If it woke her, she pretended pretty well like it hadn't. But I'd bet my money she was still passed out from the stress of the night.

Dragging a hand through my tousled hair, I quietly slipped from the bedroom, leaving the door only slightly ajar.

Outside of the bed and the warm, soft woman next to me, the rest of the cottage felt fucking freezing. I needed to get the fires going. *And coffee.* I picked up my phone from where it sat on the ottoman to see it was almost nine thirty in the morning.

Holy shit. I hadn't slept in or slept that soundly in a long while.

Walking to the window in the small dining nook, I peered outside and assessed what the storm had left us with.

The snow had collected in giant mounds from the wind, pristine and untrodden, sitting like little hills near the surrounding trees. The morning sun already glistened off the top, slowly melting layers of snow. The light was out in the lamppost, confirming the lack of power.

I'd guess there was somewhere between fifteen to twenty inches out there—more where the snow had drifted.

It wasn't ideal for snowmobiling, but maybe in a few hours, if the sun held up and I got the generator going, I could go get my snowmobile.

I went to the living room and tossed a few fresh logs on top of some kindling in the hearth. I cracked the lighter several times until the tiniest flame caught.

My hands moved by muscle memory, while my memory moved back to her kiss.

So hesitant. So soft.

She didn't kiss me because she was afraid. She kissed me because she'd been afraid to do it earlier in the living room, and her fear had won out. But after her panic attack, there was no fear left to stop her.

"*Shit,*" I swore and jabbed the poker against the log, sending small sprays of sparks up in the air. My dick was rock solid in my jeans—like it had been for most of the night, like I was thirteen instead of thirty-six.

And then the feel of her pressed against me all night.... My jaw clenched. *I missed it.* I hadn't slept with a woman in a long time. I mean, I'd had sex with women... a few... since Eleanor left me almost a decade ago, but I'd never slept with them. It was too close... too intimate. And until I felt comfortable that the twins were settled and okay, I wasn't going to entertain any situation that would jeopardize my family. I'd pick my family every time, and women tended not to like that. At least, Eleanor hadn't.

In truth, I couldn't blame her.

But even sleeping next to Eleanor hadn't felt the same way Violet had last night.

Sleeping next to Eleanor was like lying next to all the things I'd have to give up. But holding Violet as she nestled against me, reminded me of all the things I was missing—*and all the things I wanted.*

Things that were less physical but just as tempting as the way her tits pressed against my chest, full and puckered against the shirt she slept in, and the way the curve of her ass began to rise against the very edges of my fingers at her waist, my thumb getting a tease of her warm, silken skin in the chasm between her shirt and her pajama pants.

Fuck.

I shifted on the ottoman.

I needed to get out of this fucking cabin before I exploded.

My gaze locked on the flames and I prodded the logs once

more; this was the only fire I could stoke in this cottage, not the one with my gorgeous guest.

"Did you get it?"

My head whipped to the side, finding a sleepy but curious Violet.

"Get what?" I rasped, quickly drinking in the sight of her.

My fingers remembered the feel of those clothes and the sensation of the flesh underneath them. The only difference now was that she had my flannel wrapped around her instead of me.

And I wanted to burn that goddamn shirt.

"Whatever piece of the log attacked you," she replied and one corner of her lips quirked up, revealing a small dimple.

I'd seen it before, but now it taunted me. Now that I'd tasted her lips, I wanted to taste everything about them, including that tiny, teasing dimple.

"You looked like you were stabbing the fire instead of stoking it," she continued when I didn't respond because I was a lust-stunned idiot who sat regarding her rather than replying.

Grunting, I forced my eyes to the fireplace, more gently pushing at the wood one last time. "I think I got it."

Her grin flooded into a smile, one that I kicked myself for ruining when I stood and asked, "How are you feeling?"

Her head dipped in embarrassment and she turned away from me. *Guess talking about last night was off the table.*

"I'm okay." Catching sight of the clear window, she asked, "Did the snow finally stop?"

"Yeah. But it'll still be a little until the power is back. We're on the outskirts of Friendship, so I'll have to get out to the generator and get that running."

"Oh, you have a generator?" Her tone was hopeful.

"Yeah. Out back in the shed. Just wanted to get the fires going and some coffee before I head out there."

"Then what happens?" She chewed on her lip, and I read her thoughts.

How much longer were we going to be trapped here?

"I'm going to see how deep the snow is and if I can make it back to my snowmobile," I replied. "With the power out, I'd rather get you into town—to somewhere with electricity and running water, if I can... as soon as I can... I'm sure you don't want to be stuck here for any longer than you have to be."

I finished my assumption with a little laugh to disguise how much I didn't like the thought. I wanted her trapped here with me. I wanted her trapped here because then it meant I could avoid admitting that I really just wanted her *here with me*.

Her face fell for a moment before she looked away with an obligatory nod. "Of course, I appreciate it."

She moved to the side, allowing me a broad path by her. I had to force my hands into fists so they didn't reach out and pull her tight to me so I could confess that she'd worried me. My instinct was always to take care of the people I felt responsible for, and while we'd only known each other for a short time, she triggered that instinct like no other.

Clearing my throat, I grabbed a small pot and headed for the front door.

"What are you—"

I heard her teeth clatter together as a rush of frigid air blew into the cottage. Crouching, I slung the pot through the drift of fresh snow outside. Turning back to Violet with snow piled, I smiled. "Making coffee."

Her eyes rounded.

There wouldn't be running water until I got the generator going. Thankfully, most times that the power was out, it was because there was fresh, partially frozen water to be found right outside. Setting the pot on one of the two burners, I reached along the side and turned the knob that fed gas from a small propane tank to the flame.

I purchased this stove for that reason. The wood-burning element helped to heat the room, along with the oven, but it also had two burners attached to a small gas tank on the side so I could get highly concentrated heat.

Even once the generator was on, I wouldn't connect the stove to its power; it would be too much of a drain on the small supply which I needed to run the water and electricity.

"Seems like you've done this once or twice before," she murmured, flipping over the mugs we'd used yesterday, which sat drying by the sink and pulling out a new filter and some fresh ground Ocean Roasters brand coffee from the cabinet.

"Once or twice."

The only downfall of this method was the snow took up far more space than the water it provided. So, I reached for one of the mugs to gather more snow and brushed Violet's fingers in the process.

She pulled back with an inhale, heat and electricity igniting between us in a space that was definitely lacking both.

"I'm going to grab some socks," she declared, crossing her arms and disappearing back into the bedroom.

With a drawn breath, I took the mug and gathered another cupful of snow and dumped it in the pot, repeating the process two more times until there was enough water for a few generous cups of coffee.

Minutes later, the repurposed snow was boiling, and I poured it over the coffee in the funnel, filling both mugs to the brim.

I opened a single packet of sugar in each.

"How did you know?"

I glanced at Violet, picking up her mug and handing it to her.

"Know what?"

"That I like one sugar?"

Oh.

"I saw how you made your coffee yesterday." I shrugged. "I'm good at remembering details."

Or just remembering details about her.

"Thank you," she said softly and took the cup, refusing to avoid or pull away when her fingers rubbed against mine.

"Coffee is the least I can do." I picked up my own mug and

took a sip. "Plus, I think it was somewhere in the rental agreement."

Pulling out one of the dining chairs, my chest swelled with pride as she admired the craftsmanship for a moment before taking a seat.

"I believe you are correct. *'Fresh-made Morning Coffee by Mysterious Woodsman' was* the perk that pushed your cottage to first choice." Her smile dimmed. "But that's not what I'm thanking you for."

I held my breath.

"I'm talking about last night," she continued with a softer, less certain voice. "Thank you for helping me. I'm not... used to dealing with panic attacks. Anxiety attacks, yes. The panic ones..." She paused, and I just waited patiently for whatever it was she needed to say. "Those have been a more recent development."

My jaw ticced.

This was the Violet I wanted to know more about, the one she tried to hold back. Carefully, I rested my hip against the counter, afraid any sudden movement might send her running from this conversation once more.

"My younger brother, Kit, used to get them all the time," I offered. Her eyes instantly locked with mine. "He was in the military and when he came home... after his last tour in the Middle East... Well, let's just say I've seen them once or twice."

"I can't imagine." Her fingers fumbled with her mug as though it were a stress ball rather than a coffee cup. "I mean, I can because I get them, but I don't have as good a reason."

Shit.

"No one deserves a panic attack *more*, Violet, because no one deserves a panic attack."

I took another sip of coffee when her tongue appeared again over her lips.

In the few seconds before she spoke again, I felt the weight of the silence—*the stillness.* This morning, there was no storm. No wind. It was as though the snow had covered the earth so heavily that everything had no choice but to just *be still.*

"I've had anxiety all my life," she began. "I've been afraid of the dark all my life." I heard the exhale of her small, pitiful laugh. "But lately, with work and family stress, it's gotten much worse. In fact, it's why I'm up here."

She drank from her mug but it was one of those sips taken not because she needed coffee, but because she was trying to swallow back words she was ashamed to admit.

But confessions are like Mother Nature; they can only be held back for so long before they have to be unleashed.

"Last month, I had my first real panic attack—or at least, a really bad one." Her thumb rubbed along the lip of the mug. "I was at home making dinner, and I got a phone call with some news... sort of work... sort of family... and, like last night, every-thing just started fading away into nothingness. My heart racing. I couldn't breathe. Truthfully, I thought I was having a heart attack and so did my best friend. And that's how I ended up in the hospital for over a week."

She took a moment to compose herself before her gaze wavered unsteadily as it looked for mine. "How did your brother stop them?"

My head ducked, and my grip tightened on my mug. Kit had never been the type of kid to look back at the reason for some-thing; instead, he was the type to just power through and beat whatever part of him that wasn't cooperating into submission.

"I don't know that he did," I admitted painfully. Unfortu-nately, it was hard to help someone who didn't want it. And Kit —Kit didn't want help. "He moved out and won't talk about that part of his life."

She reached over and grabbed my hand without hesitation. "I'm sorry."

I never said anything, but it fucking killed me that my younger brother suffered and wouldn't let me—hell, wouldn't let anyone—help him. And if there was one lesson I wasn't sure I would ever learn, it was that you can't help those who don't want to be helped.

I stared at where our fingers connected, wondering how the universe worked in such a way to bring two people together like this.

Not that we were together, but there was just something... something I didn't know how to explain. Like those "spot-the-differences" picture games. I *knew* there was something different with the way I felt about her, but I hadn't found the actual difference yet.

"What happened that the panic attacks started?" I asked, holding her fingers just a bit tighter to make it clear that I was the one giving her support now, if she wanted to accept it.

I watched her swallow and the way her pulse picked up against her neck. She stayed silent for so long I thought she was bound to tell me it was none of my business—*and it wasn't.*

"Do you really want to know?" she asked quietly with a shy smile. "I don't think I saw *complimentary psychotherapy* on the rental agreement."

"It was right after the section about coffee."

Each of her small smiles was like a glimpse of the sun through the clouds.

"My family owns Royale Hotels." When no recognition crossed my face, she elaborated. "It's a luxury hotel line. Up in these parts, we own the Harbor Hotel down by Kennebunkport."

I nodded, now recalling why it had sounded familiar. The Harbor Hotel was where the richest of the rich stayed when they vacationed along the coast of Maine.

"For years now, I've been basically running the show along with my father. My mom spends her time with the typical New York City socialite schedule, and my younger brother spends the family's money on tabloid-worthy parties and everything that goes along with them."

Bits and pieces—*details*—about her began to develop in three dimensions.

Her relationship to the hotel business. Why she wore designer clothes but didn't seem like the kind of woman who would purchase them. *And why she'd chosen to vacation in a cottage instead of a resort.*

"We've been going through a huge acquisition phase over the last two years. I scouted almost a dozen properties that I convinced the board to purchase, and with their success, I was sure my father finally saw my value." She paused with a small shake of her head, realizing she had forgotten a piece of information. "Let me back up. I guess I should clarify that my parents always planned on having my brother, Gerald, take over the business. I was the one who was supposed to follow in my mom's footsteps and win over the social scene, marry someone with equal wealth and influence... all that good stuff."

When my eyebrow rose, she tacked on, "Yes, that is still a very real thing in some circles." She sighed. "Anyway, with my brother sowing his wild oats, they needed someone to show interest in the business, so I was the backup plan. Meanwhile, all I wanted to do was be a part of my family's legacy.

"With the success of my suggestions, I thought things were going well. I was taking on more responsibilities, and I thought..." She licked her lips before sighing with dismay. "Whatever I thought, I was wrong. Now, looking back, I see how things began to change about six months ago. Meetings that were being held without me. Things happening that I should've been a part of but wasn't..." Her head drifted from side to side. "Hindsight is twenty-twenty, right?"

I could only manage a swift nod.

"Maybe I would've seen it except that I came home from a week-long trip to one of our newest properties, performing a six-month review, to find my fiancé of four years sleeping with the manager of housekeeping."

Violet jumped in her seat as my mug came crashing down on the table.

My nostrils flared. It felt like I was breathing pure fire and exhaling the hottest steam. *Who the fuck in their right mind would cheat on this smart, gorgeous, captivating woman?* I'd never had the urge to kill anyone—save for the joking attempts I threatened my siblings with—until that moment.

"Violet—"

"He wasn't that great anyway," she interjected and admitted. "But he fits all my parents' qualifications, and he was nice, and good-looking. But I really should've known from the start. I was just too wrapped up in trying to be both children my parents wanted."

Jesus.

"I'm sorry," I ground out, even though I was far more than that.

She gave me a brave smile. "Don't be. If he was really worth the effort, I'd go after him with that poker myself." She nodded over her shoulder to her weapon of choice. "So, I think that was what started the symptoms, but I just pushed through them because I didn't have another choice."

Her eyes caught on our hands still linked together and she reluctantly pulled hers back to her mug. The flush of embarrassment stained her cheeks, realizing how long we'd sat holding hands was too long for two people who'd only just met.

"But that day, my father called to tell me he was retiring. *Called.* Even though I'd seen him several times in the office earlier that day..." Unlike when she spoke about her moron of a fiancé, her voice here became strained with hurt and disbelief. "I knew it was coming soon. I knew the purchases we'd made were to set up the business for its next stage of growth—the one that would happen without him. But I hadn't expected him to announce it to me with the added information that upon his retirement, the corporation would be left in Gerald's control."

The wind came out of me. *Motherfuckers.*

"What?"

She'd done all the work, and they were going to give the credit and the reward to her brother.

Motherfuckers.

My grip tightened, and my face must have looked ridiculous because she let out a sad laugh.

"Yeah. That's exactly how I felt. Working so hard for so long... being responsible for the promising direction we were headed in... only for everything, all my hard work, to be bestowed upon my younger brother who, no offense to him, but he can't even manage to have a party in a hotel without the cops being called and everything going to shit, let alone know anything about running an entire conglomeration of them."

My ears buzzed, pressurized from the anger building inside me.

Sure, my family was wealthy up in these parts with Stonebar Farms, but my mother and uncle would never pass the business to someone incapable of running it—*to someone with no interest in running it*—just because of their gender.

"They left you with nothing?" Christ, what a fucking disgrace.

"Well, not nothing. They're not *that* coldhearted." She downed the last of her coffee. "I would be... Well, I guess I am... well-off because they didn't cut me off. They left me lots of things: my name, my association, and heaps of residual income." She let out a long sigh. "Everything except my pride, basically."

Everything except being valued for who she was and what she'd accomplished.

"Jesus, Violet, I'm so sorry. I don't—I can't imagine—" I didn't know what to say because I couldn't fucking imagine. I couldn't imagine betraying anyone in my family like that— ripping their hard work and dreams right out from under them.

"Yeah. I couldn't really process it either." She stood and took her mug to the sink while I stayed fuming at the table. "It only took about ten minutes after he hung up for the panic attack to start. Next thing I knew, I was in the hospital, with my best friend, who's also my assistant, railing at me for giving her a heart attack."

I pushed my chair back and stood to face her.

"She was the one who booked my retreat up here," Violet confessed, connecting her past to our present. "I needed to get away and regroup. To figure out what the hell I'm supposed to do now."

I closed the distance between us, finding her gaze as I set my cup on the counter.

There it was again—that look of vulnerability threaded with steel. And I couldn't stop my hands as they found her shoulders and squeezed.

"I'm sorry, Violet," I offered. "You're worth more than that. You *deserve* more than that."

I wished I could show her. I wished like hell I could be the one to give her what she deserved. Instead, I'd have to settle for whatever moment this was because the borrowed time the snowstorm had given us was rapidly disintegrating.

My hands were meant to be supportive—to show her my gratitude for opening up to me and to lend her my strength even though I wasn't sure she needed it, but the second I touched her, everything about the moment changed.

Her mouth parted and her eyes dipped to my lips, both of us instantly recalling the kiss.

A kiss we hadn't talked about.

A kiss I wanted to elaborate on.

And, instead of supporting her, I felt myself pull her closer. Her hands reached up to my chest, but she didn't push me away. She gripped my shirt and tightened her hold on me until we were flush.

"Violet..." Her name rumbled from my chest like a new storm brewing, warning that a deluge of desire was going to come crashing down if we didn't separate and seek shelter.

One of my hands slid up along her neck and threaded into the thick of her hair while the other tipped her chin up, angling her mouth to mine.

"About last night..." I trailed off as my thumb began to brush over her plump lower lip that begged to be tasted. *"About the kiss..."* I trailed off again with a groan as her mouth opened ever so slightly and the warm velvet of her tongue slipped out and licked the tip of my finger, effectively informing me everything I needed to know about that kiss: *it wasn't going to be our last.*

And if that wasn't invitation enough, she rose up on her tiptoes.

It wasn't responsible to kiss her now, but I didn't care.

Whatever attraction was between us had been brewing from the moment I'd walked into the cottage the other night and like the storm, there was just no fucking stopping it. It needed to happen. I needed to fucking kiss her. And once it was done, I'd figure out just what kind of situation it left us in.

My head drifted down to meet hers, smelling the sweet lavender of her skin and the rich aroma of her coffee.

And just as my lips touched down on the sweet softness of hers, the door of the cottage flew open with a crash and the cold chill of reality.

"Jamie! Holy shit!"

CHAPTER SEVEN
VIOLET

I SPRUNG BACK from Jamie with a gasp, one hand covering my mouth, the other cinching my shirt—*his shirt*—over my front.

With the snowsuit and helmet, the person who crossed the threshold looked like an alien. The mirrored black panel over the eyes caught the glint of the fire as it swung back and forth between Jamie and me.

The woman, given away by the muffled pitch of her voice, tugged off her gloves and pulled the helmet from her head.

Long, caramel waves unraveled over her shoulders, and I found myself staring into familiar, rich-brown eyes.

"Holy. Fucking. Shit," the woman repeated, sounding much younger now without the mask to alter her voice.

"Frankie—" Jamie's rough reply confirmed she was his sister. "What the hell are you—"

He broke off again as two more suited bodies thumped through the door, pushing Frankie farther into the room.

"C'mon, Frankie. Make room for all of us," the one male said.

"Jeez, Nox, I told you to wait with the bikes," she huffed and flipped her hair.

"Who are you?" the other unidentified male asked in my direction, his helmet also swaying between Jamie and me.

"Christ," Jamie swore next to me, running a hand through his red hair before extending it out to the motley crew. "Guess this is happening now, then." His throat clearing sounded suspiciously like a growl. "The tall one is Max Hamilton, brilliant businessman and owner of MaineStems flower delivery service; another joker in my family. And his brother, Lenox—or Nox, too charming for his own good, he works with my mom and my uncle, his father. They're my cousins."

As he spoke, the two men took off their helmets, revealing similar sandy-brown hair and matching brown eyes. Max's eyes raked over me shrewdly and then to Jamie, assessing both of us and this situation. Meanwhile, Nox just gave a half-quirked smile in greeting, and I wondered just how many women in Maine had expired from the sexy curve of that mouth. Though I could appreciate it, it didn't invade my body with goose bumps like Jamie's did.

"And the ringleader"—Jamie pointed directly at the female in the center—"is my sister, Trouble."

The hand at my mouth now covered my chuckle as his sister glowered.

She huffed and balled her fists on her hips, tossing instructions over her shoulder for Nox to close the door, before turning to me and introducing herself. "In his old age, Groucho over here sometimes forgets things." A smile and a fighting glint flashed in her eyes. "I'm Francesca Kinkade but just call me Frankie."

There was a tense beat of silence where the siblings' stares warred in the space between us.

"Sorry to just barge in, Jamie," Nox said as he crossed his arms, his eyes making all the right connections about the situation they'd walked into. "But Frankie insisted she needed to head out here to find you because all of Friendship is without power, and we all know you never like to turn on the generator you bought for exactly these situations."

I glanced at Jamie, but my attention quickly returned to Max when he butted in and asked bluntly, "Sorry, I didn't catch your name. Not sure if Jamie thought I might be able to read it off his lips or something—"

"Max," Jamie practically growled in warning, and while I should've been embarrassed, instead I found myself holding back another laugh.

"I'm Violet Royale," I offered, stepping forward and extending a hand with a practiced ease from a life I might never live again.

"It's a pleasure to meet you." He whipped off one glove and shook my hand.

Nox took it a step farther, eyeing Jamie as he took my hand from his brother and brought the backs of my knuckles to his lips —lips that cracked into a smile as they barely touched my skin, more entertained by the way Jamie was staring daggers.

"Hi, Violet." Frankie immediately claimed her introduction. "It's so nice to meet you." She beamed innocently at me.

My mouth opened but before I could reply, Jamie broke in with, "Don't you mean finally meet her in person?" he bit out with an angry, arched eyebrow. "I assume you already talked to her when you told her about my cottage."

Again, I opened my mouth to remind him that it had actually been my assistant whom Frankie would've been communicating with, but one look at Jamie and my lips snapped shut.

"Uh-oh," Nox mumbled, stepping back as though a fight was about to happen.

"Shit, Frankie, what did you do?" Max turned to her and demanded, pointing a finger. "I knew it. I knew we were walking into one of your schemes. I knew something was up when you blew out the door this morning. Didn't even leave time for me to put fuckin' long johns on underneath my snow pants and now my balls are fucking freezing off—"

"Max!" Jamie snapped. His eyes reminding everyone that there was an outsider there—*me*—and talking about balls falling off wasn't appropriate conversation in front of company, even though I didn't mind.

Even though I enjoyed watching their family's interaction too much, as though I were a part of it.

"Sorry, Jamie. But seriously, Frankie, what did you do?"

"I didn't do—"

"She put my cottage up on VRBO without telling me," Jamie informed his cousin with a firm voice. "So, imagine my... *our* surprise when I came home the other night and was greeted by a poker-wielding Violet who thought I was an intruder... *in my own home.*" His voice grew harder with each word, though it seemed his anger was more on my behalf than his. "What a crazy thought to believe she had the place to herself—*that she'd rented it from its actual owner.*"

He put heavy emphasis on actual, and Frankie had the decency to flush.

The room fell so quiet I swore if a single snowflake blew from the roof, I would've been able to hear it land on the piles of snow below.

"Jesus, Frankie," Max groaned and shook his head. "That is balls—"

"Can we please stop saying balls?"

My shoulders shook as I bit into my lip to stop any sound from escaping. I knew Jamie was upset. He had every right to be. But that didn't change how comical their exchange was.

"It's really fine—" I tried to tell him.

"No, it's not," he insisted firmly. Any thought of disagreeing with him vanished under his hot stare.

A red-hot shiver ran up and down my spine like one of those carnival games—the one where you hit the target as hard as you can to try and get the marker all the way up to ding the bell; well, Jamie had swung with all his might and now my need ricocheted up and down my body. He didn't need to stand up for me. He didn't need to do any of this for me. But I knew without a doubt that he was, and I felt desire flood between my thighs.

God, my woodsman was certainly protective.

Even when he wasn't my woodsman. Even when he wasn't my anything...

"It's not fine, and what you did..." He turned on Frankie as his hands sank into his hips.

Meanwhile, Frankie whipped to face Jamie and insisted, "I didn't mean for this—"

Jamie held up a hand that stopped her instantly, and I realized this was a situation the two had encountered before, and judging by the look on Jamie's face, Frankie knew when to step down.

Jamie then sternly informed her, "We'll talk about this later."

Whether it was the tone or the words, it left me curious as to the age difference between them since Jamie almost sounded like a father. And with that thought in mind, I had to guess the difference was significant.

Her head fell, and for all the moments I might have cursed the prank that felt like it changed so much of my life, I felt bad for the woman in front of me as remorse bled into her openhearted eyes.

"Well then," I said with moderate cheerfulness, attempting to break the heavy tension in the air. "It's nice to meet you, too, Frankie. You can call me Vi, if you want."

The younger woman raised her eyes to me and sent me a grateful smile, and I could see behind her very heartfelt remorse still lay the same spark of mischievousness which caused this whole situation in the first place.

Clearly, no matter what Jamie said, it didn't deter her spunk.

She stuck out her hand and, with a smile, I reached out and shook it. What caught me off guard, though, was when she held tight for an extra second and said, "Vi. I like it." Her grin widened. "And I really like your shirt." My gaze darted down to Jamie's flannel as Frankie's attention went to her brother. "It looks almost exactly like one that Ja—"

"Jamie," Max broke in with a laugh, elbowing Frankie as she released my grip and changed the subject. "We passed your snowmobile about a mile back. What happened?"

"Couldn't make it through the storm the other night. So, I packed it up and trekked the rest of the way."

"No shit," he swore. "Well, we got ours here."

"I see that." I felt Jamie's eyes settle longingly on me for a split second before he went on, "Well if you made it, let me change, so I can take Violet into town and somewhere with power."

Frankie snorted. "The whole town is out. I mean, except the few places on generators. But most are holding out now that the storm stopped." Her eyes lit and she smiled. "Mom's generator is on. You could bring her to the house."

The stare down between them was so palpable, it felt as though I could actually see the tug-of-war pulling through the air.

I cleared my throat, deciding that since this conversation was about me that I should have a say. "I'm sure there will be some-place in town I can stay. There's no need to—"

"I'm taking you to my mom's house," Jamie declared before I could finish telling him he didn't need to do that. "This way you can shower and relax, and I can figure out a plan."

My lips thinned tightly as I nodded.

Truthfully, my first choice would be to return to the moment before his sister barged through the door and the kiss that promised everything. But going to his family's home with the possibility of being surrounded by more of... *this...* definitely came in at a close second.

"There won't be room for all your things," he said and came close to me. I couldn't look away from the smoldering intensity in his eyes—*protective, passionate, and a little bit pissed.* "So grab what you need, and I'll come back for the rest later."

Nodding, I slipped by him to follow his instructions.

"Violet."

I half turned as he called my name. "My snow pants are in the bottom drawer. Wear them."

Des Moines, Iowa.

With a quick nod, I darted into the bedroom and shut the

door behind me, hoping I could forget the looks on their faces when hearing Jamie instruct me to put on *more* of his clothes.

What the hell was happening to me up here?

I groaned.

Was this what happened when I relaxed? When the world was too demanding to be worried about work or stress? I got drunk with strangers, asked them to hold me while I slept, and then kissed them?

Okay... not them... him.

I got drunk with him. I wanted him to hold me. I wanted to kiss him.

I froze at the doorway, my essentials stuffed into my tote bag.

I was doing something for myself—that's what this was.

And that was why it was so foreign.

I didn't know whether to be proud or distraught that it had been so long since I'd done something for myself, I almost didn't recognize the notion.

I braced myself and reached for the doorknob.

At some point, I was going back home to face my parents and my vastly different future. No fiancé. No family—not really. If I was going to get comfortable being just a little bit selfish, I might as well start now—*start here.*

Because there was a good chance I wasn't going to find an auburn-haired woodsman with muscles like mountains back home in New York...

And definitely not one I wanted the way I wanted him.

Silence reigned over the group when I came out into the living room. Silence reigned on the short circuit we took to where Jamie's snowmobile was half buried in the snow. But the silence stretched taut with desire as I straddled the snow-traveling bike behind the rock-solid man who maneuvered it, which was the most uncomfortable.

With my arms wrapped around Jamie's middle, clinging tight

as we sailed through the fresh white powder, I took in the scenery as it flew by from underneath the orange-tinted panel on the helmet he'd given me to wear, and tried to ignore how it felt to be pressed so tightly against him.

I'd never been on a snowmobile before, but after the first few minutes, the anxiety was crushed with excitement.

I squealed as it felt like we lifted off the ground, sailing over one mound of snow. When Jamie slowed and turned to check on me, seeing the giant smile on my face, the whole tone of the ride changed. No longer was it just minutes of transportation from one shelter to the next as we began to carve through the snow, speeding up and sailing through it until I was laughing so hard my helmet began to fog and my cheeks began to hurt.

When Jamie slowed down, I peered over his shoulder and saw we were approaching a house from behind. *The Kinkade home.*

Jutting out from the white landscape was a multifaceted yellow-sided farmhouse. The two-storied home sat amid several fields, a few bare trees rising up as lone markers near the corners of the building. The style was definitely colonial, but the unshuttered, large-paned windows suggested it had been modernized relatively recently.

Instead of pulling up to the house, our small train of snowmobiles veered to the right and I turned my cumbersome, helmeted head just as we came to a stop in front of a gray-paneled barn a few yards from the main house, a covered walkway adjoining the two.

I winced as Jamie helped me off the snowmobile. My legs must've been clamping down on the sides of the seat, and I didn't realize.

Seeing my discomfort, he ushered me toward the path. "Let's get you inside and get a bath going."

I would never argue with a warm bath.

His hand was at the small of my back when I felt him pause. "Frankie, we'll talk inside as soon as Violet is settled."

It wasn't a question. And I could feel the fire in Frankie's gaze as she bristled from her brother's command.

"Your mom and Gigi are in the addition getting baskets ready," Max's voice echoed behind us as Jamie steered me toward the house.

Addition. That was why the house looked like two joined together.

Holding my bag to my chest, I murmured my thanks as Jamie opened the door for me, the words trailing off as I entered what had to be the most stylish farmhouse I'd ever seen. If Maine had a home style magazine, this place should've been on the cover.

Light caramel wooden beams and rich iron hardware and fixtures accented the variety of pale-neutral walls. The numerous windows lit the space with a warm light that made you feel like you'd come home. In spite of its size, the house only felt welcoming.

I didn't have too much time to take in the decor as Jamie ushered me up the stairwell, the steps accented with deep-navy paint along the sides. From what I could see, there were countless photos of the Kinkade family—a fact I could ascertain since Jamie's hair stuck out like a flaming-red thumb. There was also original artwork and various antiques decorating so many surfaces.

Being in the hotel business, my eyes were always catching on the decor and then focusing on the details. Even the way each of the beams was unique and almost hand carved, I had to wonder if Jamie was responsible for them.

I caught glimpses of two fireplaces along the trek upstairs. Rich leather couches. Blankets and quilts draped over the back of every seat.

"In here." I turned toward the sound of his voice.

Jamie opened one of the doors in the upstairs hall and revealed a bedroom. *A guest bedroom, I hoped.*

Framed with windows on two sides, the sloped ceiling rising to match the A-frame on the roof, a full, four-poster bed claimed the center of the space with a matching mahogany dresser in the far corner.

"This house is beautiful," I blurted out, spinning in the space.

He paused, caught off guard by the compliment as he realized it was usually customary to give a guest a tour of a house rather than practically dragging them through it without so much as a word.

"Thanks." He dragged a hand through his hair. "I can... ahh... give you the full tour after..."

After my bath.

And after he warned the rest of his family about me.

He shot me a hint of a smile before opening the door next to him.

My gasp was almost as loud as my jaw dropping to the floor as I entered the bathroom to face a huge freestanding pedestal tub set in front of a two-paned window with its white curtains pulled to the sides to provide an unobstructed view of the winter wonderland beyond.

Heaven.

My skin prickled at the thought of a nice, long soak in that tub after the last few days.

"Candles. Towels. Soaps," he spoke gruffly, opening the doors to the antique wood cabinet, revealing a spa-like assortment of goods.

The mention of candles flared my nostrils, and I realized the spiced wood and warm berry scent that pervaded the house had subliminally encouraged my brain to feel at ease in the space, bribing my senses to feel at home.

"And bath bombs," he added, holding up a brightly colored round orb as though it had been left by a UFO. "Never understood the stuff, but my sisters claim it's critical to the calm, so I had to buy boxes of the damn things..." It looked small, perched in the tripod of his fingers as he scrunched his face endearingly and put the wrapped bath accessory back into its spot.

I pulled my lower lip into my mouth again, unsure if I was

stopping a chuckle at his expression or suppressing a sigh at the way he cared about his sisters.

I wondered how many times Jamie Kinkade ran to the store to buy his sisters tampons or ice cream—because the kind of man who would do that was the same who would purchase aromatic and effervescent bath bombs even though he'd rather not know about either.

"Thank you." My cheeks flushed with how husky my voice sounded.

Instantly, his eyes darkened to the stormy depths they'd been earlier when he was about to kiss me.

I still wanted him to kiss me.

More than I wanted this bath.

I pulled my lower lip between my teeth and heard the soft hiss of his breath in response. My bag slid to the floor next to me, but Jamie's eyes never left mine. He hardly knew me, but he looked at me like I was his.

And dammit if that didn't make me squirm with how good it felt.

But when I took a hesitant step toward him, his eyes dropped and he shook his head—*and his desire*—away.

"Take your time," he rasped. "I'll be downstairs when you're done."

"Thank"—the door closed behind him—"you," I finished with a quiet huff and turned back to the tub.

My consolation prize.

For now.

Chapter Eight
Jamie

My feet rooted to the barnwood floor in the kitchen.

"Francesca Olivia Kinkade," I growled at my younger half sister, who'd entered the room. I glared at her, rightfully concerned yet obstinately defiant face.

She was still wearing her snow pants, but her jacket and winter wear had vanished, leaving her Patriots tee tucked into her waistband. She'd pulled her hair up and piled it in a high mess on her head and stood with her feet planted apart and her arms crossed, her expression ready for battle.

"What the *hell* were you thinking?"

My voice wasn't raised. Volume never made a difference in making a point.

Her back straightened and her eyes, the color we'd both inherited from our mother, glinted as I gripped onto the edge of the kitchen counter, fighting not to tear into her for the thoughtless, careless, and downright illegal—

"Look, Jamie," she huffed as her shoulders sagged. "I didn't mean for—"

"Didn't mean? How could you *not mean* to list my property on a home rental site?"

"Okay, well, I did mean to do that," she conceded with a flat tone that had me tipping my head back and staring up at the beams I'd hand carved and finished, wishing I would've added some sort of inscribed pep talk to refer to when dealing with Frankie's antics.

Rubbing my hands over my mouth, I let out an exasperated growl.

"Why the hell would you do something like this? I get that you think I'm too serious. I *get* that you think I work too much. And I know you're just as entertained as Gigi when it comes to matchmaking in this town..." I shook my head. "But this? This is too far. You're twenty-three, Frankie. You can't list my *home* on a website and trick an innocent fucking person into renting it without my knowledge!"

My head dropped with a ragged grunt when I saw her eyes glaze over. I shouldn't have cursed at her, but it wasn't just me her little stunt affected. Whatever Frankie was pissed at me for had nothing to do with Violet, but Violet had become a casualty of her charade.

"I can't believe you," she hollered at me, her lip quivering and full-fledged angry Frankie about to erupt from her chest. "Work too much? Too serious? I think it's a little beyond—"

"Francesca? Jamie? Is that you?" The voice that cut Frankie off was followed by the distinct, commanding steps of our mother coming up the basement steps.

"Christ," I muttered, accusing Frankie with my stare for alerting our mother to our presence.

"I didn't, I swear," she muttered, knowing just as well as I that CI-Ailene was about to get involved.

"It is you two," our mother's voice hummed as she rounded the corner, wiping her hands on the bottom of her berry-stained apron.

Ailene Kinkade was a petite, round woman with large twinkling eyes, perpetually reddened cheeks, and a smile that made you feel like it was Christmas morning every time it beamed—*and she smiled a lot, especially in relation to her children.* Nine times out of ten, if she was home, you were likely to catch her wearing an original Stonebar Farms apron, stained with various fruits and jams, no matter how many times it had been washed over the decades. Her short brown hair was pulled back in a clip and her feet were always clad in fuzzy red slippers inside the house.

"What's all the commotion?" Her hands disappeared into her waist as she looked between the two of us.

I arched an eyebrow at Frankie, waiting for my sister to confess.

When seconds of silence passed, she turned to me without the slightest falter in her smile. "Jamie? Would you care to explain what you two are arguing about in my house?"

I let out a long breath and repeated my accusation. "Francesca listed my cottage on an online home rental site." Our mother's eyes widened and her head slowly turned toward Frankie. "And a woman from New York rented it for two weeks. Needless to say, when I got home the other night, I wasn't planning on a guest, she wasn't planning on an intruder, and *neither of us* was planning on being trapped by the storm with a complete stranger."

"*Francesca!*" Ailene gasped and rounded on Frankie, and I gave my sister the look that said this was her own doing. "Is this true?"

"Yes, it's true, alright?" Frankie bit out. "But it was an unfortunate, fortunate coincidence that it turned out to be a blizzard the night she arrived, and you ended up stuck there, okay? I couldn't have planned *that*."

Our mother raised both of her hands to stop Frankie from continuing and shook her head. "Francesca, why would you do it in the first place?"

My sister's defiance grew harder while her lip wavered in trepidation.

I braced myself for whatever rationalization brewed inside my little sister's active mind. It took her a few moments to find the courage to speak, and when she did, she leveled me with an accusation I didn't expect.

"We were trying to set you up, okay?"

My mouth dropped.

"Set me up?" I choked out. "*We?*" Frankie shifted under the lasers in my stare. "Who else decided my own life wasn't my own?"

She huffed.

"Well, obviously, mostly me. Lou was just there telling me it was a bad idea like she usually does, which is how I knew it would be a good idea," Frankie mused coolly.

I held up a finger, stopping both my sister and my mother from speaking. As the victim of this little plot, I was the one who got to speak first.

"So, the two girls I *raised* decided I didn't know how to run my own life? That's what you're telling me?" I demanded, the question making me wonder what the hell kind of job I had done helping our mother raise them if Frankie thought it was okay to do this.

"To be fair, Jamie, I think the whole town can see you're too concerned about being there for everyone else and not taking any time for yourself."

The fact my sister was so concerned about my love life warmed the older-brother part of my heart, but as the man who took pride in putting my family and our town first and taking care of myself second, I wanted to dunk Frankie's head in the snow outside.

"Who gave you the notion it was acceptable to play with peoples' lives like this?" I asked with a low voice threaded with thinly restrained anger.

"Seriously?" she cracked, folding her arms across her. "You're almost forty, Jamie, and you never go out. You never go on dates. I *never* see you with a woman. I mean, at this point, I'd wager that the last time you got laid was back when that revolutionary-era bed frame in your museum was still in service—"

"*Francesca!*" Our mother scolded, though I caught how she had to cover her mouth to hide the smile that fought to escape.

Great. Even my mother was concerned about my dry spell.

Almost forty... My thirty-six-year-old fingers were tempted to throttle Frankie for that alone.

"You can scold me, Mama, but you know I'm right," she quipped, hazarding a glance at Ailene before raising her hand and returning her attention to me. "He's always working. Always helping me or Lou or this person or that business. And I get that I'm your sister—*your younger sister*—and I shouldn't really be too concerned with your dating life or... anything else... that comes with that, but I am because you're my brother and I love you and I'm worried that you're missing out on life and love."

I couldn't have been more shocked if Frankie had announced she'd gone and gotten married. I couldn't have been more shocked because I'd practically raised the damn troublemaker since she was five. I knew her favorite movie was a tie between *Gone With The Wind* and *Tangled*. I knew her favorite food was anything pickled and that she only liked tuna fish when it came in a macaroni salad. I sat and did her homework with her even though I could see she was too smart to be book smart—counting myself as right when she graduated high school and opened her own candle-making business. I *knew* my family, and I *knew* Frankie.

But this? This I had no fucking clue.

Sometimes, there really was no fucking telling what went on inside a woman's mind.

"Oh my..." our mother breathed out with a firm shake of her head.

Even though I was shocked to my core, I couldn't argue that Frankie was wrong.

I had my family and my work. They were the most important things to me, so yeah, I didn't make a whole lot of time for anything else, and I really had no interest in dating anyone because, after family and work, there wasn't a whole helluva lot left of me to go around.

"So, you... rented my house?" I pinched the bridge of my nose, trying to connect the dots.

"Look, Jamie, you weren't dating on your own. Lou and I tried to get you to meet some of the women she works with at the Squeeze, but you had zero interest—no, make that negative interest. Dating apps were out of the question because, again, that would require cooperation on your part. So, I had to resort to drastic measures."

She shrugged, like all of this was entirely fucking rational.

"Drastic measures?" I hurled at her. "Francesca, my dating life is none of your damn business!"

Her gaze sharpened. "I listed your cottage in the dead of winter because, obviously, you need someone who can handle Maine during the times when White Walkers and north of the Wall look like a tropical vacation compared to our situation."

"But you can't just pick... how do you even know..." My voice died off because I had no idea how those sites worked, but Frankie got the gist of my questions.

"I listed it as needing to contact for availability. So, I was able to screen out anyone who was coming as a couple. And then, for individuals, I just asked them questions and said it was because the cottage was very old and I liked to know a little about the renter and why they were coming..." she prattled on. "And I asked for a license photo to verify identity—and if someone could look good on a driver's license..." She shrugged.

Christ, who the hell raised this girl to be so creative and conniving and curious?

I groaned.

Me. I did.

And CI-Ailene.

Yeah, this shouldn't have come as a surprise at all.

"What exactly did you think was going to happen when I got there and realized there was a stranger in my home?"

Her lips pursed. "I assumed that a city girl wouldn't know how to light a fire or work your stupid stove. And that you, being your usual overbearing and protective self, would be forced to help her and check up on her and generally spend some time with her out of guilt alone for this happening. The snowstorm... that was just pure luck—pure genius on Mother Nature's part."

"My word, Francesca..." our mother muttered under her breath.

For a second, I wasn't sure if I was more shocked at what Frankie had been thinking or that her plans had stunned our mother to silence.

I heard the water begin to drain and knew Violet was done with her bath. The idea of her getting out of the bath, naked, with water sliding over every inch of her—

"And did you think about the other person?" I bit out, forcing my attention back to my sister and what she'd done. "Did you think about Violet at all during this?"

"Of course!" she exclaimed.

"Really? Because I don't think a woman coming up here to escape was looking to do that with some random guy she'd never met."

Frankie pffted me and scoffed, "And why not? I mean, obviously, I was thinking more about you because you are my brother, but you're a good-looking guy. You're kind—except when I hide your tools or move your stuff—and successful and sometimes funny." I rolled my eyes at her edifications that, at any other time, would've made me laugh. "Who wouldn't be interested in a guy like you? I mean, most of the women in town would be if they thought there was ever a chance you'd be interested in any of them."

I groaned, struggling to believe I was having *this* conversation with my sister in front of our mother.

Frankie shrugged in a way that made me tense with foreboding. "Plus, I googled Violet when I realized it was her assistant who was making the reservation, figuring she had to be someone pretty important if she had her own assistant."

I drew up to my full height, letting my arms fall to my sides, sensing what she was about to say before it came out but knowing there was nothing I could do to stop it.

"Aside from her family and business, I saw that she'd been dumped by her fiancé a few months ago, so I figured that you could be like the dashing rebound—"

"*Frankie!*" She jumped as I snapped her name, tired of her reasonings. I almost wanted to shake her. Or beat my own head against the wall...

Of course, she could have no idea of the encyclopedia of disgraceful things Violet's family had done to her, in addition to losing her fiancé. *But that was the point...* Frankie couldn't just go around trying to manipulate people and their lives when she didn't know the whole story...

"Jamie." Both our gazes looked to Ailene as she swiveled to look at me, her head tipping to the side. "Where exactly *is* this Violet?"

Shit.

My mom had come into the kitchen right in the middle of our argument, I hadn't even told her that she was the one now with a houseguest.

I opened my mouth to reply, but a female voice sounded instead from the entry to the kitchen.

"Right here."

All three of us turned. Violet stood in the doorway, wearing black leggings and an oversized sweater, her damp hair braided down over her shoulder. The first thought that crossed my mind was that she was naked because she wasn't wearing my flannel.

And then I wondered just how much of our conversation she'd heard...

CHAPTER NINE
JAMIE

"VIOLET."

Frankie watched me like a hawk as I stepped around the island in the kitchen to usher my guest into the room. The worst part about all of this was I remembered what Frankie had walked in on —*or almost walked in on*—back at the cottage earlier this morning; I knew it would only fuel her misguided imagination that she'd been right to do this all along and that her plan was working.

It didn't matter if it was working.

It didn't matter if I was attracted to the woman tricked into staying at my cottage.

It didn't matter because, in principle, *it was still wrong.*

But I'd have to figure out how to make that point clear and deal with Frankie later.

"Violet, this is my mother, Ailene Kinkade." I glanced at my mother. "Mom, meet Violet Royale."

If she heard anything, Violet didn't let on as she stepped forward and reached out to shake my mother's hand.

Ailene put her hands on her stomach and chuckled before reaching out and pulling Violet in for a hug.

"So nice to meet you, dear." She gave Violet a squeeze. "But we're huggers up in these parts."

Violet's cheeks bloomed with pink and a warm smile spread over her lips. Regardless of how she got here, the one thing I could count on was my family to make her feel welcome.

"Thank you so much for letting me use your bath. After everything that happened, I needed a good soak."

"Of course, of course," my mother tutted as she raised her eyebrow at me.

"The cottage lost power, but even with the generator, I figured it would be easier and more comfortable if I just brought her here," I explained, not having gotten that far in the conversation yet.

"Well, you are certainly welcome to stay as long as you like. I'm sure Jamie's cottage isn't the pinnacle of luxury out there, but there is always a room open here."

"Thank you so—"

"Ailene!" Everyone turned at the loud screech coming up from the basement, and I sent another silent prayer up to the heavens. "Ailene! Where did you go? I'm out of labels!"

Frankie and I groaned at the same time, but our mother's smile stayed constant.

"Up here, Mom!" she called and then turned back to Violet. "Looks like you're getting to meet a whole handful of the family today, I hope you don't mind."

"Of course not—"

Violet was cut off again as Gigi hobbled into the room wearing a bright-green sweater and dark slacks, topped with an apron similar to my mother's, except instead of stains, it was covered with Stonebar Farms labels haphazardly plastered to the fabric.

At almost ninety-two, she was permanently hunched and had a staggered walk. Though the doctors had given her a cane years ago, it became clear pretty quickly that Gigi Ford would never assent to a walking aid, relegating the cane to an extension of her hands. And since her hands were prone to causing mischief, the cane was quickly disposed of.

I'd swear Gigi was where Frankie got her penchant for brazen schemes from.

Her hair was always permed, and for the last three years since Frankie and Lou had convinced her, it was streaked with one color or another. Right now, with Christmas coming, there were vibrant green strands curled among the bright-white ones.

Clear blue eyes squinted as her arthritic and knobbed fingers adjusted the large rhinestone-lined frames on her face.

"You didn't tell me we had company, Ailene," she sassed, walking straight up to Violet and taking one of her hands with one of those warm, old-granny smiles that completely belied how sharp and purposely kooky she was. "Aren't you a lovely fresh face..." She patted Violet's hand. "Since none of these ninnies are going to introduce me, I'm Gigi. It's lovely to meet you."

"Oh, Mom," Ailene huffed and stepped forward. "Of course, I was going to introduce you, but I just found out we had a guest, too."

Gigi's eyes squinted as she followed with, "She looks like she just got out of the shower. How did you not know there was a guest showering in your house?"

"Because I was down in the basement with you—"

"Well, with those damn ears of yours, I'm surprised you didn't hear," Gigi retorted, holding up a hand that was already cupped from old age and half whispering to Violet. "All I wanted was a cookie the other night, and this one heard me searching and sent me back to bed as though I hadn't slaved all day labeling jars and jars..."

Her hand then rose to rest dramatically on her forehead as though the lack of a cookie meant certain death.

I couldn't take my eyes off Violet. If she hadn't known from the simple circumstance of her arrival, usually about thirty seconds in the presence of my mother and grandmother was enough to give any outsider the sense of just how crazy my family was.

My mother rolled her eyes. "Mom... you'd already had two,

and you know what the doctor said about your sugar. Now, let's not trouble Jamie's guest with all that."

I wasn't sure I'd ever seen Gigi's eyes go so wide. I was afraid her eyeballs might fall out of their sockets.

"You're Jamie's girlfriend?"

"Christ," I swore under my breath. And the shit just kept coming.

"My name is Violet," she said decisively, and following my mother's instruction, bent forward and pulled my grandmother in for a hug. Over Violet's shoulder, I caught Gigi's wide eyes and almost maniacally beaming smile.

"It's lovely to meet you, Gigi, however, I'm just a guest, not a girlfriend," she continued smoothly, the pink in her cheeks the only hint of the awkwardness she must have felt.

"She's my guest, Gigi," I repeated, knowing it would take at least twenty repetitions before my grandmother would believe it. "And actually, she's going to be yours for a bit until I can get the power back on at the cottage."

"Oh no," Violet finally broke in. "That's not necessary." She shook her head. "I don't need to intrude. I'm sure I can find a place in town where I can stay for the rest of my trip—"

"Absolutely not—"

"Goodness no—"

"*No,*" I growled with the finality of the decision over the protests of my mother and grandmother.

One Kinkade was overwhelming, but three of them? That was a force of nature Violet smartly decided it was better not to mess with.

"Well, I really appreciate it," she said gratefully.

"Of course, of course," my mother tutted again, wrapping an arm around Violet's shoulders.

"Yes, good." Gigi nodded, her head looking like a green-streaked cotton ball bouncing on a toothpick neck. "As I was saying, Ailene, I'm completely out of labels. I don't know how this keeps happening—"

"Well, Mom, perhaps because you have a good dozen labels stuck to you rather than the jars," Ailene said sweetly as the rest of us fought back a laugh.

In addition to the wild inscriptions she placed on the labels, Gigi also managed to get an inordinate number of them stuck to her, to the dog, Jelly, and to her general surroundings.

Gigi looked down and gasped, "Well, goodness me, how did those ninnies get there?"

Frankie reached up and covered her mouth, trying to hide her snort.

I let out a long sigh and dragged a hand through my hair. I thought I'd been doing the right thing, bringing Violet here because it was warm and had electricity and running water. I hadn't considered that exposing her to my family might not be as relaxing.

"Look, I need to go back and check on the generator and then stop in at my shop and make sure everything is okay," I said, directed mostly at Violet, though all three sets of eagerly eavesdropping ears were tuned in, lost labels completely forgotten. "You're welcome to go back out with me, or you can stay and relax here, or—"

"Ooo, yes," Gigi exclaimed. "She can help us with the labeling!"

"Gigi," I pleaded. "She's on vacation up here—"

"Oh, posh. No one vacations in Maine in the middle of winter. Plus, we women always need to keep ourselves busy."

I groaned.

"Or you can come with me, Violet," Frankie interjected and offered with a chipper voice. My jaw tensed as I dragged a hard gaze to her, wondering what part of her plan this was and what she had in mind.

"I'm heading out to deliver baskets, if you want to come," she continued with a smile and a twinkle in her eye that I really didn't like.

The last thing I wanted was Frankie to make Violet feel like she was obligated to be attracted to me.

"Or you can just stay here and rel—"

"Thank you, everyone," Violet cut in, learning quickly that in order to get a word in for herself around here, she had to just take it. "I think I'll go with you, Frankie, if that's okay."

My eyes narrowed, and I clamped my teeth together to stop the urge to bark orders at a woman I had no business ordering around.

"I'd like to see if I can get a little cell service in town to make a few calls back home and let them know I made it... that I'm still alive." Her eyes slid over to mine with an apologetic smile.

The women in my family chuckled with her. Meanwhile, I stood still save for the tic in my jaw.

"Awesome! You're going to love it!" my devious little sister exclaimed, giving me a side-eye of complete success as she linked her arm with Violet's and pulled her back toward the stairs. "Let's get you all bundled back up!"

"Alright, well, be careful out there, Francesca. Tell the boys, too!" my mother called up after them with a resigned shake of her head as she turned back to me and smiled. "I like her."

"*Mom...*" I warned.

"I just said I liked her, Jamie. That's all."

Gigi harrumphed. "Well, you can be a ninny and not say it, but I refuse." And then, turning to me, informed me with one pointed, crooked finger waving in my face, "I think she's a keeper, Jamie, and that you should marry her."

"*Jesus, Gigi.*" This was what happened when you didn't date or bring a woman home for years. The first one who walked through the door with me was automatically destined to be my wife.

"You know, I had a feeling this storm was bringing something," she went on, completely ignoring my outburst and denial as she scanned down the front of her label-covered apron. "I had a feeling and... aha!"

She chortled and plucked one sticky from the bottom right corner of the fabric and held it out to me.

"There's a jar waiting for it downstairs, but since you're here, I'll let you do the honors."

"Alright, Gigi," my mother said, giving me the "you know your grandmother" look as she tried to corral her back toward the basement entrance.

Unamused, I reached out and took the damn label from the tip of her finger, knowing she wouldn't let it go until I did.

"I'll be back later," I said gruffly.

My mother waved me off as she and my grandmother quickly fell into a conversation about my love life—and lack thereof—as though I wasn't still standing right there.

Only once their voices faded into distant echoes on the steps did I pull out the drawer for the trash can. Gigi gave us labels all the time. Most times, they were nonsense—amusing but uninformative. It was the family joke to save them and try to finagle an explanation for *how* they had come true. Most times, it was a stretch.

My eyes flicked over the label, about to toss it, but then I did a double take. Slowly shutting the trash drawer with my knee, I stared at my grandmother's wiry scrawl underneath the Stonebar Farms logo.

Purple Princess.

I swallowed hard.

Violet Royale.

As I stalked out of the house, my step faltered briefly when I remembered that though Violet had introduced herself, she'd never told Gigi her last name...

CHAPTER TEN
VIOLET

AFTER BUNDLING me up in a mass of her and her mother's winter gear, I trekked behind Frankie out to the barn.

Jamie's snowmobile was already gone, but the rest of the crew was ready and waiting—Santa hats attached to their helmets and sleds hooked up to the backs of the bikes. My steps slowed as I looked between them all, unsure just what exactly I'd agreed to join in on.

"Alright, Max, Nox, you guys are heading up north toward Stonebar," she instructed her cousins, who'd just finished strapping down the last white tarp over the back of their sled.

I wanted to ask what was underneath, but I knew I'd find out sooner or later.

She whipped out two walkie-talkies, handing them each one.

"Alright, Rudolph," she told Max, giving him a red nose as well.

"Seriously, Frank?" He rolled his eyes. "Can't I be like Blitzen or something?"

Her glare shut him up.

"Nox, you're Frosty," he grunted in response.

"Alright." Max huffed, snapping his nose on over his mask. "And let me guess, you're Santa?"

"Of course." She smiled sweetly.

He rolled his eyes. "Ridiculous."

"You're the one who wanted to help this year."

They shook their heads and turned to the loaded bikes.

"Don't forget to pick up Lou and Harper," she reminded them, turning to tell me that Harper was their younger sister.

"Yeah, yeah," Max grumbled back, cranking on his snowmobile.

Frankie just smiled pleasantly as they pulled away from the barn slowly before she motioned to me.

"Let's get sleighing!" she joked, pulling on her Santa hat with a wide smile. "We've got the most ground to cover."

I nodded and followed her lead, climbing onto the snowmobile behind her.

Frankie drove slowly due to the giant wooden cart turned sled we pulled behind us over the peaceful, snowy terrain. It was so beautiful and untouched. The world felt like we were the first people in it for several long minutes before a few houses came into view, and she pulled the bike to a stop.

"I think I'm starting to get the hang of this thing," I commented with a degree of surprise as I hoisted myself off the back of the snowmobile. The bath had done wonders, so this time my muscles weren't screaming.

Frankie grinned at me as she brushed her hair back from where her helmet had stuck it to her face. "You're doing great."

The snow crunched under my boots as I walked around the back and examined our tarp-covered mass.

There were a slew of reasons why I'd opted to go with Frankie toward Friendship, and cell service had only been a minor one.

Catching only the tail end of Jamie's conversation with Frankie and their mother was like being given the end of a string I wanted to tug until everything about Jamie and his family unraveled.

More than that, I wanted to know just a little bit more about Frankie's reclusive older brother...

And the way his mom welcomed me... Well, let's just say my family didn't hug. *Ever.* In fact, if curtsies were still a thing in upper social circles (aside from in an audience with the queen), I was certain they were what Carmella Royale would've required.

But Ailene... she'd pulled me in like I was a longtime friend, and the way they offered a place to stay and to help them work... I chuckled at the memory.

My profession was hospitality. I *knew* what exceptional service meant when it was paid to be provided. But this? My eyes fell. Sadly, it made me wonder if I ever really knew what having a family felt like because nothing and no one had ever made me feel like that.

"You okay, Vi?" Frankie's worried question broke my train of thought.

Realizing I was staring off, lost in thought, I smiled and nodded.

It didn't elude me that she'd called me by my nickname as though we'd been friends forever. Only Leslie called me "Vi." Not my parents. Not my brother.

She sighed and her chin dropped. "Before we get going, I want to apologize to you for what I did," she began. "I wasn't really thinking. I mean, I was. But I was thinking about Jamie and how he's always too busy taking care of everyone else to take care of himself, and when I saw your name on the rental request, I just... I don't know. I wanted him to meet you." She shook her head and repeated, "I'm sorry if it ruined your vacation. I'm sure it wasn't what you planned..."

"No, definitely not," I broke in to admit. "But... it's okay. I'll survive."

For some moments, *specifically those in Jamie's arms,* it was even more than okay, but I wasn't going to admit to that now.

"He likes you."

I balked at her bluntness and covered, "He's... just being polite and extra considerate... given the circumstances."

Her snort of disbelief made my blush deepen before she

turned with a grin and singsonged, "If that's what you want to believe."

"So, what are these again?" I changed the subject as she began to unlace the ropes that tied down the mass of goods on the sled. We'd jumped right into getting ready to leave and zooming off through the snow so I hadn't gotten a chance to ask outright.

"We call them storm baskets, but really it's just more of a tradition than actually necessary," she began.

"When Lou and I were younger, Jamie and our mom needed a way to keep us entertained during the worst of our winter storms. It was right around the time when Santa Claus was still a big thing for us."

She threw back the cover to reveal woven baskets upon baskets filled with goods.

"I don't remember if it was me or Lou who said we wanted to be Santa, but Jamie, probably going crazy trying to entertain two young twin girls—because there were only so many of his nails we could paint—told us we could be Santa if we wanted; Snowstorm Santa."

She laughed at the memory, meanwhile all the parts of me that thought of Jamie in ways I shouldn't, pictured him with his sisters, and then with his children... *our children.*

I suppressed a groan.

Topeka, Kansas. Frankfurt, Kentucky.

"So, we made up these baskets, filled up with jams and snacks and little notes and drawings that Lou and I did, and when the snow stopped, Jamie pulled us behind his snowmobile around Friendship and delivered our little disaster delights," she said with a laugh and held up one of the baskets for me to take. "We were the talk of the town."

I laughed with her as my gaze dropped to the basket's contents. "I can imagine." And I really could... a red-haired woodsman with his two little elves, doling out goods to neighbors trapped by the snow and stuck without power.

"The following year, he built a sled similar to this." She

tapped her foot on the edge of the sled. "A few years after that, he built this bigger one. And then, we started adding special jams and crackers, along with little crafts and games for families with kids. In high school, I started adding my candles into the mix."

My mouth fell open in surprise.

"Wait, you made these candles?" I asked, picking up the one in the basket, reading "Maine Blueberry and Vanilla." Above the scent in block font was the name "The Candle Cabin."

The same name on the mug in Jamie's kitchen.

"These are the same kind that were in the bathroom upstairs," I went on, recalling the evergreen and cinnamon aroma I'd indulged in earlier.

"Yeah." She beamed proudly. "They're all mine."

Next, I pulled out the jar of jam and stared. Stonebar Farms.

"Wait a second..." I blinked in both confusion and recognition.

Stonebar Farms.

I'd heard when Jamie told me his mom and uncle ran a jam and preserve business up here. He might have even said the name, but it wasn't until I saw the logo embossed into the label that it clicked.

His family owned *the* Stonebar Farms.

They were a huge corporation, sold in almost every grocery store in the country, and used at most well-known wineries in their tasting rooms.

"I didn't realize... I didn't realize your family owns Stonebar Farms."

Her eyebrow rose. "Really? I'm surprised Jamie didn't mention it."

My head ducked. "Well, he did, but he didn't. If that makes sense."

"For Jamie? It absolutely does." She chuckled.

I stared another second at the picnic basket of goods, instantly thinking what a good welcome basket this would be for our

Harbor Hotel in Kennebunkport, and then winced when I remembered it wasn't ours.

No, it wasn't mine.

"Everything okay?"

"Yeah." I nodded and slapped a smile back on my face. "Just thinking what a nice idea this is."

Her white teeth flashed as she handed me the basket and picked up a second one.

"We're a small community. It's just a nice way to be able to check on everyone after the storm. Things can get pretty wild up here," she said ruefully. "I'd say this weekend was about a four on a scale of ten as far as Maine blizzards go."

I blinked twice.

Less shocked by the rating than by the desire I felt to experience a ten.

"I liked it," I blurted out as I followed in her footsteps toward the three houses behind us. "The fires burning. Comfort foods. Feeling like there was nothing and no one else in those moments..."

Nothing to do but appreciate the present. No one to answer to... no one to disappoint... no one to disappoint me...

She looked over her shoulder, grinning. "I was hoping you'd say that."

Before I could ask what she meant, two young children—maybe around five or six—tore out from the front door of the first house in full snow gear.

"*Frankie's here! Frankie's here!*" they squealed in delight, plumes of snow bursting up like cold clouds as they tried to run through the drifts.

She turned toward me with laughing eyes. "Duck!"

"Duc—oomph!" My question ended in a grunt of assault as a snowball sailed straight into my stomach and tipped me forward, the impact mostly dulled by the armor of snow gear.

"We surrender!" Frankie yelled as another cold cannonball sailed over her head and landed just to my left.

When I looked up, Frankie was laughing hysterically as the little rug rats latched on to her legs with the biggest, partially toothless smiles on their faces. "I'm here, I'm here." She looked to me. "Johnny and Meg, this is my friend Vi."

"Hi, Vi!" they exclaimed in unison, releasing the younger woman to crowd around me and similarly wrap their arms around my legs.

"Oomph." I began to giggle as I tried not to stumble backward. "Hi there."

The little girl, Meg, looked up and added, "Sorry about the snowball." She grinned. "It was for Fwankie." With her two front teeth missing, I bit back a laugh at how it changed her pronunciation adorably.

"Alright, guys," Frankie drew their attention once again. "I'm running late today, so I don't have time for a snowball fight." There was a chorus of whines. "But I do have *two* baskets to make up for it."

The kids squealed as they each took one as Frankie instructed them to wait until they got inside to open them. As though they'd been given Christmas presents, they barely blubbered their good-byes before they were off again toward the house to open their treats. I followed Frankie's lead and waved to their parents smiling from the front window.

I was barely getting over my amusement and the effusive warmth of this community when Frankie knocked on the next door and was greeted warmly by Eva and Brian Fuller, local farmers who distilled spirits in the winter. Here, we delivered a basket and received a huge bottle of moonshine in return.

Then it was onto Miss Lenore Rito, owner of the local pet store, which was *not* inside her house, though the number of cats milling about her faded floral furniture suggested otherwise. Frankie quickly stressed our need to exit just as Miss Rito was about to introduce me to all fourteen members of her feline family.

With a shared laugh, we were back to the sled and buzzing

down another trek of untrodden snow that only a local would know contained a road underneath it.

An hour later, it felt like we'd traversed over every inch of Maine, including straight down Maine Street in the center of Friendship.

"What's that?" I asked and pointed to a two-story colonial stone house set back from the road. Beautiful decorative iron lamps lined a path that was currently doused in over a foot of snow, and there was a sign hanging from an ornate stone post at the very front of the yard, however it was too covered in snow to be able to read what it said.

Judging by the subtle creep of decayed ivy peeking out from underneath the roof and the overall sense of abandonment, whatever business was housed there hadn't been running for some time.

Frankie looked over her shoulder as she hauled out more baskets. "The Lamplight Inn."

There was a moment of hollow aching in my chest. These were the kinds of places I'd been hunting down over the last year for Royale Hotels, homesteads with history and character that were more than just cookie-cutter lodging. It hurt to see places like this fade away.

With the rise of services like VRBO and Airbnb, I tried to explain to my father the benefits of branching out into smaller B&B-type places, but he wasn't hearing it. Royale Hotels were luxury *resorts* through and through, and he didn't have the perspective to see how that could translate into smaller, more boutique lodgings.

"I take it it's no longer open," I mused.

"Well," she handed me one basket and then another, "rumor has it, it's haunted. I've yet to be able to either confirm or deny that fact."

I chuckled because I was sure she'd spared no effort trying.

"They actually wanted to tear it down a few years ago when the original owners passed away, and their son, who hadn't stepped foot in town since he was eighteen, was going to sell it to some condo developer—one that had no idea where Friendship was or the inn's history."

I sucked in a horrified breath.

"So, we bought it."

I blinked and reared back. "What?"

"My mom and my uncle. They bought it instead. You know, to save it." She tied the sled back up, lifting her stash of baskets and we began the trek down Maine Street in the opposite direction of the inn.

I couldn't stop myself from glancing back at it as we walked.

"But with Stonebar Farms getting busier and having to reconfigure their production line last year, they just haven't had the time to be able to put into restoring it, let alone running the finished product," she went on, sighing as we stopped at the front door of Sweets Street. "They'll get to it eventually."

I smiled, wondering why I still felt unsettled.

"Ginny! Special delivery!" Frankie banged on the door and a few seconds later, a woman with bright-pink hair pulled into two buns on either side of her head opened the door.

"Frankie." The woman I assumed to be Ginny greeted her with a smile and a voice that was nothing short of sugarcoated as she pulled Frankie in for a hug. "I was wondering when you'd get here!" She looked to me. "Is this the one—"

"Ginny, this is Violet. She's staying at Jamie's cottage for the holiday." She tried to be subtle, but I caught her little wink as she spoke.

"How exciting!" Her eyes twinkled, and I had a feeling this wasn't going to be the first or last time I ran into someone today who knew exactly who I was, as well as Frankie's ulterior motive for bringing me here. "Please, come in, come in."

Once again, we were welcomed inside with open arms and friendly chitchat. In this case, plied with delicious chocolate treats and fresh hot chocolate before heading back out into the cold.

After a few stops, I excused myself from the deliveries and

pulled out my frozen cell phone, hanging on to its last leg of battery and dialed Leslie's number. Even in town, the service was *really* spotty—so much so it was probably better that Les didn't answer and the call rang through to her mailbox.

Hoping my message came through clearly, I left her a brief but informative voice mail highlighting several times that I was perfectly fine and she didn't need to worry. Otherwise, next I knew, there would be a SWAT team breaking down the door of Jamie's cottage for no reason.

"You really are like Santa Claus," I exclaimed with a laugh after we'd hit almost every house and business along the most populated two blocks of town.

"Santa Frankie and my sled full of jelly," she joked right back as we climbed onto the snowmobile once again.

"Where to now?" I wondered, not that it made any difference to me.

"My brother's place."

"Jamie's?" My brow scrunched.

She laughed and swiveled her head. "No, my other brother, Kit. Looks like you'll get to meet the whole family today."

"Gotcha." She revved the engine and we pulled out into the snow. "Where does your brother live?" I couldn't help but ask, feeling as though we'd made it all over Maine at this point, with daylight beginning to dim.

I thought I felt her torso shake, but it could've just been from the ride.

Her voice drifted back to me just as she cranked on the accelerator.

"In the lighthouse."

Looming on the edge of the frozen sea, the Friendship Lighthouse stood like an ancient tower out of the crusades rather than a beacon on the colonial coast.

Wisps of ocean-white spray washed away the snow that clung to the edge of the rocky gray crags. As we approached, Frankie slowed the bike considerably, and I realized why when the earth narrowed into a slender natural bridge out to the flickering beacon atop a whitewashed brick pillar. Beneath it sat a matching single-story brick house with beaten blue shutters and dim light pulsing behind the glass. It seemed a small defense against the sea that surged and crashed feet from the doorstep.

When we hopped off the bike, I followed Frankie's exact steps up to the door, which opened when we approached.

"Kit."

Frankie threw her arms around her brother's black-sweatered shoulders. His body tensed but then appeared to remember how to respond as one arm came around and patted her on the back.

While they embraced, I took a quick once-over of the room. It was practically empty, save for the lounger, lamp, and small table, which sat haphazardly shoved close to the fireplace. On the mantel sat a line of Frankie's candles, like soldiers standing at the ready. The wood-paneled walls were littered with nails that no longer held pictures on them. In short, the room was bare—and even that was a generous term.

My attention refocused on its owner—*could one own a light-house?*—as Frankie drew back from his embrace and stepped to the side to introduce me to the black-bearded, whiskey-eyed stranger.

It was the eyes that gave the Kinkades away, I decided. Though the resemblance between the brothers was much greater than that between Jamie and Frankie.

Kit wore a knit cap over his head, and though it was warm inside compared to out in the snow, I had a feeling the house kept a good chill, being so close to the ocean regardless of how many fires were lit.

Aside from the hat and beard, there were noticeable dark streaks on his cheeks and a hint of previous ones on his forehead. Like war paint—if it had been done by a child. Combined with everything, I got the sense this man was in hiding. Hiding his person in the lighthouse perched on the edge of the world. Hiding his face underneath hats and hair. There was nothing clear about him except his eyes—the one thing he needed to see if anyone was getting too close.

"Kit, meet Vi. Vi, this is my other older brother, Kit. He's the more bearded, broodier of the Kinkade boys." She grinned and patted the muscled expanse of her brother's arm.

His eyes scanned over me—not in a possible attraction sort of way, but more in the way the 3D scanner at the airport whips around you, searching for any threats. *That was exactly it.* He looked me over to assess what kind of damage I could do—*what kind of threat I was.*

And when he grunted a low greeting, I caught the glint of the dog tags that moved with the rumble of his chest.

"Nice to meet you." It seemed not everyone in the Kinkade family was a hugger. "And thank you." I tacked on, "For your service."

His eyes narrowed and then ignored me as he switched targets, shifting his attention to his sister. "And how do you know each other?"

Frankie, unfazed by the interrogation, grinned as she pulled the basket from my hands and shoved it against her brother's unflinching chest, replying with a sheepish shrug.

"Well, it's a long story. But basically, Vi rented Jamie's cottage, but with the power going out, she's now staying at the farm."

"Jamie rented his cottage?" His voice was a steady steel line.

Frankie hesitated a split second, her hands in the midst of unpacking the larger basket she'd dumped into his arms.

"Well, I rented his cottage for him."

I snorted. *Man,* this girl was toeing the line of the truth.

"Trouble," Kit grunted, reminding me of how Jamie had introduced Frankie to me.

He dumped the basket in the chair and disappeared into the hall at the back of the room.

"You're welcome!" Frankie shot back even as she continued to unload what looked like at least a dozen candles onto the small table and the mantel.

"Sorry," she apologized. "I used to tease Jamie that Kit was the fun brother. Jamie was the oldest, so he was always more dad and less brother, but Kit?" Even her smile was sad. "Kit was the one who'd suggested riding out on the snowmobiles to deliver these baskets. He was the one who'd let me drive the bike when Jamie wasn't looking. He's not—" She broke off, her voice losing its footing before plowing ahead. "He hasn't been the same since he came back from Iraq."

The ache in her voice was heartbreaking.

"You don't have to apologize," I cut in. "I can't imagine... I just hope I didn't upset him by thanking him—"

"Oh, no." Her head drifted side to side like the sad sway of the ocean. "Truthfully, whenever anyone mentions anything about the war or his service, Kit shuts down." She stared down the dark hall where her brother disappeared. "Almost like the war broke him into two people: the inside and the outside. And the outside is the only one who made it back."

I swallowed over the lump in my throat. The past several years, I'd chosen to work personally with the Wounded Warriors Project, hosting dozens of events at our hotels across the country to help support soldiers who'd returned home injured both physically and mentally. My heart broke for them and their sacrifice, just like it did now for Kit and his.

"Has he talked to anyone?"

Frankie chuckled softly. "He hardly talks to his family." She sighed and pulled out the smaller box inside the basket and opened it. "But things seem to be getting better since he moved out of the house... out here." She pulled out two jars of cherry jam. "Well, I guess I should say things haven't gotten worse."

She strode over to the edge of the room and called out, "Momma made a special batch of your favorite jam!" No response. "I'm going to leave it in the kitchen, along with jars of pickled green beans that Lou made." Again, no response.

"Is he..." I followed her into the equally sparse kitchen.

"He's okay." She sighed. "I mean, he's okay for Kit. His workshop is back there—or I guess it's a studio." Her free hand waved away her confusion. "He paints when he's not manning the lighthouse."

"Oh." That explained the streaks all over his face.

It ended up that there were two more large baskets of supplies that Frankie and I unloaded into the house. Mostly candles and food. I learned that because of where it sat, the lighthouse rarely had stable electricity in the winter and only one fireplace, which explained the larger five-wick candles that Frankie hoisted out and stacked by the door.

Once everything was unloaded, she added another log to the fire and poked it a few good times before lighting the candles, which sat on every other step in the stairwell. She picked up the empty mugs on the floor, opened the door and filled them with snow, then melted it next to the fire before taking them into the kitchen and soaping them clean.

Meanwhile, my eyes drifted to the passage, wondering how long he'd lived like this, and then back to Frankie, who was clearly doing everything she could to help her brother even though he hardly acknowledged her presence.

"Alright. I think that's it," she said mostly to herself before shouting, "We're leaving, Kit!"

A distant echo of a grunt entered the room, which we both took as a goodbye.

This time, it was more moonlight than sun, which reflected off the snowscape in front of us as we climbed onto the snowmobile for the last ride back to the Kinkade farm.

"Does everyone around here call you Trouble?"

Frankie laughed and answered as she revved the engine back to life one last time, "Pretty much—though it's all Jamie's fault."

I didn't wait to see if she would elaborate before asking, "Oh?"

"You know how most people joke that their middle name is Trouble?"

My helmet bumped against hers as I nodded.

"Well, when I was younger, Jamie joked that when Trouble himself went walking around, he—or I guess she, would cause disaster, smirk, and then tell everyone Frankie was her middle name." I could practically hear the way her eyes rolled from her tone as the bike pulled forward.

"Because my level of misbehaving was something for Trouble to aspire to, I guess. And you know how the story goes... Friendship is a small town, so that name stuck like a warm tongue to a frozen ski pole."

Her hand sank heavily on the gas and we took off. My laughter fogged up the inside of my helmet for a good part of the ride back home.

CHAPTER ELEVEN
JAMIE

"WAS YOUR SHOP TOO COLD?"

I turned my attention from the dram of whiskey in my glass to CI-Ailene. Her question wasn't as simple as it seemed. *Not even close.*

When I'd left the farm earlier, I rode toward the old barn on the property, which I'd turned into my woodworking shop when Mom and Uncle George had the new barn built. It had taken four months for me to gut the colonial remnant and completely redesign the interior.

But it was still a barn.

And while I had several gas heaters installed to keep it warm while I worked and a cot to sleep on when I worked late, I couldn't bring myself to stay there, even though it had been my plan.

"I haven't had the heat on for a few days. It would've taken a lot to warm it up now."

Even though Frankie insisted I worked too much, I closed up shop about two weeks or so before Christmas in order to finish up projects and make sure they all were delivered in time for the holiday, usually allowing me a few days of solitude at the cottage before Christmas Eve.

A tradition that Frankie had hijacked.

"And your cottage?"

My eyes narrowed, and I let the silence settle between us. I heard what she asked, but I listened to what she was really saying.

'Are you staying at the house because of Violet?'

"Couldn't get the generator on."

It wasn't exactly a lie. It was just that I hadn't tried. After all the stops I made, by the time I got back out to the cottage, my mind had already spun so many variations of what my mischievous and matchmaking little sister could possibly be saying to the woman I really fucking wanted to kiss again, that the thought of not being here when they got back was too damn much.

"I see." She nodded with a knowing smile.

That was the special bond I shared with my mother. Even though I was her son, I was also the boy who'd helped take care of my younger brother when our father died. And then, when Fuckup Jason came along and subsequently disappeared before the twins were born, I grew out of a boy real quick to raise those girls while my mother worked day and night to keep her jam business afloat.

"Violet seems like a nice girl," she continued, sitting next to me. "She had a great time with Frankie today. Told us all about it tonight at dinner. Oh, and Lou really liked her."

A short laugh escaped me. "I can only imagine."

"Don't be too hard on Frankie. Her heart is in the right place," she said softly as she took a sip of the whiskey.

"Yeah, well, I'm just worried about where her head is..."

I didn't just check on my shop earlier. The snowstorm had put me a few days behind on deliveries. So, even if I hadn't needed to, the distraction of packing up various pieces and trekking them all over Friendship was a welcome task, even if it involved crossing over the tracks made by my sister and Violet.

It had taken all of my restraint not to follow them and see how they were doing – *to see how she was doing.*

"Francesca worries about you. And Kit."

I sighed because I knew it was the truth. *Plus, we all worried about Kit.*

Kit coming home would first and always be a blessing because there were many who hadn't. But it would be a lie to say the man he'd come back as was the man who'd left. The twins took the change the hardest, but Frankie was just the one to show it on the outside while Lou held it in.

"She shouldn't have done this," I insisted. "I don't understand *why* she did this."

I knew what she said. But I'd raised Frankie for all twenty-three years of her life. I knew when she was holding back something.

"She'll tell you. She always does."

I grunted, taking the glass back and pulling down another burning sip. This wasn't the first-time Mom and I had sat in front of the late-burning fire and shared a glass of alcohol together. It was comforting even when it was discomforting.

But that's what family was, a rock when you were in a hard place.

She reached over and patted my knee. "Well, what's done is done, Jamie. We will make it right... We will make it up to Violet the best we can, and that's all we can do right now." She snagged the glass once more and took the last sip. "Unless you think she deserves more..."

Hell yes, I thought she deserved more.

More than her shitty family.

More than her shitty fiancé.

I knew exactly what she deserved. *Loyalty. Devotion. Adoration. Love.* I just couldn't be the one to give it to her. And that was what pissed me off.

The shuffle in the kitchen drew my attention. Once again, the remnants of raising teenagers still flowed through my blood and kept me alert at all times of the night.

"*Gigi,*" I murmured.

We both sighed and shared a quiet laugh.

"Good thing I hid the newest bottle of Fuller moonshine Frankie brought back in the hamper in my room," she whispered back conspiratorially.

It was no secret in the Kinkade house that Gigi woke up in the middle of the night—*or around eleven*—in search of two things. Cookies and a nightcap. And she would always find both, no matter where they were hidden.

So, CI-Ailene had to outsmart her—planting doctor-approved sweets along with watered-down spirits in various spots around the kitchen for Gigi.

I watched my mother's head tip so she could listen carefully. She usually gave my grandmother a few seconds to find what she was looking for before ushering her back to bed.

"Jamie..." Her eye caught mine, and she gave me a small smile. "It's not Gigi."

My brow furrowed.

"Which means I'm not on duty," she said with a grin, raising the empty glass in mock cheers as she rose and wandered back to the wing of the farmhouse where she and my grandmother slept.

"Violet?"

She let out a small cry as she jumped and whipped around to face me, her eyes bulging wide.

"*Holy*—" she gasped as her hand smacked against her chest. A second later, her eyes clamped shut and she began murmuring to herself, "*Baton Rouge, Louisiana.*"

"Did you... did you just use a state capital as a swear word?"

Her eyes met mine once more, realizing the words had escaped from her head and out of her mouth. "Not as a swear word." She took another steadying breath. "Sorry, you just scared me."

Realizing the lights were off and the full moon reflecting on the snow provided only a ghostlike glow in the room, I reached for the light switch, knowing how she hated the dark.

"No!" she exclaimed as her hand clamped down on my arm to stop me. "I'm okay. I don't need..." She trailed off, her cheeks darkening. "There's enough light in here, but thank you."

I held her eyes prisoner for a moment to make sure she was telling the truth before I brought my arm back to my side and took a good look at her.

I didn't know what was worse, seeing her in nothing but my shirt, or seeing her in a set of Frankie's pajamas. As Frankie was taller and leaner, Violet's shorter form with her generous curves stretched tight what should have fit loosely over the swells of her breasts and the arch of her hips.

Fuck.

"Everything okay?" My voice took on a huskier, more strained tone now that she was close to me again. Touching me. *And looking like that.*

I drew blood from my tongue when the timbre of my voice turned her nipples into hard little peaks against the thin cotton shirt.

Violet nodded and crossed her arms which only seemed to put her tits on further display.

Forget working myself to death, Frankie's prank... and surviving Violet was going to be the death of me.

"I just needed a glass of water. I forgot to bring one with me after dinner."

Instinctively, I slid past her and opened one of the cupboards to grab a glass and fill it at the refrigerator.

I didn't do it because she was my guest. I didn't do it because I felt bad for what Frankie had done.

I did it for the way she looked at me when I turned to hand it to her—as though no one ever did simple things for her.

"Why the state capitals?" I asked as her fingers brushed over mine to take the glass.

I heard her small laugh. "When the anxiety attacks started, my doctor recommended finding something unemotional to focus on, to try and keep calm. I couldn't do numbers; they felt like a waste of time. So, I picked the capitals." She took a small drink. "I figured if I was going to repeat something, it might as well be something to learn."

I stared at her for a moment before I found myself laughing. "You really don't know how to relax, do you?"

Her white smile flashed in the shadows as her head gave a sad shake while she laughed with me.

"From what I hear, you don't either."

My laughter died off. "Is that what Frankie told you?"

She gulped. "Something along those lines."

"Well, I wouldn't believe everything she says," I said ruefully, clearly indicating the exact predicament we were in was because Frankie hadn't revealed *everything* to either one of us. "Obviously."

"It's okay, Jamie," she assured me with a softer tone, her eyes drifting down to stare a burning hole through the center of my chest.

"No, it's not," I replied gruffly, tipping her chin back up to me. "This wasn't what you planned—what you came up here for. And I'm sorry for the role my sister played in that."

Her lips parted and my own began to tingle under her gaze. "Don't be sorry," she said thickly, the air between us electrifying and pulling us back to the moment I'd been about to kiss her early this morning. "I'm not sorry."

Her tongue moistened the plump lower swell, and my whole body buckled.

She continued, "It wasn't what I came up here for, but it might be what I need."

I couldn't stop my head from drifting closer to hers, like a ship pulled toward its dock.

I needed to kiss her. I needed to taste her.

"What do you need, Violet?" I rasped.

I thought the day apart would quell the desire from the morning. Even if I couldn't bring myself to leave her alone for the night with my family, I thought I'd gotten past this.

Her breath fluttered against my skin. Her pupils swelled with desire as she swayed toward me and one hand curled into the front of my shirt right near the neckline as though she were about to drag my face down to hers.

The finest barrier of space that existed between us was no more as she stepped between my feet and her body pressed flush to mine. I grunted as the softness of her stomach cradled my aching cock and her generous tits pressed to my front.

My heart hammered like it was claustrophobic, fighting against the impinging walls of my chest.

"Another kiss," she murmured.

Two words. Barely a whisper. But fuck if they didn't rocket through my body like a sonic boom just before my mouth crashed down and claimed hers.

This wasn't the kiss ruled by comfort like the one she'd claimed the other night. This kiss was pure unstoppable need. Like the snowstorm. It didn't care what my thoughts or plans were, it didn't care whether it was right or wrong for blowing through my life, taking away my ability to walk away and my power to keep my rational mind lit. Nothing mattered except its release.

I grabbed the glass from her hand and set it on the counter before cupping her face with both of my hands, tipping her head back and demanding every inch of her sweet mouth. With a moan, she opened underneath me and her tongue speared against my lips, searching for mine.

She tasted like snow. Fresh and crisp. Untouched and begging to be ruined. *And dangerous... so fucking dangerous.*

As I sank deeper into her mouth, I found myself swallowed up by the beautiful force of nature that was her need. And like the storm, desire continued to tear down the rest of my defenses until there was nothing except her.

Her arms twined around my neck, a small moan escaping from her mouth and swallowed by mine.

"*Violet...*" I groaned as my hands trailed down along the soft column of her neck.

I couldn't stop myself. For all my restraint. For all my control. The way she molded her curves against me and stroked her tongue against mine, I couldn't stop myself from indulging in the woman who'd wound up in my cottage.

My dick jolted against the front of my jeans as my palms cupped over the weight of her breasts, the soft flesh spilling from their grasp.

Fuck.

Fucking fuck.

Feral sounds broke from my lips as my hands feasted on her tits, palming and kneading them until she arched and whimpered against me for more.

"So fucking perfect," I rasped, pulling her lower lip between my teeth as my fingers pinched together, trapping the buds of her nipples between them.

Her eyes flicked open, misty and drunk with desire.

"I want you, Jamie."

A growl tore from my chest, and I devoured her mouth once more. I couldn't hear those words. I couldn't hear her want because if I did, I'd end up fucking her in my mom's kitchen with my whole damn family sleeping in the house.

And there were some lines this storm hadn't decimated... yet...

But they came dangerously close as I toyed with her nipples, pulling and rolling the tips between my fingers. She mewled, a deliciously vulnerable sound, as I sucked on her tongue like I wished I could do to her tits. I wondered if they tasted like fucking lavender and vanilla, too.

"I was jealous of my shirt," I growled to inform her. "Jealous it got to touch and rub against these beautiful tits for days now."

She gasped and arched herself harder against my palms in response. But it was when her hips began to rub and roll against mine that I saw stars. I could feel the heat of her pussy as she pressed against the length of my cock, desperate for the same release I was.

With a growl, I tugged on her nipple before releasing it to clamp my hand on her waist and hold her back from me before I came like a fucking teenager in my jeans.

"I shouldn't," I rasped against her lips, sucking in a breath where I could to try and refuel my sanity.

Meanwhile, my fingers realized they were poised on the island of skin between the fabric of her shirt and pants, and they stroked and rubbed over the spot as though it held buried treasure.

I watched as heat flooded her cheeks, but instead of pulling back, she murmured, "But what if I want you to?"

"You're so fucking perfect, Violet." I loved the way her body arched and shuddered with the compliment. "Just the thought of touching you is driving me insane."

Her moan made my hips jolt as my angry arousal dug into my jeans. *God, this woman deserved to be adored.*

Why the fuck couldn't she live here?

Why the fuck couldn't she be mine?

As though sensing my torture, her warm fingers closed firmly around my wrist as I began to pull away.

"So then touch me," she said breathlessly, pushing the very tips of my fingers underneath the waist of her pajama bottoms.

My long groan sounded as though I'd been run through with a sword rather than been given the green light to take what my body wanted. Even there, I could feel the heat of her.

I slid my other hand up to spear my fingers through the silk of her hair, holding tight as I pulled back to bare her neck to me.

"*Fuck.*" My other hand dove lower beneath the layers of clothes, searching for her hot center.

Violet's hands gripped my shoulders as her knees weakened when my fingers found her core, hot and soaked with desire.

"*Jesus, Violet,*" I swore and squeezed my eyes shut, trying to block out the merciless desire that ravaged my own body, feeling how she wanted me. "You're so wet, beautiful."

She cried out as my fingers found her clit and began to pull and tease the swollen, sensitive nub. *God, she was so sensitive... so responsive.* With every brush, she shuddered against me and warm desire slicked my fingers even further.

I wanted to savor her.

I wanted to touch and tease her until she was crying with pleasure, and then I wanted to taste her until she came all over my tongue.

I wanted to bury my aching cock inside her until my name was the only thing she knew how to scream. *And I wanted to do it every fucking day.*

But I couldn't have what I wanted. I couldn't even come close.

But I could have this stolen moment. In Mom's kitchen. With the woman who'd invaded my wooded sanctuary.

And I would take it.

I pushed away every other sense except how her body came to life under my touch.

My lips latched on to her neck as I found her entrance and sank my middle finger deep inside her slick cunt, feeling the way her inner muscles clamped around me. I pressed against her front wall, right behind where my thumb began to work over her clit, hitting both of her sweet spots at the same time.

She gasped so quickly she choked on the breath. Instantly, her body began to convulse against mine, her strength seeping from her limbs and funneling her body toward release.

I shifted my arm to support her back as my mouth covered hers, capturing the moans that grew greater in both frequency and volume.

I felt her sag harder against me, relying on me for every support as my fingers worked over her needy pussy.

"You feel so good, Violet," I rasped. "So damn good, beautiful. I wish it was my cock inside you, so I could feel you come all over me."

I barely got the words out—the only release I could give my own need—before I swallowed her cry as she came. Her pussy gripping my finger as her climax gushed down my finger and into my palm.

For minutes, we both stayed unmoving, only allowing our lips to break apart so we could gasp for the same space of air between us.

Slowly, I slid my finger from her body and righted where her underwear had been shoved to the side. Resting my hands on her hips, I dropped my forehead to hers and groaned.

"Violet—" I didn't even know where to start. I wanted to curse. I wanted to apologize. And then I wanted to tell her I wasn't sorry at all and do it all over again. But she didn't let me.

"Good thing that wasn't on the listing," she cut me off breathlessly, her lips delectably swollen and her face warm and flushed against the cool midnight moonlight.

I arched an eyebrow.

"If mind-blowing orgasms had been advertised along with handsome woodsman, fire stoker, and personal chef, I'm pretty sure I would've tried to buy your cottage rather than just rent it," she murmured with a throaty laugh.

A smile tugged at my lips, but only a groan escaped.

I couldn't laugh when she joked about buying because buying meant staying, and staying meant she could be mine.

And it only took another second before I saw how that same thought waded through the fogginess of her release, and she dropped her gaze from mine.

With a low growl, I released her and turned to face the island, grabbing her glass of water and offering it to her once more, saying, "You should get to bed. You've had a long day." I caught her eyes as they flicked down to where the front of my jeans was stretched. "And there's more time to be spent with my family tomorrow, so you'll need your rest."

Her tongue darted out over her lips, and my balls tightened painfully. "But you—"

"Are sleeping down here," I informed her with a tight smile. I'd deal with my raging arousal on my own. "Good night, Violet."

Dragging a hand through my hair, I walked out of the kitchen and away from temptation herself, hearing only the warm and wanting thread of her voice as it followed me toward the lonely living room, wishing me a good night in return.

Chapter Twelve
Violet

"You must have slept like a baby after all that excitement yesterday."

I choked on the cracker and jam I'd just been handed to taste, barely getting a napkin in front of my mouth before I spit blueberry all over everyone.

Gigi blinked at me, her eyes comically large underneath her round, thick-lensed glasses.

"Are you alright, dear?"

I nodded even as I felt my face turning bright red. I'd drifted off in thought for the umpteenth time that morning as soon as Ailene mentioned that the Maine blueberry jam I was tasting was Jamie's favorite.

Naturally, at the mention of the gorgeous man who'd had his tongue down my throat and his hand down my pants last night, I slipped quickly back to the memory of being in his arms. Which is why, when Gigi remarked I must've slept like a baby, my first frightening thought was that she'd heard us—or worse, seen us.

My vision dimmed and the air tasted heavy.

Augusta, Maine. One breath. Annapolis, Maryland. Two breaths.

"I'm sorry," I said in a strained voice. "That was really delicious, by the way. So delicious, I missed what you said, Gigi…"

She smiled at me with a smile that bordered on too innocent to be innocent. "I said you must've slept like a baby after the excitement of the day yesterday."

"I think we all did, Gigi," Frankie jumped in and replied with a smirk.

It was a gathering of the Kinkade women down in the basement of the farmhouse as we set to wrapping and labeling several dozen jars of jam.

I'd woken up to the smell of a full country breakfast coming from downstairs, though the way my mouth watered when I walked into the kitchen in the morning light had nothing to do with the food.

Ailene and Lou, who was Frankie's *identical* twin sister, worked like an assembly line at the stove, turning out eggs, bacon, hash browns, and toast, complete with a selection of no less than seven Stonebar jams and jellies. Gigi set the table, humming as she went, and Frankie doled out generous mugs of coffee. When she caught my searching stare, she'd declared that Jamie had gone out with their cousins into town to help some of the businesses that'd gotten power back but had some damage from the storm.

I wasn't sure if I was more relieved or saddened, I did know we needed to talk about what happened last night.

Having a fling was definitely *not* on the short list—or even the long list—of ways I'd thought to relax and recover on this vacation. Until last night. And now, it seemed to be the only thing on the list.

"More labels, Elouise," Gigi said, attempting to snap her bent fingers.

Lou was definitely the yin to her twin's yang. Her quiet shyness and kind smiles transformed her appearance into the astute observer, making it impossible to confuse the two though biologically they were identical.

I cleared my throat to disguise a chuckle. For every label Gigi placed on a jar, another one was scribbled on and stuck on a beam for *"later."* I felt her eyes shift to me, so I kept my gaze trained on my task: hand tying the twine around the slip of checkered fabric that covered the lid.

"So, who wants to take bets on how long Jamie is going to stay mad at me?" Frankie mused with a sigh. She, Lou, and Ailene scooped out raspberry, strawberry, and blueberry jams, respectively, into empty jars and capped them for Gigi to label and me to cover.

"Oh, Frankie, you know he'll be fine soon," her mother hushed.

"I told you it wasn't a good idea," Lou murmured.

Frankie rolled her eyes. "You tell me all my ideas are bad ideas, Lou. I've learned to not listen to you if I ever have a hope of having some fun."

Lou didn't respond.

"Well, he's got six more days because he better be over it by Christmas." Frankie tried to hold on to the playful bite in her tone, but it was easy to hear how forced it was over the very real fear that her brother was going to be mad at her for the holiday.

My eyes fell to my fingers as they fumbled with the tie I was working on, the fabric and twine fluttering off the jar lid completely and the sudden urge to cry throwing me completely off guard.

Frankie was so worried about Jamie being upset with her for the holiday, meanwhile, my family hadn't even bothered with more than a phone call and an email while I was in the hospital. Forget wondering about Christmas together. I couldn't even remember if we'd ever had a Christmas as a family. The holidays were one of our—*their* busiest seasons and time was spent at one hotel and one event after another.

"You're staying up here over the holiday then, Violet?" Ailene asked me, but when I looked up, she wasn't watching me at all. Yet, it felt like she *saw* me—and the emptiness I'd come up here with.

"That was my plan, yes," I confirmed as nonchalantly as I could.

"So, you don't celebrate Christmas with your family?" Lou asked, her eyes wide, making her appear much younger than twenty-three.

I worked up a brave smile before focusing my attention on tying my bow on the jar as I replied, "No, not really. I mean, we celebrate Christmas but not so much together. My family..." I swallowed hard, realizing I didn't know how to explain them or how they were because, up here, around this family, I found myself having a hard time understanding it. "They aren't like that," I finished lamely.

"You don't celebrate Christmas with your family?" Frankie blurted out. "That's like celebrating Christmas without Santa Claus."

"Frankie..." Ailene chided.

I knew she wasn't trying to be insensitive. In fact, I'd been that same person—living in the bubble of "how could my father *not* ask me to take over the business on his retirement when I've worked so hard and done so much?"

But sometimes the bubble pops and you learn that not everyone acts the way they should—or the way you think they should.

My small laugh turned into a sigh as I found myself starting to agree with her. "I didn't say it was what I wanted... it's just how they are. How we were raised."

"Well," Ailene interjected with the tone of a judge making the final ruling on a case. "I'm assuming Friendship will be back up and running by the end of the day, so I don't know what that means for you, Violet, but we'd love it if you wanted to spend Christmas with our family."

Thank God, I was done with the damn bow and had just tucked the jar alongside its siblings in the case, otherwise I would've dropped the whole thing on the floor and really turned into a blubbering mess.

"Thank you," I replied, blinking rapidly to pull back the tears that threatened to fall.

What did I do to deserve this?

"I'll think about it," I added a moment later, knowing there was really only one person whose opinion mattered, whether I'd be welcome at such an intimate family gathering—and he wasn't in the room.

I jumped as there was a slap to the center of my chest, and I looked down to see a Stonebar label crookedly attached to my sternum.

Home.

My brow furrowed, and I opened my mouth to ask what it meant when Frankie gripped my upper arm and said, "Gigi likes to give out little notes while she works."

"They aren't *notes,* Francesca." Gigi scoffed. "They are *fortunes.*"

Frankie's lips pursed as she met my intrigued stare with her laughing one. "Yes, yes. Sometimes, Gigi's little fruity fortunes only make sense in the future."

Gigi tsked. "You laugh, but there's a reason everyone wants one of my labeled jars."

The way Frankie shrugged said she couldn't exactly deny that fact. Meanwhile, I wondered what kind of fortune "*home*" was.

Was I supposed to go home?

Was it a hint that I was unwelcome?

Pain bloomed in my chest at that thought as I pressed the label firmly to my chest, trying to disperse the hurt and went back to work. Meanwhile, Gigi continued to bop along to her internal beat as she scrawled out labels with an eccentric flourish.

"Francesca," she drawled, bestowing the wild twin with her own label.

Frankie took a quick glance at the singular word before eyeing her grandmother.

"So how come I keep getting the same fortune then, Gigi?" she pressed, holding up the label for me to see. "This is the fourth or fifth time you've given me *"chandler"* and I started my candle business years ago, so if that's the case, you're late on that account. The only other option is a name, but there is no one in Friendship named Chandler."

"I don't get to pick the word," Gigi scolded. "I only write it."

I met Frankie's gaze again and grinned, finding myself sinking deeper and deeper into just how special their family was. Between Santa Frankie and fruit fortunes, I told myself anyone in my shoes would be wishing they were a part of the Kinkade crew right about now.

"Well, you let the jelly god, or whoever picks the words, know that I'm requesting a new one," she sassed.

Gigi paused and pretended to think for a moment before she retorted, "The god of jelly says *'frankly, Frankie, I don't give a jam.'*"

There was that classic, split-second pause before all of us doubled over with laughter, Gigi clapping gleefully at her clever *Gone with the Wind* pun.

"Keep this fun in mind when you decide about Christmas." Ailene chuckled with a smile and an expression that told me this was a common occurrence around here.

Laughter. Love.

Even while they worked.

The stark difference to my own life wasn't lost on me—not for a single, belly-clenching, side-stitching moment.

"Plus, Jamie will want you here," Frankie singsonged with a gleeful nonchalance as though she'd heard my earlier thought. "No matter what he says."

I flushed and repeated, "I'll think about it," adding, "but I will have to ask him."

It was his family, after all.

Gigi chimed in with a gleeful shrug. "Men don't know what they want. Even if it breaks into their house and stands naked in the middle of their living room."

I began to choke on my breath just as she continued, "Which

is what I had to do to your grandfather to get him to notice me. Damn man was as stubborn as a mule." And with a wicked glint in her eye began to add, "But he was hu—"

"*Gigi!*" Both twins exclaimed in unison, their horrified looks swiftly bursting into laughter that sucked the rest of us in like a tornado until I was crying happy tears.

Our efficient accomplishments over the last few hours quickly deteriorated into a fit of laughter, inappropriate jokes, and sampling far too much of the jam we were supposed to be bottling.

At some point, meats and cheeses appeared in the center of the giant worktable in the basement, and paired with the jam, it was a charcuterie board to rival the ones served in our finest hotels. As we nibbled and chatted, trying to find our rhythm again, I completely lost track of time—of everything, really, until I heard my name bellowed.

"Violet!"

Ailene chuckled, "She's down here with us, Jamie!"

Moments later, the heavy thuds of his footsteps beat into the stairs. The steps slowed almost to a halt when his flame-topped, fierce eyes locked with mine, first marking me safe and sound in his mind before they deepened, recalling the previous night.

Vivid memories and vibrant sensations caused heat to erupt throughout my body, and I sucked in a small breath, quickly checking to make sure no one—especially Gigi—noticed.

"I told you not to ask her to work; it's her vacation," he growled.

"I offered to help," I broke in, wiping my hands on my apron and folding my arms. "Don't worry. They did as they were told and gave me a whole list of all the relaxing activities the Kinkade Retreat has to offer."

"And you chose to bottle jam?" he gaped.

I swallowed my laugh, though the rest of our company didn't. "What can I say? I chose to come to Maine in the middle of winter for vacation, too." I shrugged. "I'm weird."

"I think she fits right in," Frankie chimed from behind me as Jamie sent her a hard glare.

"What's going on in town?" Ailene set down the jar in her hand and instead spooned a heaping portion of blueberry jam onto one of the few remaining toasts and handed it to her eldest son.

He grunted and ate the snack in one bite.

"He gets hangry," Frankie informed me in a whisper.

"Power's back on. Max and I fixed the porch at The Maine Squeeze; the roof collapsed under the weight of the snow."

"Oh no," Lou said.

"It'll be fine," he assured her and then turned his attention to me. "The power is back on at the cottage, too."

I swallowed over the lump in my throat. "Oh."

The cottage.

Where he was going to take me back and leave me. Alone.

It hit me suddenly that the very thing I'd chosen this particular location for was the very last thing I wanted.

"So, it's okay to go back?" I asked dumbly, trying to disguise how saddened I was by the prospect.

"Well, you can't take her back right now, Jamie Kinkade," Ailene scolded and handed him another cracker as though bribing his firm sense of duty to chill out for a few minutes.

"Why—"

"Dinner, you ninny!" Gigi exclaimed and tossed a cracker at his head.

"*Christ!*" He ducked but not before the carb cannon bounced off his damp curls and onto the floor. "Gigi, what the—"

"You can take her after dinner, Jamie," Ailene interjected, sending her mother a scolding glance. When he looked uncertain, she added more quietly, "It's the least we can do."

His lips thinned into a line of disgruntled acceptance, and I couldn't tell whether it was because he didn't want me here or he was afraid I didn't want to be here.

"Next time, I'll throw the whole jar," Gigi threatened as she hobbled by him, flipping her head, the green and white cotton candy mass of her hair unmoving. At almost ninety-two, you better believe there was a whole can of hairspray holding that perm to perm-fection.

I had to bite into my cheek to stop from laughing as Jamie looked thoroughly put in his place.

As we began to file up the stairwell, I felt a soft touch on my arm and Lou's cozy smile greeted me when I looked to my right.

"It'd be nice if you were here for Christmas," she said softly. "I've never seen my brother look at someone the way he looks at you."

"And how's that?" I said, my voice thick with uncertainty and hope.

"Like you're too good to be true."

CHAPTER THIRTEEN
VIOLET

I'D NEVER LAUGHED at the dinner table.

I'd never made inappropriate jokes at the dinner table.

And I'd certainly never thrown bits of food at a family member when they were about to say something embarrassing.

But these were all things I'd either done or seen done tonight, and I felt like Aladdin walking into the Cave of Wonders.

For the entire ride back to Jamie's cottage, which was doused in silence underneath the starlit sky, I flipped through my memories like I had them on a Rolodex but had yet to come across a time when I'd enjoyed dinner so much—not because of the food, though that was excellent, too, but because of the people.

Dinner had always been about etiquette in the Royale household—and the pun in that statement wasn't lost on me and neither was it inappropriate.

No one rested their elbows on the table like Gigi did. There was never the tossing of dinner rolls between guests like there was between Frankie and Nox. And there were *definitely* no inappropriate discussions like how many new members of Friendship would make their appearance nine months from now, and who their parents would be.

Of course, there was normal conversation, too—but normal

for them didn't feel *normal* to me when it felt like I was welcomed into this secret little club, the kind all the cool kids would want to be a part of in high school. The kind people would extort, bribe, trick, or threaten to be a part of.

I might consider doing all those things... if only I weren't an outsider.

If only I weren't leaving.

The snowmobile rumbled through the last bit of woods, over the small hill, and down into the hidden glen where the familiar building sat. The lights in the windows and the lamppost outside glowed like they had the first night I arrived, only now it felt different.

That night I felt relieved when I arrived at my refuge.

Tonight, it felt like coming home.

"Thank you," I murmured as Jamie swung off the bike and helped me up.

The snow, which melted some during the day and had now frozen in the frigid night temperatures, made my feet slip as I stood, sliding me the handful of inches it took to bring me up against his body.

The impact was hardly measurable; still, the air whooshed from my lungs like it had stolen my breath.

I felt his hands on the side of the helmet he'd had me wear, pulling it off me.

His red hair was dark and damp from the ride, strands sticking together like glazed embers. His eyes locked with mine, the look in them the same one I'd caught on and off all evening, only this time, it was unguarded.

This time, the desire in his eyes was free.

Just as my lips parted, he spoke, "Sorry it took so long."

I barely swallowed my small whimper as he kept me steady with one hand and stepped away.

"Please, stop apologizing," I said, my frustration getting the better of me. "I enjoyed my time with your family... at your family's house..."

I wasn't trying to allude to what had happened in the kitchen last night, but that's all it sounded like.

His jaw ticced. "I lit the fires earlier so it should be nice and warm in there for you. I'll be back in the morning to keep them going."

This time, I couldn't stop my jaw from dropping. "Wait... you're not staying?"

I didn't know what I felt dumber about, assuming he'd be staying at the cottage because it was his home, or asking him about it.

His head jerked in response.

"But it's your house," I insisted. "Where are you going to sleep?"

Stop being nosy, Vi. It's none of your business.

"I have a loft in my shop where I usually stay."

"You usually sleep where you work?" I winced as soon as the question left my lips because the truth was, I did, too.

I'd lived out of Royale Hotels all my life. A hotel had never been a home away from home because a hotel had always been my home.

"It's really not a big deal, Violet," he told me. "You rented my cottage for yourself; the least I can do is hold up the end of the bargain my sister made." He stepped around me, about to get back on the snowmobile, and murmured, "Good night."

"That's it?" I blurted out, spinning on my heel and almost losing my balance again.

"Is there something else you need?" His brow furrowed. "The water and electricity are back on. I put fresh towels in the bath and—"

"What about last night?"

The pools of his eyes deepened to bottomless.

The longer he stared, the more my anxiety rose, spreading like a wintery frost over my cells, and for the first time that night, though I'd been out in the freezing temperature for almost half an hour, I felt cold.

"Last night shouldn't have happened," he said with a low, definitive voice, and each word felt like it stripped me bare. "I shouldn't have... you're a guest here... it's not respectful..."

Augusta, Maine...

I gasped as even my trick to ward off my stifling anxiety backfired into a sharp, slicing pain in my chest.

Looked like I was going to have to switch to names of prior presidents from now on. Either that, or the US was officially going to have only forty-nine states in my mind...

I wasn't sure I even heard all of what he said. It was hard to focus on anything except how it felt like I was standing butt naked in the middle of a snowstorm—it was hard to focus on anything except not letting my heart freeze to death.

"Please, stop," I heard myself say, swallowing over the snow-ball-sized lump in my throat.

"*Shit.*" I heard him curse, the word sounded much rawer in the dry stillness and frozen landscape of our surroundings. "I didn't mean—"

Annapolis, Maryland. Boston, Massachusetts.

"It's fine," I said with a nod, too afraid to hear what else he was going to say. "I'm going to go inside now."

Turning toward the cottage, I could feel his frustration pulsing with each of the few steps I took to the front door, stalking me like a wolf through the snow.

His low growl only added to the sensation of his boots crunching behind me.

"Vi—" He broke off as I opened the door and swung around to face him, determined to stand tall, even if the few inches that separated us still made my knees weak in spite of how I rationally knew I'd just been turned down.

Once again... Violet Royale... The queen of Not. Quite. Enough.

Even though a part of me whispered that he was doing no less than what I expected from the Jamie Kinkade I'd come to know over the past three days—the one so bound by duty and misguided chivalry that he'd sooner strangle himself with the ties than let them slacken—it didn't dull the sharp sting of rejection.

"Good night, Mr. Kinkade," I cut him off, fishing for my hospitality mask that had hidden far more perturbation than this before. *Far more... definitely...* "Thank you for your help."

In life, there was only one thing more satisfying than making your point by slamming a door in a man's face.

And that was the rare opportunity to slam his own door in his face.

I sniffed and my brow furrowed.

I sniffed twice more before my eyes shot open.

Bacon.

There was no mistaking the scent of bacon—*ever.* And since I was currently still lying in bed in the same exact spot I'd collapsed into it last night, ignoring the tears that leaked out of the corners of my eyes, I knew I hadn't cooked bacon in my sleep.

Jamie...

The heat that rushed through my body was quickly doused by the fresh reminder of his rejection last night.

With a groan, I tossed off the covers, ignoring the fact I'd chosen to sleep in his flannel shirt. I mean, at this point, it was basically mine.

Dragging on my sweatpants, not wanting to seem more desperate than I had been by walking out to greet him half-naked *again,* I stalked out of the bedroom door, only to come to a fast halt when it wasn't Jamie I found in the kitchen but Frankie.

"Morning, Vi," she shot me a quirked grin. "How'd you sleep?"

"Fine..." I said slowly as I approached her to check out the breakfast spread she'd laid out.

"Hope you don't mind I'm making you breakfast," she went on with a light tone, turning the spitting bacon in the pan. "Jamie showed up at the house at butt crack o'clock this morning and asked, in his not-so-asking way, that I bring you breakfast." She broke off and chuckled, "What'd you do to him?"

My eyes widened. "Excuse me?"

She slid me a conspiring glance before dumping the thick strips of bacon onto a plate that already contained what appeared to be a vegetable omelet.

"He looked like he'd spent the night sleeping outside in the doghouse." She laughed and handed me my plate before crossing her arms and resting her hips on the edge of the stove. "Which is a look I don't think I've ever seen on my always-do-the-right-thing brother... a look like he'd done something wrong."

I flushed and my eyes dropped to my plate. "Nothing." I shrugged nonchalantly. "He brought me home last night... and that was it."

She hummed. "Well, whatever it was, I'm just glad *I* wasn't the one in the doghouse this morning."

"Is he still mad at you?"

The laughter in her eyes dulled a bit.

"I don't think so." She shifted her weight and sighed. "I mean, he's still displeased—which was why I was tasked to bring you breakfast even though Lou is definitely the better cook—*but not by much*," she clarified. "Anyway, of course, I was planning on stopping by here on my way into town to check on you, so it worked out."

I gave her a grateful smile, digging a fork into the omelet and then quickly checking, "Are you eating?"

"Already ate." She nodded for me to go ahead. "Just going to wait for the coffee to finish up here. Don't know why Jamie insists on this ancient contraption, but don't worry, I worked part-time at The Maine Squeeze for two years." She winked at me. "Just wait until you taste what I can do with a cup of the famous Ocean Roasters brew."

While I ate, Frankie cheerfully talked on about how much they'd enjoyed having me for dinner last night and that she hoped

Jamie didn't scare me away from spending Christmas with them. I kept my head nodding every few seconds just so she would move on.

"Anyway, I've got to get to my cabin. I'm *so* behind on Christmas candles it's not even funny," she finished as she set a piping hot mug of coffee on the table.

There was only one thing in the world more appetizing than the smell of bacon—*and that was fresh, strong coffee.*

"What is the age difference?" I blurted out, the question lurking in the back of my mind for days now. "Between you and your brothers."

I said brothers, but she knew I meant Jamie.

"Well, Jamie's thirteen years older than Lou and me. And Kit is seven."

My eyes widened a bit. "My brother and I are only two years apart, but he's younger," I offered; I wasn't sure why.

"Well," she went on, tying her hair back up into a ponytail, "Jamie and Kit are our half brothers, so that's why they're basically old men."

My eyes shot up to hers. I hadn't realized they weren't full siblings.

"But you have the same last name?"

She blinked as understanding—or my lack of it—dawned on her. "Well, Jamie and Kit's father passed away not long after Kit was born. So, Jamie helped our mom with Kit—*even at that age*—while she really brought Stonebar Farms to life."

My stomach turned. Of course, I assumed something had happened to his father when the only man he mentioned in his life was his uncle, but I didn't realize it had happened so long ago.

"Stonebar wasn't even close to what it is now, but it was still worth a lot when our mom met my and Lou's dad." I noticed the slight edge that sharpened in her voice. "She held off marrying him because of my brothers—Jamie and he didn't get along at all, and it worried her. But when she got pregnant with us, she decided to finally say yes."

I held my breath, my lips poised at the edge of my mug, but unable to take a sip knowing the other shoe was about to drop.

"Until he-who-shall-not-be-named realized there would be a prenup agreement and that every piece of Stonebar Farms would be hers until her death, at which point it would go to her kids. So, he left."

The mug landed on the table with a thud that echoed the way my jaw dropped.

"He left?"

"Yeah. What a dick, right?" she scoffed and reached for my shoulder, giving it a squeeze. "Don't worry about it, Vi. We never met the man, so I'm not sorry for it."

She made a good point.

"Plus, we had Jamie and my uncle George to fill the void. Which, in retrospect, sometimes feels overfilled with Jamie's over-protectiveness, but I'll keep him," she teased. "For now."

I laughed and stood as she donned her snow gear and made her way to the door.

"But wait, how did you end up with the Kinkade last name?"

Frankie turned on the front stoop, the snow crunching under her boots. "Oh, right." She flipped the visor of her helmet up. "We had our biological father's name until Lou and I turned eighteen. But family means something up in this neck of the woods and that man was never family. But Jamie... he'd been a brother and filled the role of father without being asked."

I felt my throat thicken with emotion and I pretended like the shiver that swung up my spine came from the cold

"So, for our birthday, we went over to the courthouse in Augusta and legally changed our names. For our mother. For Jamie. And for us." She beamed at me and finished with, "We're obviously far too crazy to be anything but Kinkades."

❄

I finished my coffee in a strange state of happy sadness. I wanted to cry for what had happened to Ailene—to their family and to the boy who'd quickly stepped into the role of a man. But I also felt nothing but happiness because I couldn't imagine their family any other way.

No wonder Jamie always did the responsible thing.

He'd never had the opportunity not to.

Not that it was irresponsible to pursue our kiss further, but it was certainly questionable.

After a quick shower, I ambled about the cottage, reading, relaxing, and generally feeling anxious that I had nothing to do.

I wasn't sure what was worse: stressing because you had so much to do or stressing because you felt like you should be doing something.

Sinking into the couch, I pulled my knees to my chest and resorted to staring out the window as though I could will my handsome woodsman to ride up on his snow-skimming steed and save me from myself.

All of a sudden, alert after alert began to chime from my cell in my purse—a contraption I'd completely forgotten about in its uselessness.

Digging through my things, I pulled out my phone to see over a dozen calls and messages flickering on my screen as bars of service stood tall in the upper corner.

Maybe there was service out here and the snow had taken that out, too.

I didn't have to look to know all the messages were from Leslie. I didn't bother to read them before tapping on her contact once more and letting out a small sigh when I heard the call ring through.

"Jesus, Mary, and George Washington!" Leslie bellowed on the line. "Is that you, Vi? Are you okay? Is this your kidnapper calling for ransom because whatever it is, I don't have it—"

I snorted. "Thanks, Les."

"Holy shit. What happened? Are you okay?" she repeated. "I

mean, I got your crackled voice mail the other day—*my phone didn't even ring!*"

"I'm fine," I cut back in before she really got herself worked up. "I landed in the middle of a blizzard. No service. No electricity. And technically, no place to stay."

I winced at the sound that came from the other end of the line.

From there, the next hour passed in a blur as I filled her in on everything that had happened, from the moment I stepped into that fateful Uber to being rejected by the man in whose cottage I was currently residing.

"Holy. Shit." I put her on speaker as she repeated the words a handful—or two—of times. "But you're okay though? I can't believe you had another attack. Well, I can't believe a lot of things about that story but shit..."

"Yeah. I'm fine." *Thanks to Jamie* went unsaid.

"Wow."

I sighed. "So, that's where I'm at. I guess you could say my vacation is officially starting today—or the vacation I envisioned when you decided to make me take one."

"You have to sleep with him."

I choked on my sip from my second cup of coffee for the day. "Excuse me?" I shook my head like she could see me. "Les, I'm not going to sleep with him. I'm not that kind of—"

"Okay, I'm going to stop you right there. First, there is no *that kind* of woman. There are women. And women have wants. Period."

Wants?

I only had one—and he didn't want me.

"Okay, fine. But it was a stupid thought anyway. I'm on vacation. I'm leaving after the holiday. I was caught up from the stress of the storm and living with him for like a day, and then spending time with his family like I was one of them..." I trailed off, hating the burn in my throat. "I wasn't thinking clearly."

"Okay, Vi, I'm claiming my right as your best friend to tell you that you haven't been thinking clearly for a long time," she replied as kindly as her firmness would allow. "A long time, as in all the time and effort you put into working for your family who never appreciated you and then agreeing to marry a man who couldn't keep his dick in his pants if Trump built a wall around them."

A sound slipped from my lips that was part laugh and part groan.

"Have you slept with anyone since Dick—I mean, Rick?"

"No," I grumbled, leaving off that I hadn't even slept with Rick very often leading up to our recent breakup. It made more sense now that I knew he was getting some on the side, but that was beside the point.

"All I'm saying is that your vacation was not just for you to take a break from work, it was for you to actually do something for yourself for once. And I'm all for that *something* turning into *someone...*"

"Right, except he said it was a mistake."

She huffed. "Vi, a kiss is a mistake. His hand finding its way into your pants is not a mistake," she snorted. "I don't even need to meet this man to choke on his sense of chivalry from all the way down here. Of course, he thinks walking away from you is the right thing. He has sisters. He's probably doing what he hopes someone else would do for them."

I sighed.

"Of course, he thinks it's the responsible thing to do to leave you in peace. But he's completely wrong. *Shocker.*"

I gnawed on my lower lip, hearing Leslie audibly speak what the little voice inside my head screamed.

"I don't know, Les..." I trailed off. "I don't know what to do."

"And that's exactly why you have me." I could hear her grin on the other end of the line. "Obviously, your best course of action is to slather your naked self in blueberry jam—*that was his favorite, right?*—and watch his reservations melt away."

Had I really gone so far as to tell her I knew his favorite flavor of jam?

"Wow, you are *so* helpful." I burst out laughing.

"I'm just saying, don't be afraid to try again, Vi." A more serious note entered her voice, which caught my attention. "I know you've been let down by a shit ton of people recently who *never* should have... but don't let yourself be one of them. If he wants you even half as much as how you talk about him makes it seem, you'll regret not taking another chance."

"I don't like chances..." I grumbled. "Plus, I don't know if I'll see him again now."

Also true.

The fridge had been stocked and Frankie had left me with directions to town. There was a very good chance he meant to leave me to my solitary vacation at his cottage just like I'd booked it.

"Oh, you'll see him again, Vi," she promised me. "He cooked for you. He took you to meet his family. And he gave you an orgasm without getting one in return. Trust me"—she chuckled—"he'll be back."

My heart thudded heavily in my chest, hoping she was right.

Chapter Fourteen
Jamie

"Shit." Coffee splattered over the edge of the travel cup and onto the counter.

"You alright there, cuz?" Max drawled with far too much entertainment in his voice.

"I've got it under control," I bit out, wiping up my spill.

"Yeah, I disagree."

I whipped around to catch his grin. "Why are you here again?"

"To watch you make a mess out of Aunt Ailene's kitchen because you're too dick distracted."

"I don't even want to know what the hell that means." Though I had a pretty good guess.

"I don't know why you're torturing yourself, Jamie," he went on, lifting his arms to cup his hands behind his head. "If you like the girl, go see her. It's not like she's staying in your own damn house or anything."

I clenched my jaw.

"Seriously, you've been nothing but a scrooge for the past two days."

"She's here on vacation. Not to make friends. Or meet guys.

Or deal with my insane family," I informed him, though it was only part of the reason I steered clear of my cottage.

The more troubling reason was that I'd walked away from her once. I wouldn't be able to do it again. And after the mess I'd made walking away that first time, there wasn't a snowball's chance in hell I'd be welcomed back, even if I came on my knees.

"I hope you know we take that as a compliment," Frankie retorted from the doorframe and I wondered just how long she'd been standing there.

"Take it however you want. I have to go finish up orders and deliveries."

I'd been staying at my workshop—which was great for getting shit done and avoiding conversations like this. It was not so great for avoiding all my thoughts that somehow worked their way back to Violet.

"Alright, well then, Max and I are going to stop in and check on Vi and see if she wants to come with us—"

"Frankie..." I warned.

"She's a grown woman, Jamie. Just like I am," she retorted with a defiant flip of her hair. "If she wants to be alone, she is welcome to tell me. I'm not just going to assume it like some people..."

My eyes narrowed.

She couldn't know what happened the other night, could she?

My head jerked. *No, she couldn't.* And I wasn't assuming; it was what she came for.

But then I caught the sly look between my sister and cousin and knew the first things out of their mouths would be tale after tale of how I'd been a grouchy asshole since dropping her back off.

And that was the last thing I needed.

"No," I bit out. "I'll check on her. I left some plans over there anyway that I need for a project."

I turned back to putting a lid on my travel mug before I had to see the knowing look they'd share at my obviously blatant falsehood.

"Have a good day," Frankie hummed as I walked by her with a mumbled goodbye.

"And do us all a favor and relax a little!" Max hollered after me.

The sound of the door shutting was the only response he received.

The sound of my snowmobile cutting off was the end of the time I'd had to figure out what to say.

I'd helped raise my brother.

I'd helped raise my two sisters.

I'd helped run Stonebar Farms, and then started my own business.

I had answers to a lot of things. When you're the one people rely on, you have to. But as I climbed off the snowmobile, I had to accept I didn't have an answer for this—for what to do.

And that was unsettling, to say the least.

Clearing my throat, I made it through the second knock before the door opened underneath my knuckles.

My breath stumbled into my chest, seeing Violet in a pale-blue tank, her gray yoga pants, and my flannel shirt. Surprise flitted over her face before she quickly tamped it down.

Maybe there was hope after all.

"Hi," I rasped, bringing my arm back to my side.

"Hey." She licked her lips. "Is everything okay?"

I gave a quick nod. "Yeah. Fine. I just... I left some plans here the other day that I need."

"Oh." Disappointment flashed over her face as she stepped back and motioned me inside. "Of course."

Propped in the corner of the kitchen sat the round case that held plans for a new desk for Frankie's Candle Cabin. It was her Christmas present.

And it was almost done.

I didn't really need the plans, but I did need to see Violet.

Grabbing the strap, I slung it over my shoulder and turned back to Violet. "And I wanted to check on you and apologize for the other night."

Instantly, the energy changed between us.

She glanced down at the coffee mug in her hands. "It's okay. I'm sorry I slammed the door in your face."

A sharp laugh escaped me. "I deserved it."

"Well, thank you," she said softly and then, lifting her mug slightly, added, "And I'm doing... good."

She didn't sound too confident.

"Are you sure?" I stepped toward her and it felt like my body rose another ten degrees.

"Yeah." She shook her head in that adorable way where she was trying to convince herself and not just me.

"What are you doing today?"

She looked around as though she'd been avoiding that very question.

"I guess the same as yesterday... Read. Check my emails. Call my friend, Leslie—oh, I have service now, by the way," she added before trailing off, thoroughly unenthusiastic about everything she'd just mentioned.

"How about you?"

I cleared my throat. "I've got to stop back at my shop and take care of a few things, and then I've got the last of my deliveries to make."

I told myself it was the way her eyes brightened that made me ask, but really, I was grasping for any excuse to spend more time with her.

"Did you want to come?"

Her mouth parted, and she stared as though she couldn't have heard me correctly.

Shit.

"With me. I mean, do you want to come with me?" I followed up, seeing how she'd misinterpreted my question.

"Do you want me to?"

I cursed myself. Seeing the way she doubted herself because of me was the worst fucking feeling in the world.

So, I did the only thing I could to make up for it.

I told her the truth.

"Yeah, I do."

VIOLET

"This is really incredible, Jamie," I gushed as he finished his tour through the artifacts he'd collected over the years, which were proudly displayed in the loft of the old barn.

"Wasn't just mine," he insisted, shifting his weight because he was unwilling to take the compliment. "I'd set my sights on the barn, knowing I needed space to work and this had it in spades, but it was mostly Uncle George's suggestions, along with Max and Nox's help—Kit was deployed at the time—that we'd turned this part here into a small museum and made room for my workshop in the back."

"Such a wonderful idea." My eyes couldn't stop from wandering along all the old furniture and farm equipment, some dating back to the Civil War era and earlier.

"We acquired this hotel down south last year," I began, the thoughtfulness of the idea reminding me that for every person as considerate as Jamie, there was one equally as careless.

"It was filled with Civil War-era antiques. I'd wanted to keep them and put them back in the space once we renovated. Instead, my brother hosted a private party once the building was closed for renovation and almost all of them were destroyed." My voice broke right at the end.

I wasn't sure why I was so emotional about furniture. It was pieces of history—pieces of lives gone by. Or maybe it was because those pieces were made the way Jamie made his—with the specific customer in mind. With the care and detail as though he were carving his own children from the wood.

"Jesus..." he breathed out.

"He told me no one would want to stay in a luxury hotel full of relics," I added with a weak laugh.

"Sometimes people are too focused on what could be, rather than appreciating what has been." His voice echoed the heaviness in my chest.

I turned back to him, letting my eyes linger on the way his hip was propped against the support beams, outlining the narrow taper of his waist, which flared up and out to wide, solid shoulders as his arms locked across his chest.

"I'm sorry."

I shivered.

Most men would have taken the easy road and claimed that my brother was a heartless moron. *And maybe he was.* But Jamie... Jamie had this way about him—a way that when I spoke, he wasn't just listening to what I said, he was hearing the woman who was saying it... the woman who felt sorry for her little brother who didn't know how to make his mark on the world except in all the wrong ways.

"Me too." And that was why there was no bitterness in my tone, only sadness.

"So, anyone can come see this?" I changed the subject back to the small collection we were still walking through.

The main level of the barn was Jamie's space. We'd entered through the front and right into his showroom of sorts. The way he'd laid out the ornate and well-crafted furniture was meant to make a statement, and it did. I was speechless until we entered the back half of the barn where he actually worked, and I had a litany of questions that bubbled over and out.

He shrugged and nodded. "Most times they call first. It's not an official museum or anything, just something the locals know about. For the most part, it's the schools who bring classes through during the year for some local history, but I'm not sure what's going to happen over the next year."

"What do you mean?"

Jamie sighed. "Just with how my business is growing, I'm

going to need the space soon, so I'm not sure where all of it is going to go."

I rested my hand on the door to an old armoire, running my fingers along the hand-carved scrolls and feeling like if I opened it, it would take me right to Narnia.

"A lot of these would be perfect for the Lamplight Inn," I said without much hesitation, the thought springing to my mind from out of nowhere.

I'd found myself going back to the quaint image of the run-down inn several times since I'd seen it for the first time the other day. The character of the building sticking with me like a fire on the brink of dying, the embers pulsing and popping, begging to be brought back to life.

Jamie cleared his throat and drew my attention. "Take it Frankie told you about that?"

"We walked by it when she took me into town the other day."

He nodded, understanding. "That place used to be a real Friendship gem, but when the Barons passed away, it just... fell apart."

"I'm glad your mom bought it so they didn't tear it down," I said. "Those kinds of places deserve to be preserved."

Again, he nodded. "Just need to find someone to get her back up and running. With the Farms blowing up, the project just went on the back burner."

"I'm sure she'll find the perfect person to take it on." I smiled, a twinge of jealousy taking me by surprise as I wandered over to an old china cabinet in his collection. "But I think putting some of these pieces in it when it's done would really bring out that colonial feel."

When I looked back, Jamie was watching me with a look in his eye that I couldn't quite put my finger on.

"I mean," I stammered. "I'm sure whatever they decide to do will be great." I shrugged. "Just being in the industry, I've seen a lot of historic hotels lean heavily on incorporating history into their decor when possible. It just brings another layer to the experience and the stay..."

I trailed off, feeling heat bloom in my cheeks because I was rambling about work, and Jamie was still staring.

"Sorry," I said sheepishly. "I haven't taken off from work in... a long time. Seeing the inn the other day, and now this... it's switched my brain into work mode."

"It's a great idea, Violet," he said firmly, looking as though he wasn't sure why he hadn't thought of it. "Perfect, really..."

I beamed but then ducked my head, a strange sensation pinching my chest.

"What is it?" he asked, his brow pinching with concern.

I smiled and shook my head.

"Tell me." The words were a demand, but the tone was a plea.

My hand dropped to my side. "Sometimes, it feels like that snowstorm was... magic." I broke off with an embarrassed laugh, unsure how else to describe it. "Like it trapped me—us—in the cottage and when I came out, it was to a different world than I'd lived in when I walked inside."

"In a good or bad way?"

"Oh, a good one," I rushed to assure him, adding more quietly, "Too good of one. That's why I said magic."

Jamie's stare intensified, making me feel as though fire was being slowly wrapped around each of my limbs.

His gaze tore from mine and he said, "I guess I'll have to add that to the listing then."

It took a split second for me to catch the joke, but then I was laughing with him.

"I think there are a few other *magical* things you could add to —" I broke off, pulling both my lips back between my teeth as I realized just what I was about to allude to.

He closed the space between us, and though the barn was several thousand square feet and several stories tall, I hadn't felt small until that moment. Jamie—and my desire for him— assaulted each of my senses.

"Like what?" he rasped, his eyes locking on my lips where my tongue had just wet them.

I gulped. Leslie's encouragement echoed in the back of my mind, but I didn't heed it.

"Like jam," I replied with a nervous laugh and stepped to the stairwell back to the main level. "Of course."

He paused and repeated my lie, "Of course."

After a minute of walking around in silence, Jamie following a few steps behind me like a sinfully sexy shadow, I rounded the table saw and came to one of his current projects—almost done by the looks of it.

"What's this?" I nodded to the desk as I hesitantly reached out and touched it, the wood feeling like the softest velvet underneath my fingertips. "It's beautiful."

He replied with a low, rough voice, "Thanks."

There was no doubt Jamie had been complimented thousands of times on the craftsmanship of his work, but the way he beamed at me, the expanse of his chest swelling, made me feel like I was the first and only one.

"It's Frankie's Christmas present," he revealed, holding my stare as he ran his hand along the same stretch of wood until his fingers bumped into mine.

I sucked in a breath, glancing down to see if the spark had left a mark on the piece like it had done to me.

Jamie cleared his throat. "She just bought her own building this summer—a small cabin up off Maine Street to sell her candles. Nox and I have been helping her remodel it, but she needs a good desk. She's been using my old metal one from here, but it doesn't suit her."

My hand tightened on the wood.

"Frankie needs something that makes a statement..." he trailed off with a grunt and I chuckled.

"You mean like she does?"

He laughed, the sound like the crackle of a fire, an unexpected and necessary release. "Frankie makes a statement like Kanye West at the Grammys."

I raised an eyebrow. I didn't take Jamie for the kind of man to know about the whole Taylor Swift and Kanye West drama.

"I have two younger sisters," he grumbled as an excuse. "Of course, I know about things like that."

I nodded, drifting back to a sadder thought... no one had ever made something for me in my entire life. Hell, *Dick* couldn't even be bothered to make me dinner, let alone craft something as thoughtful as this.

"Took me a bit to get it right," he went on, his expression like he was reliving the desk's fabrication in his mind. "This was the third top I made for it. First wasn't big enough. Second one I just didn't like. But this one... this one took me forever to get this smooth..."

As Jamie spoke, my mind drifted to the image of him making the desk. The precision. The expertise. And then to the way his muscles would tighten and flex as they positioned the pieces together and sanded along the grain.

I turned away in case it was too easy to see how my mouth dried up and my cheeks flushed.

His hand on my elbow stopped me from completely walking away.

"I have to go drop off a few things from the front." He nodded to where a few plastic-wrapped and packaged cubes sat. "I can take you back to the cottage, if you want, or—"

"I'll come with you," I said hurriedly.

Whatever magic was in that storm, I hoped it would hold on a little longer...

CHAPTER FIFTEEN
VIOLET

TWO HEADBOARDS, a rocking chair, dining table, and a toddler's rocking horse later, we pulled back up to the barn in Jamie's giant white Ford F150 with a now-empty trailer hitched to the back. Our trek through town had gone a bit differently than delivering storm baskets with Frankie. This time, I got to see how everyone (or everyone I'd met thus far) in Friendship admired Jamie Kinkade, and flat out loved the Kinkade family overall.

Since it was a few days out from the end of the storm, the roads had been expertly cleared and the town was back to business as usual.

We stopped at The Maine Squeeze, where Lou was working behind the counter, along with two other women, Lauren and Tess. A quick detour turned into a half-an-hour intermission when Gigi strolled in with Nox trailing behind her; two minutes later, a crowd had formed around her and her basket as she doled out fortunes—*I mean, jam.*

Jamie drove slowly, giving me the unofficial tour of Friendship, the town out in full force, preparing for Christmas. The storm had knocked down most of the lights and decor, so it was a community-wide effort to get them back up for the holiday that was three days away.

I stared out the window, watching in awe as we drove by the commotion. Lights, garland, reindeer and Santas—*And lobsters.*

So. Many. Lobsters.

Jamie informed me that adding red lobsters to holiday decorations was a Maine tradition. And nowhere was it more evident than the Stonebar Kitchen store where the two small Christmas trees that framed the entrance were covered in lobster ornaments with names written on them.

Even though Stonebar Kitchen was a national company, its founding store was tiny—*like closet tiny.* It reminded me of the first Starbucks coffee shop in Seattle or the Twinings Tea store in London—able to fit maybe fifteen people before there was a fire code violation.

Ailene welcomed me with a hug, giving me a quick tour of the shelves lining either side and informing me that they had a larger company headquarters a few miles north in their namesake town of Stonebar Ridge, but that this was their local baby. I had a feeling not many tourists wandered into Friendship; the town hadn't even qualified for a dot on the map.

By comparison, New York City was always decorated for the holiday, every lamppost, street sign and storefront competed as though they gave out Spirit of Christmas awards, complete with a free trip to the North Pole.

Our hotels were always picked and photographed for their Christmas decor, but *we*—the Royales—never decorated. Not the hotels. Not our homes.

"You hire someone to do that, Violet," my mother's words from decades ago rang out. Not condescending, just fact—a fact which made me feel like I had so much but not enough of the right things in my life.

We'd returned to his shop with pizza we'd picked up along the way, sharing dinner over his worktable before he'd reluctantly nodded to the snowmobile and said he'd better get me back to the cottage.

The ride back seemed so much shorter than I remembered. Then again, I always felt the ride home from anywhere always was.

"You okay?" Jamie asked as he pulled me off the bike.

I stepped close to him as I stood, wanting to hide the way the day with him made me long for so many things I couldn't have.

I nodded quickly and assured him I was fine, grateful the helmet still hid my eyes.

"Did we get all of your deliveries made?" I asked, worried that my presence had set him behind. "I hope I didn't slow you down too much."

I shuddered when his hands brushed under my chin to undo the strap. The hesitation in his fingers told me he felt the same. Releasing it, I felt the weight of the helmet slowly release my head, sending my hair tumbling down over my shoulders.

"All done," he said with a low, rasped voice. The hint of a dimple appeared on one cheek for a second before it set like the sun into something much deeper. "Hope it's alright I kept you out all day."

My head jerked to nod. "Truthfully, after one day alone in the cottage, I think another would have driven me crazy." I smiled, though I wasn't sure if it would've been from solitude or separation from him. "I'm glad you invited me."

"Me too."

My breath labored in my chest. If I'd thought an entire day with him would acclimate my body to his presence, I was wrong. Instead, it felt like I was walking around a room drenched in gasoline, afraid any wrong movement would strike a spark that would send me up in flames.

"Jamie—"

"Violet—"

We both broke off, having spoken at the exact same time. Neither of us laughed. My throat was far too dry for that. And

Jamie... he stared down at me, his brown eyes deepening to rich pools of desire.

Lansing, Michigan.

"Go ahead," he instructed.

St. Paul, Minnesota.

It was a miracle I remembered what I wanted to say, standing so close to him—so close to what I wanted.

There were a million ways I imagined this exact moment—many starting the way I had the last time we'd stood here when he'd walked away. But I no longer cared about what happened in the kitchen or how he thought it was the gentlemanly thing to leave me be. I cared about tonight.

I cared about now.

And I cared about being with him.

"I wanted to ask you to stay," I informed him, pleased with the steadiness in my tone.

His gaze drifted over my face, searching my eyes and then every inch of my skin before finally settling on my lips.

"You won't find it," I blurted out.

"Find what?" His voice was threadbare.

I licked my lips and felt the temperature in the air around him rise.

"Uncertainty." I winced when my voice broke over the word. "I'm sure I want you to stay."

Coming to Maine was about doing something for myself—it was about putting myself first. Not what my parents wanted. Not what the family business needed.

I came here to find what I wanted.

And Jamie? Jamie was it.

"I'm just not sure it's what you want," I finished more softly.

And it was okay if it wasn't. I told myself I would survive one more rejection just like I had all the ones before.

But I didn't have to worry about that.

A small cry erupted from my lips as I found myself hoisted into the air, just registering Jamie's strong arms around me, holding me, when my back was against the door to the cottage.

His gaze captured mine, my breath coming in small pants.

His face was only inches from mine as the hard wall of his body trapped me against the door.

"Ask me," he commanded.

The need that rumbled from his chest caused a shiver to run down my spine, pebbling my nipples against the layers of clothes that separated us and pooling between my legs which were wrapped around the back of his.

"Ask me, Violet," he growled once more.

My hands slid from the corners of his shoulders along his neck as I wrapped my arms around him.

Tipping my face closer, I held his eyes and I murmured, "Will you stay with me?"

I heard the clatter of the helmet as he tossed it onto the snowy ground at our feet.

His mouth answered with a fiery crash onto mine, branding the word *yes* to my lips.

His kiss epitomized everything about this place. Powerful and wild. Beautiful and addictive.

And I melted into it because it was everything I wanted: *this woodsman in a winter wonderland.*

Opening my lips, I let out a moan as his tongue slid demandingly between them to stroke against mine.

I liked Jamie like this. Unrestrained. Not needing to be the man in control, though he would always be the man in charge. I liked when he gave me his rough edges, the ones ignored for the sake of being the head of the family; it felt like he gave me a piece of himself no one else saw.

And I liked that a whole lot.

With one arm locked underneath my ass, I felt the door give way behind me, letting us into the cottage once more.

It had only been days, but it felt like warmth and support and love. It felt like home.

Kicking the door shut behind us, he carried me straight toward the bedroom. This was the second time he'd carried me into this room, but for an entirely different reason.

Our mouths tore at each other's, knowing full well where this was leading… having known for a long time now.

As soon as my feet hit the floor, he had one hand in my hair, locking my head tight so he could continue to devour my mouth.

Breaking free with a gasp, we both worked to divest the other of the layers of winter garb that separated us.

Boots thudded into a stack on the floor. Snow pants swished into a pile by the empty fireplace. Clad in only our final layers, it was only the bright light from the moon shining through the window that illuminated us in a magical silver glow.

I sucked in a breath at the first touch of my fingers against the hot steel of his chest, sliding them underneath his shirt and dragging it up over his head.

The smattering of hair in the center of his chest was more rusted than the color of his hair and it quickly tapered off over the hard ridges of his abdomen before disappearing, along with those V-marked slices beneath his pants.

Desire pooled low in my stomach when I caught the hard outline of his erection straining against the fabric.

Without thinking, I reached out and flattened my palm over his length, enjoying the low curse that erupted from his lips.

"Violet…" he grunted and grabbed my wrist, sliding my hand up until my palm was against his lips.

His eyes rolled with desire as he pressed a kiss to the center of my hand, and it was a kiss I felt all the way down in my core.

"Touch me like that and this'll be over far too soon," he

warned against my fingertips before dipping his head to mine. "I've been dying to be inside you from the second I saw you wearing my shirt."

I sucked in a breath and shuddered at the memory.

His mouth found mine once more, giving my need an outlet as his hands went to work stripping the rest of my clothes away.

Goose bumps coursed down my back as he pulled my shirt up over my head. With his hands on my waist, his kiss became more demanding, taking bits and pieces of my heart and soul with each stroke of his tongue as he backed me toward the bed.

When the mattress hit the backs of my legs, he tugged at the waist of the leggings I'd layered underneath the snow pants Frankie had let me borrow. As soon as they cleared my thighs, Jamie released me with a gentle push so my ass sank onto the bed.

Dragging in air while I had the chance, I planted my hands on the mattress, steadying myself back as Jamie peeled one leg and then the other free from the fabric, leaving me in nothing except the matching deep-purple lace of my bra and thong.

As soon as my pants were added to the scattered mess of clothes on the floor, Jamie froze when he looked back at me; positioned between my legs and kneeling, his gaze had a straight shot to my core and then up my chest.

"Jesus, Violet..."

I shivered as the rough timbre of his voice felt as though it reached out and rubbed right over my clit.

With a low growl, his head turned and his teeth sank into the sensitive skin on the inside of my thigh just above my knee.

"Jamie," I moaned his name and my head tipped back.

"You could kill a man wearing that," he growled against my skin, each word inching higher up my leg.

I gulped, holding my breath as I felt the warmth of his exhale release over my aching pussy.

"Well then," I said with a sultry voice. "You better take them off."

His eyes whipped to mine.

"For your own safety," I added huskily.

My core clenched and soaked my panties further at the feral growl that escaped him. But even though I ached for him to, he didn't start with my underwear.

Instead, he rose up and captured my mouth ravenously as his hands unclasped my bra.

I arched into his bold kiss, plunging my tongue into the warmth of his mouth, tasting the hint of whiskey we'd shared before trekking back into the snow earlier tonight.

Freeing each of my arms, the bra hit the floor with a soft clink.

Jamie pulled back slowly to look at me and murmured, "You're so damn beautiful, Violet."

He made sure to say it only as he was holding my gaze so I'd know he was talking about all of me, including the parts deep inside it felt like only he could see.

Reverently, he drew back, drinking in the sight of my bare breasts and savoring each second.

My nipples stood hard and studded in the cold air. There were no fires in the cottage. But even though I could feel the chill in the air, I didn't feel cold.

In fact, the more skin he bared, the hotter I felt.

I watched his body tighten and his jaw clench, absorbing each inch of me as though he claimed it for his own.

A thought that made my heart beat harder.

Jamie's palm began at the notch in my waist, sliding up over my ribs before molding over the weight of my breast. But even though his touch sent electricity straight down to my core, it was the look on his face that made my body feel like it was choking on the verge of an orgasm.

The raw need in his eyes. Primitive and feral as his fingers cupped and kneaded my flesh.

With unsteady breaths, I arched against him, feeling as though I'd been waiting forever for his touch. His thumb rolled over my pebbled nipple, and I moaned.

There was a very good chance I was going to come before he even touched my sex.

"Jamie," I whimpered.

Freed from his trance, he growled and his head dipped to tug my nipple into his mouth. Firm, demanding lips and his hot tongue glided back and forth over the sensitive peak. With a cry, I bucked against him as his lips locked and sucked hard. My head dropped back as stars began to fill my eyes.

His tongue and teeth worked a whole new kind of magic over my skin. Biting and soothing the tender flesh until I was thrashing against the covers, sure that I wouldn't survive the torture.

When his mouth slid to my other breast, I felt his finger trail down to the waist of my thong.

If I were able to sigh in relief, I would have as the fabric inched over my hips and down my thighs.

I closed my eyes for a moment, realizing what it was about him that drove me crazy. It was the way that every touch was more than skin deep. Every brush of his fingers or kiss of his lips was more than praising my body, it was worshiping my soul.

"Been dying to taste you," his lips rasped over my quivering stomach, moving lower so he could free my legs from my underwear.

I moaned, losing all capacity for words.

Rich—Dick had never gone down on me. It 'wasn't his thing,' and the very mention of it brought out this disgusted look on his face that, truthfully, made me too embarrassed to think of asking again.

I thought I knew what to expect from memories of previous relationships a long time ago until I felt the warm pads of Jamie's fingers spread my folds wide, his tongue carving a path between them, and I realized I remembered nothing.

No. Not remembered.

I knew nothing.

The way Jamie's tongue worked over my clit was nothing short of mind numbing.

I let myself fall the rest of the way onto the bed so my fingers could spear through his hair, locking him against my needy pussy. His obsessive tongue flicked over every inch of that nub of nerves as my head pressed back into the mattress.

"Fuck, Violet," he growled, lapping at my desire that rushed against his lips. "So fucking sweet."

The thick locks of his hair looked like fire seeping between my fingers and the sweep of his tongue felt like pure flames against my core as it dipped inside me before tracing up to swirl around my clit.

He took his time with me, as though I were one of his creations. His hands and mouth carved and sanded over each aching inch, molding me into something that was exquisite and his own.

I heard myself moan his name, begging for so much more, even though it seemed as though he was searching for his own release between my thighs.

My muscles clenched in rapid succession as his mouth became more demanding. I tried to command my fingers to pull his head away but instead, they only crushed him closer.

I choked in air as the waves of my orgasm grew too tall to stay afloat.

"I want to taste you come, Violet," he growled against me, his lips moving furiously with the effort. "I need to..."

My body broke with a scream—one that I imagined echoed out over the silent, snowy landscape all the way into town.

But the only thing I heard was the way Jamie growled his appreciation, greedily licking every drop my body gushed out.

"Jamie... what are you doing to me?" I pleaded breathlessly.

What should've sapped all my strength only made my need stronger. What should've sated my desire only made me crave him more. And what should've made my body lifeless only brought it to life.

His eyes were wild when they met mine, his lips glistening

with my juices as he licked every last drop before rising up in front of me.

I didn't feel my arms move until I was pushing myself up on the bed so I could reach forward and stop his hands at the waist of his pants.

With a glint of warning in his eyes, his fingers moved aside so mine could do the work of releasing him.

Another wave of need crashed over me when I carefully lifted the fabric over the blunt purple head of his cock, the length pulsing angrily as I tugged his pants and boxers down over his hips.

Oh god.

My lips parted at the size of him. Feeling his arousal through his pants the other night was nothing compared to seeing it in person. The trunk of his cock was so long and thick, wrapped with veins pulsing with need; if there was ever an erection to fit a woodsman, it was this.

He stepped out of the last of his clothes as I slid my fingers around his turgid length, enjoying how every cord of his muscular thighs and each square of his abdomen rippled from my touch.

"Jesus," he croaked, his head dropping back with a ragged groan.

I stroked his cock, feeling it swell and swell until a bead of moisture pooled at the tip.

"You're going to kill me," he choked out.

A thrill of power shot through me as I bent forward and swiped my tongue over the tip.

I squealed as I felt myself being tossed back onto the bed, Jamie growling and bending over me to bite along my neck.

"Need to be inside you, Vi." I shivered at the way he rasped my nickname. It felt as intimate as what we were about to do. "Fuck. Need to grab a condom."

I tightened my arms around his neck, meeting his curious gaze. "I'm on the pill..."

He reached up and cupped my cheek, his eyes darkening with possessive need. "You trust me?"

My heart lurched. How could I not trust this man?

I nodded as my knees tipped wider, welcoming him between them as he scooted me fully onto the bed. Gripping one of my shins, he bent my knee toward my chest and began to rub his erection against my slick center.

I moaned, feeling the way my desire coated his throbbing length, letting him press and glide easily along my entrance and over my clit.

My first orgasm was a distant dull memory compared to the way I needed him right now.

Just like the last time he'd held me in this bed, I felt safe and so adored. But this time, those feelings were unhampered by my fear and his restraint.

I arched against him, whimpering when I felt the blunt tip of his cock positioned at my entrance.

My breath caught like an animal when it realized it was about to become prey. Prey to desire. Prey to need. *Prey to him.*

With a single commanding thrust, his cock drove deep and spread me wide. My lips parted only to be filled with the warm velvet of his tongue, plunging inside my mouth the way he wanted to do to my body but instead, holding himself there, pinned to the deepest part of me.

I felt stuffed full of him—consumed by the sensations ravaging my body. His cock began to pulse inside me, and he let out a pained groan; he held it all at bay so my body could adjust.

His hands slid warmly along my calves up to my knees, rubbing and squeezing impatiently as my body acclimated. "Christ, you feel so good," he murmured.

When my lower muscles clenched around him in response, the last of his restraint broke and he pulled back an inch before pushing deep once more.

Over the next few minutes, I forgot about breathing as his

thrusts worked me into a frenzy. Each one drawing him farther out of me only to return even deeper, rubbing against my front wall, which was tender and greedy for more pleasure.

"*Jamie.*" I hardly recognized myself—not who I was in this moment, but the person I'd been before him. That woman, I didn't know. But this Violet... *this was me.*

And this me wanted him, and everything he could give me. But I knew he'd hold himself back if he thought it was the right thing to do.

So, once more, I took what I wanted.

Digging in my heels, I lifted my hips to meet his, daring him to keep his control. Grabbing his wrist, I slid his hand to my breast, moaning as his fingers flexed over my skin.

"*Violet.*" My name ripped from his lips as he released my breast to hinge forward, locking me between his forearms.

His control was done. His thrusts were no longer measured but deliciously brutal. He speared into me over and over again, the faint moonlight glistening on his sheen of sweat as he grunted above me.

My fingers curled into the hair at the base of his neck as the spiral of my release began once more, this time feeling as though it might shatter each of my muscles with how it made them tense.

He groaned, and his cock stretched me wider.

He pushed me higher and higher, each possessive thrust carrying me closer toward a second, building orgasm.

"Please, Jamie." I was going to melt every flake of snow in the entire state of Maine with this orgasm.

"I'm here, Vi. I've got you," he breathed as his head dipped so he could suck on my nipple and grind his pelvis at a different angle against me.

My clit was so swollen and aching it didn't take anything more than that. One second, I saw the path to my orgasm as clear as day in front of me, and the next, I'd stepped clear off the cliff, tumbling violently into my climax—so violently, my mouth opened, but no noise came out.

There was no building crescendo, no steady preparation for the onslaught of desire.

It went off like a bomb strapped to my chest as I dropped off the cliff of pleasure, and my body shattered. I tensed and jerked against him, stars exploding like fireworks in my vision as my core tightened so savagely around him, I was afraid I might push him out.

I heard his rough shout as the heat of his release flooded me, coating my muscles that still ricocheted from my orgasm.

"Oh, fuck..." He let out a long groan, still pinning himself inside me as his cock continued to pulse.

His head collapsed into the corner of my neck, his warm breaths soothing my racing pulse.

We stayed like that for long minutes, drinking in the cool air until it finally felt cold.

With a possessive grip on my hip, his arousal still lodged inside me, Jamie turned his head up and claimed my mouth once more.

This kiss was demanding in a different way. Instead of demanding desire, it claimed all the deeper parts of me that orgasm had touched. It marked them as Kinkade property, and I had no strength or desire to disagree.

Later, I would worry about what it meant and what the future would hold. I wasn't foolish enough to forget this wasn't my home—that I was only here for a short time longer.

But I also wasn't foolish enough to not appreciate something special when I came across it.

And this... this was something magical.

"That was..." I trailed off, wanting to say something but lacking any words to appropriately describe it.

"Don't say it," he grumbled against my chest.

"Say what?"

"*That* is not going on the damn rental listing."

A grin broke out over my face and I managed a small chuckle. "I wasn't going to suggest it, trust me," I replied. "Though I'm sure you'd make millions if you did..." I trailed off, the humor suddenly lost at the thought of him being with someone else.

Peeling himself up, his fingers caught under my chin and he held my gaze locked to his.

"I doubt it," he said with a low, serious voice, his eyes in turmoil. "It's never felt like that before."

I sucked in a breath.

I was surprised by his admission but not by what he said, because I felt it, too. I'd had sex... had orgasms before. But there was a difference between knowing how to do CPR and saving a life... and this... this had felt like saving a life.

Something deeper.

Something unexpected but more meaningful.

Something worth holding on to.

We stayed like that for what felt like a life-changing second before Jamie pushed himself all the way up and slid out of me, his cock bobbing heavily between his legs as he disappeared into the bathroom, returning a beat later with a damp cloth which he used to gently clean between my legs.

A few minutes later, we were both in front of the small bathroom mirror, still naked and brushing our teeth. Rationally, I knew I'd just slept with a man I'd only met a week ago, but it didn't feel that way.

He didn't feel like a stranger when he talked to me, when he cooked for me or held me during my panic attack until I felt safe. He didn't feel like a stranger when he touched and kissed me, or when his body claimed my own.

He felt right.

It had begun to flurry outside when Jamie ushered me into bed. He didn't join me until he'd struck up a small fire to make sure we stayed warm and then pulled me snugly into his arms.

"Good night, Vi," he rumbled as his hand stroked gently against my back.

Just like I couldn't fight the lull of sleep as it stole over me, neither could I fight how safe and adored I felt—both things that were luxuries in my prior luxurious life.

"Good night, Jamie."

And just like that, in the snow-covered cottage, nestled in a winter wonderland, I realized I was falling in love with the woodsman whose arms were wrapped around me as though he had no intention of ever letting me go.

Chapter Sixteen
Jamie

My arm reached out next to me, but the soft, warm body which had been there all night, fitted against my side, was gone.

Shit. I never slept that deeply. *Never.* I was always too worried about having to look out for someone, worry about them, protect them.

"Violet." I did a double take at my own voice as I called her name; it sounded much deeper and more relaxed than usual.

Damn, was that from sex?

I shook my head. Was that from sex with Violet?

I didn't know what happened yesterday, but it was something.

Coming back here to apologize, being unable to stay away, something about her had tipped the scales inside me, and I found it hard to focus on what anyone else needed—*not that they needed anything*—with her on my mind.

And last night... I'd never had sex bare before. I had my family to take care of. My younger brother. My baby sisters. And my mother, trying to support us all. Taking that risk was never an option, even with the pill. But Violet...

I tossed the covers off and yanked on my boxers. My thoughts warred between reliving the most incredible sex I'd ever had and worrying about why the hell she hadn't been in my arms when I'd woken up.

The fire I'd lit last night was almost completely out as I threw open the bedroom door, stopping short when I caught sight of Violet, humming away in the kitchen, her hair piled messily on top of her head, and wearing nothing but my flannel, judging by the bottom curve of her ass peeking out from underneath it as she reached in the cupboard to pull down some mugs.

My dick was instantly at attention as her eyes jerked to me and widened.

"Jamie," she greeted me with a breathless flush spreading underneath my shirt, which covered her luscious curves.

I closed the space between us, taking the mugs from her hands. I set them on the counter while trapping her back to it.

"Violet." I held her gaze. "Do you regret last night?"

I didn't have time to dance around the subject. Not when my shirt was hanging off her curves and she had that sexy, morning-after glow.

"No," she gasped. "Why would you think that?"

"Because I woke up to an empty bed." The statement was foreign on my tongue, having woken up to an empty bed—and an empty heart—for over a decade now. But one night was all it took to change that.

One night for the thought of waking up without Violet to be completely unacceptable.

"I thought I'd make coffee." She licked her lips.

I growled my approval as one hand slipped to the outside of her thigh, sliding up underneath the edge of the flannel until it rested on the bare curve of her hip.

"As much as I love coffee, Vi." I pulled her against me and felt her stomach quiver as it cradled my hard cock. "It's not nearly as energizing as the thought of being inside you," I murmured into her ear.

Her gasp turned into a small yelp at the pounding on the

front door, and she ducked against my chest as it subsequently opened—

"Jamie?" Frankie called, and I could hear her smirk of victory even before I craned over my shoulder to see it. "I thought I might find you here."

"You know, I know I didn't teach you how to rent out other people's houses, but I'm damn sure I taught you how to knock—"

"I did knock!"

"—And wait for someone to answer the door," I growled.

Violet relaxed in my arms, hearing it was only my sister, once again, barging in at the most inopportune moment.

"Well, I didn't have time to wait, and I, obviously, figured wrong about the potential for interrupting something going on in the—"

"Is he in there?"

I groaned as Gigi's voice echoed through the doorway a second before her green and white cotton-candy hair poked through.

"Oh, my." My grandmother let out a little gasp, taking in our position and lack of clothing. "Francesca," she scolded, turning on my sister and swatting her with her gloves. "I told you to wait and let them answer the door first."

I looked to Violet, who I felt shaking in my arms. I should've known by now it was from laughter and not tears of embarrassment.

"Gigi. Frankie," I cut into their bickering about whether it was better to just barge in on the act for confirmation or wait and see if I'd try to hide it. "Can I ask what brought you here—*aside from meddling in my love life?*"

Later, I could question my choice of words in that moment.

"Seriously, Jamie?" Frankie groaned and jokingly smacked her forehead in defeat. "Is *any* blood going to your brain right now?"

"We need to get the tree!" Gigi exclaimed with the urgency of needing to take someone to a hospital and then hit my sister again with her gloves.

"*Shit.*" I'd forgotten about the tree.

"What tree?" Violet asked with a soft voice as my eyes met her dancing ones.

I sighed. "The Kinkade family Christmas tree," I explained. "We planned to go last week, but with the storm and cleanup... will you come?"

Her gaze widened and I worried whatever was happening between us was slipping. I worried this was too much. Too much of my family. Too soon. We'd just slept—

"Like a *real* Christmas tree?" she asked in awe.

"Of course!" Frankie piped from the background, reminding me we had an audience. "It's not Christmas without a real tree."

I grunted. "You don't have—"

"I'd love to, Jamie," Violet replied, and from the childlike excitement in her eyes, I knew she meant it.

"Good." I grinned. Then, turning on my nosy relatives, I ordered them, "We'll be ready in five. I'd tell you to make yourself at home, but you seem pretty adept at doing that already."

Grabbing her hand, I pulled her back into the bedroom and slammed the door, ignoring the gleeful murmurs from the other side.

"How about this one?" Frankie called to the whole crew.

I'd warned Violet this was a big day for the Kinkade Brigade—the term appropriate to my extended family—and I think she got the picture when we walked out to find all of my siblings, my mother, Gigi, Uncle George, Nox and Max, and Harper, waiting in the sled.

Yes, sled.

After the whole snowstorm basket idea sprung up, someone —I honestly couldn't remember who—decided Uncle George and I should build a giant platform sled that could be hitched to the back of a pickup. Decorated with bells and garland on the sides, all of the "kids" rode on it to get the tree while my uncle George drove and my mother and Gigi rode in the climate-controlled truck cabin.

Blasting Christmas music and passing out cups of mulled wine from the container, which had its own carved-out spot on the sled, we drove through town to the sounds of hoots and cheers.

This was just a normal Christmas event for me. But for Violet... Hell... From the look on her face, you'd think we were taking her to the North Pole to meet the real Santa.

"Not that one, Frankie," Lou spoke up, her arm linked with Harper's.

Frankie led the Kinkade Brigade through our woodland trek, searching for the elusive, perfect Christmas tree, Lou and Harp not far behind, followed by Violet and me, and the parents. Bringing up the rear were Kit and the rest of my cousins; Kit because he no longer liked to be in groups, and the Ford brothers because they knew better than to try to have a say in this decision, relegating themselves to the drunken musical accompaniment to the adventure.

"What's wrong with it?"

"Well, there's a dead spot on this side. The bottom is too full. The top is too narrow. And we're going to have to cut off so much if we want it to fit—"

"Alright, Lou! Sheesh." Frankie raised both her hands in defeat and dramatically rolled her eyes. "And here I thought it had character. But fine, my dear Christmas tree snob, I'll let you find a *perfect*ly boring one."

Stalking around her more type *A* twin, Frankie set her sights on Violet.

"I can't believe you've never had a real tree before."

"Well, we did a few times—for a few hotels," Violet explained. "But we never went out and actually cut one down."

"Well, I'm glad you came with us then." My sister's eyes

gleamed deviously at me as she added with unnecessary emphasis, "I'm *so* glad Jamie had the bright idea to invite you," before she giggled and spun back to go boss Max and Nox around.

I grumbled under my breath, knowing that little matchmaking diva showed up on purpose to prove how *right* she was for renting out my property to Violet.

I glanced down at Violet, who pointed out a tree to Lou, perfectly proportioned and standing in a clearing to our right, and couldn't stop the feeling that she just belonged there.

In Maine.

With my family.

And with me.

"Did you always want to work in the hotel business?" I tried to ask nonchalantly a few minutes later after everyone enthusiastically latched on to the tree Violet picked and Frankie customarily bestowed Kit with the Christmas saw. Meanwhile, Nox and Max serenaded my younger brother with a sloppy, off-key version of "O Christmas Tree" as Kit waded through the snow and disappeared beneath the branches.

She looked up to me, her brows raised in surprise. "Yes and no," she confessed. "I always wanted to work in it because it was my family's business and I wanted to be a part of that. But I wouldn't say that manager of a hotel chain was the career I dreamed of as a child."

"So, if you could do anything, what would you do?"

Her gaze fell as she chewed on her lower lip, and I had to wonder if anyone had ever bothered to ask—or care—about what Violet wanted for her own life.

I cared.

I cared a whole helluva lot. Especially because I wanted to be part of what she wanted.

"*Timber!*" Our conversation was cut short as Max hollered out into the wilderness seconds before the tree toppled to the side, narrowly avoiding Nox, who was pulling on one of the branches to make it easier for Kit to saw.

Hoots and hollers echoed around our family circle as the annual Kinkade family Christmas tree was officially harvested.

Frankie skipped over to Violet, clapping her hands gleefully, and exclaimed, "Now, we get to decorate!"

"Hand me the twine, Max," I instructed, balancing myself on the ladder in my mom's living room, ready to anchor the top of the tree to some nearby molding in order to steady the ten-foot-plus evergreen.

In my periphery, I caught Violet's head dipping low as she talked to Lou and Mom, and my attention was diverted, wondering what they were whispering about.

"Hey, lover boy," Max jeered, tapping the ball of twine against my leg. "Your rope."

Glaring at my younger cousin, I snapped it from his hand and went back to my task, the tree tall and steady a minute later.

Gigi sauntered over and handed me a glass of eggnog a minute later in a moose-head glass mug she'd won in a game of White Elephant a few years back, the gag gift mimicking the cups from *National Lampoon's Christmas Vacation*.

Cupping her hand around her ear, she turned to me wide eyed, "Do you hear that sound?" She shushed me. "It's a funny, squeaky sound."

Every year she said those words in her two-line skit from the same movie. And every year the whole room burst into laughter at how on-point her imitation was.

"Trust me. There are no squirrels in that tree." I bent down and kissed my grandmother on the top of her head before making my way through the mass of family over to where Violet stood.

"*Grace? She died fifty years ago!*" Nox chimed in from the back in a falsetto voice.

"If only there were a Clark Kinkade," Max sighed, wiping tears from his eyes.

Shaking my head, I quickly stopped and crouched down by

Kit, who stared at the reflection of the fire in his glass of whisky. He didn't participate, but at least he was here.

"Everything going okay with the thing?" I asked cryptically with a low voice, looking around to make sure no one else heard me.

From the moment Violet told me she'd rented my cottage for two weeks—over Christmas—the thought hadn't sat well with me. And with each fact I learned about her family, and the more I found myself in awe of her heart, that pit in my stomach only grew deeper. So, I decided that night I needed to give her a gift.

It wasn't going to be big or grand; she was only my guest at the time. But still, I wanted to give her something from here because no one should celebrate Christmas alone. And after what Frankie did, I wanted Violet to have something she could look at fondly.

But as the days passed, the gift idea stayed the same, only now I realized it meant so much more. *And I hoped it would be enough to make her stay.*

"I told you I'd have it done," my brother clipped.

I let out a long breath. "Okay. Just hadn't heard from you since I dropped it off the other day—"

"You never hear from me. It's not anything new," he cut in, his gaze still on his drink. "I told you it'll be ready by Christmas."

My jaw tightened. He wasn't wrong. We didn't hear from him.

Kit stayed cooped up in his lighthouse, where Frankie blithely checked on him and reported back to the rest of us. He only came to the bigger family gatherings because Lou had pleaded with him, and while Frankie's wrath was something no mortal should have to withstand, Lou's tears could bring the world to its knees.

"Excuse me, Violet," my mother said as I approached. "Lou, can you help me with the tubs?"

"Of decorations," I clarified as they disappeared toward the storage room at the other end of the house.

"Ahh." She nodded and smiled up at me.

"We can go anytime you want," I reminded her, not wanting her to feel as though she were obligated to stay just because of me.

"I don't want to leave," she replied immediately, her eyes flicking to mine just after she spoke.

Tonight, or ever? I wanted to ask but was too afraid of the answer.

"I also have an answer for your question," she continued, taking another sip from the glass of cranberry-infused wine Gigi had poured for all the women after dinner. "I do like what I do. I like the idea of owning something and running it in a way where people feel as though they are coming to a home away from home. And my whole life, I wanted to do that even more because it was my family's business. I wanted to help them and make them happy." She let out a sad laugh. "But I never thought those two things would be at odds."

Clearing my throat, I reached down and threaded my fingers through hers, loving the way goose bumps trickled over her arm as she sucked in a breath.

"As much as you love your family, your parents, Vi, sometimes you have to do what makes you happy. It's your life. It can't always be lived for everyone else," I offered, giving her fingers a squeeze. "Although, don't tell my sisters that. God knows what 'making herself happy' will give Frankie license to do," I tacked on, air-quoting myself and drawing a chuckle from us both.

"Jamie!" Frankie bounced in front of us and into the conversation. "I know she's your girlfriend and all, but you have to share Vi."

I gaped, feeling like I should correct her but not wanting to in the slightest.

And it looked like Violet didn't either.

"We have something for you," Lou added from behind her, a bright smile on my shy and reserved sister's face.

With an apologetic smile, Violet let my sister lead her out into the crowd.

"Dammit, Nox, what the hell did you do to these lights?"

Max hollered, trying to untangle the massive ball of twinkle lights from the box.

"Last year was your year to put them back, dickhead. Don't look at me," Nox scoffed.

"Boys..." Ailene warned over her shoulder as she approached Violet. "Vi, we're so happy you're here spending the holiday with us—*however that came about.*" She shot me a poignant stare.

Reaching into the pocket of her apron, she pulled out a small, red-wrapped present tied with a Stonebar Farms ribbon.

"Since you're here, we'd like you to have this." She handed the gift to Violet, who looked like she was about to keel right over from shock.

I stepped off the landing in the hall and came toward them, needing to be close to her in case she did go down.

"I don't—you didn't have to—" Violet gushed as she took the small gift. I was the only one who saw the way her fingers trembled slightly as she peeled back the red paper to reveal her very red gift. "A lobster?" And then, a few seconds later. "My lobster!"

A watery laugh escaped her as she held up the iconic lobster ornament that had her name on it.

"Jamie carved it, and Lou and I decorated it," Frankie beamed.

"I don't know what to say." Violet pressed a hand to her lips. "Thank you so much. This is so thoughtful... I've never had my own ornament before."

My sister huffed and pulled Violet in for a hug, giving me a wink over her shoulder. "Well, you're a part of the Kinkade Christmas now, you have to have your own lobster for the tree!"

As soon as Frankie let her go, Violet turned to me and before she could say another word, I cupped my hand around the back of her neck and pulled her lips to mine, branding this moment and this magic on her skin.

She wasn't just welcomed into my family for the holiday. Somehow, she'd stumbled through the cold, stark environment around my heart, wrapped herself in its worn flannel trappings, and made herself at home.

I didn't even hear the cheers as I savored the taste of her. When I drew back, the slow claps and laughter filtered in around us.

"Thank you," she murmured.

And then she was gone, yanked by my sisters up to the tree to decorate as Harper cranked up the country Christmas tunes.

I watched as Nox and Max continued to fight over the lights. Harper and Lou relied on Violet to help them place each ornament a precise distance from the others while Frankie snuck onto the tree every inappropriate and embarrassing ornament collected over the years.

And finally—*last but not least*—Gigi climbed up on the ladder to put the angel—who had conspicuously green-dyed hair and wore a custom Stonebar Farms apron—on the top.

CHAPTER SEVENTEEN
VIOLET

I WAS LAUGHING, and it didn't look like I was going to be able to stop anytime soon.

Gigi had just popped a *very* avant-garde angel on top of the tree, and I caught Nox climbing up on Max's shoulders in order to tuck one of those tiny liquor bottles—*whiskey, of course*—into her arms.

"My brother looks jealous of his own family," Frankie teased me as she grabbed my hand and suddenly I found myself spinning to the Christmas classic, "All I Want For Christmas Is You" by Mariah Carey.

I caught a glimpse of Jamie, staring at me with the same look he'd had all night: as though there was nothing left to the world around him except me.

It made me warm in ways that spending last night with him could only scratch the surface.

Though it scratched it pretty darn nicely...

Frankie continued to murmur far more inappropriate things to me each time my turn ended in front of her until I wasn't sure if it was from twirling or the stomach-clenching laughter (*or that damn cranberry wine*) that I couldn't see straight. All I knew was at some point, she wasn't talking, and I was spinning in the direction of the very warm gaze which held me hostage.

Twirling until I connected with a very hot marble chest, Jamie's warm grip securing my shoulders and holding me steady.

His red waves swam in front of my eyes for a minute before they coalesced into the face I couldn't stop thinking about. My lips parted, but instead of speaking, I sucked in a cruel breath as I felt it happening again.

No.

My mouth dried up, and my stomach sucked in.

Jackson, Mississippi. Jefferson City, Missouri.

My chest jerked, trying to breathe without air.

No, no, no.

I wasn't afraid. I wasn't panicked. But my brain thought I was, recognizing my rapid heart rate. My breathlessness. My unsteadiness. All these things it associated with a panic attack tricked it into believing another one was coming.

"Violet?" The warm supports of his hands tensed. "Are you okay?" His voice sounded like it was coming from the far end of a tunnel.

Helena, Montana.

Not here. Not in front of all of them. *Breathe.*

Of course, that only made it worse.

Of course, that kind of thinking turned it into a real panic attack.

Sounds became vague. I wasn't sure if I was moving myself or if someone was moving me. Shadows dwarfed light, making me feel like I was in the tunnel but going in reverse. I gasped for air, knowing there was no way I could calm myself down now.

"I'm here, Violet. I've got you."

I tried to hold on to his voice, but it felt like trying to grasp a thread of floss as it slipped through my fingers.

"What's going on, Jamie? What's wrong?" I couldn't tell if it was Frankie or Lou who asked.

The voices swirled around me. I wished their concern could

make it better, but instead, the vortex sucked me deeper into the dark panic.

"*Everyone, get the fuck away from her.*" A different voice barked out the order. Low. Commanding. Militaristic... Kit. "*Get her out of here, Jamie.*"

There was more commotion, more voices, but only for a moment before the world fell away underneath me.

The dry night chill gave me some sense of awareness once more. The crunch of the snow. The soft moonlight. The hum of the snowmobile.

By the time we reached the cottage, I'd realized I was wrapped around Jamie's front, chest to chest, with my legs folded around his waist and his arms locking me steady. Their comfort fought for me—fought with me to bring me back through the darkness.

"I'm sorry," I murmured as he deftly hoisted me from the bike and carried me into the haven of the cottage.

He didn't say anything until the bed dipped beneath us, and he fit me against his chest. And when there was only him, my anxiety had its own panic and began to retreat.

"Even in the happiest moments, there's no turning it off," I whispered thickly, feeling the hot drops of embarrassment begin to fall and dampen his shirt. "I'm sorry."

His finger tucked underneath my chin, lifting my hazy gaze until it met his forceful one—the one that drove all other thoughts from my mind.

"Don't ever apologize for this, Vi," he rasped, making the tears fall harder.

I shook my head, hating myself for making him leave his family. Hating myself because they'd welcomed me, they'd made me feel a part of something—*of a family*—and this was how my body revolted.

Hating myself because even too much happiness was something to fear.

"Listen to me," he growled, more demanding than the darkness. "You've been uncomfortable and anxious and scared before, but remember how you've been strong. You haven't let this break you. You've weathered the attacks. You've survived them. And you'll survive them this time because they can't survive you."

My heart beat heavily, feeling each of his words as they flowed through my body.

"You never apologize for being a fighter, Vi. Never." He pressed his lips to my forehead, and I shook with the fierce tenderness that emanated from him. "You're going to be just fine, sweetheart. And I'll be here until you are. I've got you."

I let out a long breath—one that felt like I'd been holding it inside me from the moment I stopped twirling and my body went haywire. All the tension and fear locked in my body, trapped in the fibers of my muscles, fueled by the thunderous insecurities pumping through my blood — all released like water through a broken dam.

I sagged against the warm haven of Jamie's chest, lulled by the constant, reassuring beat of his heart.

You're going to be just fine, sweetheart.

The exhaustion that came after the panic attack hit just as hard as the anvil of anxiety itself. But now, I wasn't afraid of the darkness that came with sleep. I wasn't concerned about what fears might haunt their way into my subconscious. And I wasn't worried about what weight would be added to the strain on my heart...

Because he held me.

Because he had me.

Because he had my heart.

"Don't even think about it," the low, half-asleep voice grumbled next to me as I tried to slip out from Jamie's arms without disturbing him.

The morning sun filtered through the window, reflecting off the bright blanket of snow.

With a small smile, I retreated to relish the moment. *A new day.* And then my spirits dimmed, the comfort fleeing as I recalled what happened last night.

"I'm so sorry, Ja—"

Hard lips crashed onto mine with a growl. "I told you not to apologize."

I swallowed over the lump in my throat as his fingers began trailing lightly along my arm.

"I wish there was a switch, you know?" I murmured. "I wish coming up here, away from it all... away from my family... would've just flipped it off. But I guess it doesn't work like that."

I felt a difference being up here, maybe that was why I was so disappointed in myself after last night—because I thought with no reason for the attacks, they shouldn't happen.

Jamie pressed another kiss to the side of my head, letting his lips rest there for several long seconds as though his support could diffuse through my skull and into my messed-up brain.

"Emotions don't have a switch, Vi." His eyes searched out mine. "Sometimes, the only switch you can flip is the one that says 'keep going and don't give up.'"

I knew I'd heard some variation of what he'd said before. But there was a difference between listening to a song on the radio and hearing it being played live in concert.

And Jamie? He was definitely the live version.

He was too polite to say anything about my family, though I already knew what he thought of them, and more of the truth certainly wouldn't help their image. But I was tired. Tired of the anxiety. Tired of the insecurity. And tired of keeping quiet just because they believed how they treated me was normal and I was the one in the wrong for expecting more.

"I always thought my anxiety came from the job," I announced against his chest. "The work, but also the expectation I put on myself to succeed. And my parents, especially my mother —" I broke off with a huff. "Well, I learned to hide that anxiety pretty quickly when she began insisting I go on medication and get Botox for all the wrinkles it was causing me."

"I'm surprised she didn't tell you to quit," he said simply.

"Quitting would've meant leaving only my father and brother in charge," I replied with a bitter laugh. "And as much as she had an image for me to live up to, neither of them could deny what I was doing for the company and the kind of profit it was bringing in."

I closed my eyes, focusing for a second on the soothing touch of his hand rubbing circles on my lower back.

"I just wanted to be important enough—*valuable enough*—for them to treat me like an equal and not an accessory," I whispered against where my cheek was pressed to his chest.

His arms tightened around me, tugging me even closer into the safe, warm space.

"Sweetheart," Jamie cooed so achingly and so sweetly, tears sprung from the corners of my eyes.

"I thought I could work hard enough, make them—us successful enough to prove my worth." I swallowed hard over the shame of what I'd been willing to sacrifice to make that happen. "So, I didn't care what anxiety it created or the strain it put on the parts of my life that were still mine. I powered through."

I savored the firm press of his fingers along the small of my back, working through the stress tension which collected there.

"But the harder I worked, the more I was pushed out. So, I worked harder, and the panic grew worse. Richard cheated. And then when my dad told me, after everything I'd done, he was still handing the business over to my brother..." I shuddered. "It was all for nothing."

"Don't say that, Vi," Jamie said gruffly.

"That's how it felt," I whispered brokenly. "I'd done everything... and still, I was nothing."

A large, warm hand cupped my cheek, tipping my face up as Jamie leaned in.

"You, Violet Royale, are not nothing." I gulped, drowning in his stare. "You are the strongest, most selfless woman I've ever met. You do what is right without question. You sacrifice everything—*too much*—to help those you care about. And you've had the strength to hold on to the parts of you that crave laughter and family and love even though you've been taught it's all wrong."

My lips parted, completely devoid of words.

"Violet, you are so far away from nothing that to say you are everything still wouldn't be enough."

And sweet, Lincoln, Nebraska, I believed him.

Not only did I believe him, but I knew for certain I had fallen. I'd fallen for my incredible woodsman like a drunk college girl, looking up after the fall and wondering how it happened.

Though there was no point in wondering.

I was already knees bruised, hands scraped, and ass on the ground, in love with Jamie Kinkade.

Naturally, after a train-coming-at-you-head-on realization like that, I pulled away and averted my gaze, mumbling, "Thank you... and thanks for listening." I propped myself up. "I've never told anyone that before. Never had anyone to tell really."

"Anything you want to tell me, Vi, I'm here to listen."

I glanced back at him, offering a small smile. "I'd like to—I need to apologize to your mom—to your family for last night—"

"Sweetheart, they don't need an apology." I was distracted for a moment by the way his chest flexed as he sat up to face me. "They just want to know you're okay."

I nodded, knowing he was telling the truth. "We should get up." My nose scrunched. "Wait, why do I smell food?"

He grinned at me, and when I scanned the room a second time, I realized Jamie must have done several things while I was sleeping.

The fire was burning low and steady. Jamie wore only his boxers, and he'd stripped me down to my tee and wrapped me in his shirt. And there was the distinct smell of breakfast coming from the adjoining room.

"Jamie..." I trailed off as I climbed down from the bed, holding his eyes until I reached the door and pulled it open.

My jaw dropped.

It wasn't just breakfast. It was a buffet.

Eggs. Bacon. Sausage. Muffins. Pancakes. Fruit. Toast.

I spun to him. "When did you do all this?" I gasped and walked into the kitchen without waiting for an answer.

My stomach grumbled appreciably and eagerly, and I popped a piece of bacon in my mouth just as Jamie joined me.

"How did you do this?" I demanded.

Anxiety attacks drained me, there was never any question about that. But had I really missed a five-course breakfast being prepared while I slept?

There was no way.

He folded his arms over his chest and leaned against the fridge in a mouth-watering display of muscle. I struggled to keep my eyes from drifting down to my periphery, where I noticed the bulge in his boxers.

"I didn't do it."

"I don't underst—" I broke off as understanding hit me like a snowball crashing into my back. "Y-Your family did this?"

He nodded.

"When? How?" Really, the question I was asking was, "*why?*"

"They stopped in a little earlier. You just happened to still be sleeping, and I didn't want to wake you," he explained. "Plus, thought it might be better if you didn't wake to a houseful of people."

I blinked quickly to try and stop the tears, but it only made them fall faster.

"Don't cry, Vi," he pleaded with a small chuckle, stepping toward me to wipe my cheeks.

"I'm trying not to," I insisted with a strained laugh. "But

you... your family keeps doing these wonderful things... It's not my fault."

Jamie's wide smile and full laugh drew out my own.

I covered my face with my hands and groaned, "And I can't believe they made me my own lobster."

Slowly but surely, the other parts of yesterday filtered into my mind. The tree. Dinner. Too much eggnog. Off-key Christmas carols. Lobster ornaments. Dancing and laughter.

In the dark moments, it was easy to forget the miles of light that came before and that would come after. Back home, it was hard to find that light. But here... it was impossible not to see it.

His crooked grin sent a spiral of heat down to my core. "Well, we couldn't have you sitting under the tree tomorrow morning with everyone else's lobster on it except yours."

Yes, they definitely could have, and I wouldn't have been offended in the slightest.

Wait...

"Oh my god, tomorrow is Christmas!" I exclaimed, having lost all sense of time. "That means—"

Jamie hauled me against him and kissed me into silence. I found this to be my favorite way of being cut off.

If only it could stop the reminder that I had less than a week left in Friendship.

"Time to eat," he commanded against my mouth, and even though I swayed into him with a soft moan, I had a feeling he was referring to the real food on the table.

"So, what's today?" I asked as we sat down and began to dig in.

"What do you mean?"

I glanced at him with skeptical eyes. "Well, it's Christmas Eve. I find it hard to believe there is nothing happening in Friendship to celebrate."

His lips thinned and he took another bite of the heaping pile of eggs and bacon on his plate.

"Nothing we have to go to if you don't feel up to it."

My fingers tensed around my fork as I set it down with threatening slowness and leveled him with a stare.

"Whatever it is, I want to go," I told him decisively. "I'm not going to let my panic attacks stop me from living."

I caught the bright flash of admiration in his eyes. "Okay then." He nodded. "But you'd better eat up because there is no celebration spared when it comes to Christmas," Jamie warned with a grin. "And I hope you haven't had your fill of my cousins' tone-deaf caroling because they will be out in full force tonight."

I burst out laughing. "I haven't. Don't worry, I haven't..."

The truth was, I hadn't had my fill of anything in this town, and I doubted I ever would.

Especially him.

Chapter Eighteen
Jamie

"READY WHEN YOU ARE, but no rush," I tossed over my shoulder, taking another sip of the whiskey I'd just poured for myself, hearing Violet get out of the shower.

She was dangerous.

This was dangerous.

My whole life I'd steered wide and clear of anything remotely risky. But now, I felt like I was careening toward it without any care in the world as long as it kept Violet in my arms.

I knew what Christmas Eve meant.

I knew it signaled the final few days before she was supposed to go back home—that was why I couldn't let her say it. Because I didn't have a response ready.

For the first time in what felt like my entire damn life, I wasn't prepared. I didn't know how to tell her what she'd come to mean to me in any rational sense because there was nothing rational about it.

What I felt for Violet came on like a Maine blizzard in the middle of winter; the feelings didn't pile on slow and steady like snow would in more southern states, they fell hard and fast and unrelenting until, mere hours later, she was everywhere and a part of everything in my life.

"Jamie..."

I cleared my throat and began to turn. "You rea—" I almost dropped my glass at the sight in front of me.

Violet stood, her damp hair resting over one shoulder, wearing only my flannel shirt—*with only half the buttons done.* My mouth dried up as I scanned the creamy white expanse of her chest, the subtle swells of her breasts peeking out from the edge of the shirt, down the soft plane of her stomach until the shirt covered the magical place between her thighs.

"What are you doing?" I rasped.

She licked her lips. "We were interrupted yesterday... but if we have to go..."

With a growl, I tossed my cup into the sink and advanced on her, eating up the rest of her words with my presence as my dick hardened in my jeans.

"You keep wearing my shirt like this, and you won't be going anywhere for a *very* long time," I threatened.

"Promise?" Her voice was intoxicatingly sultry, spiked with a dash of surprise.

Hearing the question from her lips, asking me to swear to something that was more than figurative, asking me to promise something for myself felt like freedom of sorts. I'd told her she couldn't stop living her life because of her panic attacks, but in a sense, I'd stopped living parts of my own for the sake of my family.

"Promise."

But not anymore.

And I swore the longing in her eyes mirrored my own as my mouth claimed hers.

Knowing how many times I'd fantasized about fucking her while she wore my flannel only made my need that much more potent now that I was about to.

Gripping the backs of her thighs, I lifted her onto my dining table—the one I'd carved, *and the one I was about to feast on.*

There was no gentle Jamie when it came to Violet and her lush curves.

My hands roamed possessively up her sides until they were filled with the full weight of her breasts. Swallowing her cries, I kneaded and teased her, allowing the fabric to create another layer of friction against her soft skin.

My tongue stroked against hers as I dragged the shirt back and forth over her nipples until she was arching against me. She whimpered as I tormented her, begging for more.

She might not quite believe me yet, but Violet was a force of nature. *My own personal snowstorm.* She didn't come barreling in ostentatiously with booming thunder or high screaming winds. She came with quiet, determined power and brought me to my knees.

"You're incredible," I murmured against her lips, dragging my tongue along their seam.

I slid my mouth from hers, marking a trail along her jaw and down her neck. Her head tipped back with a soft cry as she shivered and rolled her hips against mine.

With a low growl, I hauled a chair behind me. Never letting my mouth leave the intoxicating lavender-vanilla taste of her skin, I sat, positioning myself perfectly between her legs with her gorgeous tits at eye level.

"Jamie..." she hummed my name as I dragged the flannel over the swells of her breasts, her nipples red and peaked and begging in front of my gaze.

Dropping my head, I pulled one turgid peak into my mouth, groaning at the delectable taste of her against my tongue. I savored every inch of her velvet skin with my mouth. Laving and sucking. Flicking and swirling. Her nipple was sweeter than any Maine blueberry I'd ever tasted.

"You are perfect," I whispered, trailing my mouth to her other breast and fastening it over the bud.

I leaned into her until she finally relaxed back on her elbows, every inch of her on display for me.

On my fucking table.

Grunting, I flicked open the few buttons on the shirt. I would've ripped them off if I wasn't so damn keen on seeing her in my shirt again, which required it to stay intact.

She seemed to float back onto the table as I dragged my mouth and several wet kisses over her stomach, which quivered when my hands slid lower, spreading her soft, slick folds with my thumbs.

The first swipe of my tongue was nothing short of pure intoxication. The taste of her... it obliterated all rational thought. Rich and sweet, she was pure, potent intoxication.

And I gave in to the intoxication.

I licked and sucked the sweet honey between her thighs until even my breath over her swollen clit made her shudder violently. Slowly, I pushed one finger and then another inside her hot pussy, stroking against that secret, explosive spot until she was gasping and pleading my name.

My dick was either going to explode or fall off if I didn't get inside her soon, so I worked over her clit, pressing my fingers inside her at the same time until her orgasm flowed against my tongue and rippled around my fingers.

I groaned as she cried out with pleasure, her body pulsing around my fingers, pushing me away and begging for more at the same time.

I kept my tongue on her, licking every last drop she wrung out against my fingers.

"I love how it feels when you eat me," she admitted, almost incoherent from her release.

"And how is that?" I murmured, taking one last lick over her clit and reducing her body to a quivering puddle.

She hummed in both relief and longing as I drew back, shoving the chair back with a screech as I stood.

"Like you could survive on me," she replied, her eyes deep

pools of stark need as she watched me unbutton my jeans, shove them along with my underwear down, and take the thick length of my cock in my hand.

I groaned as I pulled several long strokes along my dick, staring down at her naked body, framed with flannel, spread wide and waiting for me.

"I could," I said as I leaned over her, positioning the tip of my cock at her entrance. "Because you're everything."

I grabbed her hips, locking them against the table, as I slammed inside of her. A hoarse shout ripped from my chest at the impossible stretch and squeeze of her tight pussy around me.

Whether her gasp was from my words or the way I invaded her body, I wasn't sure. But I couldn't think about it now. The way she felt around me was pure fucking heaven.

And I was drowning in the unbelievable *and incredible* reality of it all.

I tried to stay steady, even for a moment, but she wriggled and arched against me, desperate for me to move.

Groaning raggedly, I slid my cock out of her heat only to shove myself back in to the hilt and stretching her to her limit.

"I want to take it slow every time," I said raggedly as I picked up the pace. "But you feel so damn good, sweetheart..."

She moaned her approval as my mouth latched back onto her nipple, sucking and nipping as I angled her hips so I could drive deeper inside her.

Violet whimpered and wrapped her legs around my waist, urging me on as the table began to groan and shift underneath the force of my thrusts. Her fingers locked in my hair, pulling my head toward her other breast and the needy nipple that wanted its turn for attention.

"Jamie," she gasped my name.

I felt the way her body tensed each time the blunt head of my cock slid deep against her front wall. She was hanging on by a thread.

So was I.

My teeth clamped around her nipple, and she screamed as her greedy pussy suctioned down around my cock and she came. This time, her release didn't happen in steady streams against my tongue; this time she came like a fucking lightning bolt carving a bright, electrifying streak of pleasure through the sky and striking her orgasm onto me.

"Oh, fuck," I grunted against her chest.

The feel of her climax as it pulled me deeper, held me tighter, and massaged down my length was too much—*was everything*.

My eyes squeezed shut as I slammed into her, once, twice, and then exploded, willing myself even deeper inside her warmth as my release pumped out of me in thick, long streams.

Resting my forehead on her collarbone, I panted, watching the unsteady rise and fall of her breasts as she did the same.

Her capacity to speak returned just before mine.

"I'm almost ready," she said huskily.

My sharp burst of laughter quickly turned into a strained moan when she chuckled with me and her muscles began to milk along my already hardening cock again.

"We really don't have to go anywhere," I offered once more for an entirely new reason.

"Mmm," she hummed and drew my face up to hers, planting a firm kiss on my lips before pushing gently against my chest. "But I'd like to."

My head hung in defeat.

"But when we come home... I'd like to have more of you," she promised with a tempting squirm of her hips.

"You're in my cottage, *in my shirt*, Miss Royale," I drawled slowly with a devilish grin. "You better be prepared to get all of me."

Violet shivered with the promise as I rose up and slid out of her.

As much as several parts of me could only focus on being back inside her, there was at least one part—one very demanding part—that clung to how she'd referred to my cottage as home.

And it was everything I wanted.

My mom and Lou had stolen Violet during our stroll down Maine Street, giving her their best crazy Christmas stories while appreciating all the twinkle lights which lit every house for three blocks straight, including the Lamplight Inn, which they'd paused in front of.

I'd been watching them carefully, wondering what Ailene was saying the way she pointed at the place and then linked her arm through Violet's.

"I was right."

I peered to the side, waiting for Frankie, who appeared next to me a moment later. I'd wondered just where she'd gotten off to.

"About what? Lenore dressing her cats up as Santa and his reindeer?" There was always a debate over which cat would get the honor of being jolly old Saint Nick and if the other would end up as either reindeer or elves.

This year she'd gone with reindeer.

Nine cats strung up and pulled the one in the red suit who sat in a custom sleigh she'd had me build four years ago. A sleigh that had "Meowy Christmas" on the back.

It wasn't my proudest moment.

"Or that Ginny definitely spiked this hot chocolate?"

Ginny sometimes babysat the Fuller kids and was bonused with bottles of their homemade moonshine, which she then worked into several of her adult-only chocolate treats.

"Oh, she did." Frankie grinned and took another swig from her own mug. "It was all my idea."

I gave her a side-eye. "I bet."

"But that's not what I'm talking about." Her teasing smile dimmed just a bit as she tipped her chin up and over in Violet's direction.

"Frankie," I warned.

"You're falling in love with her, aren't you?"

It wasn't an accusation as much as it was hopeful. Like a child asking on Christmas Eve, is Santa coming *tonight?*

I cleared my throat, scanning the crowd and searching for any other answer than the inevitable one revealing how I felt.

"And if I am?"

She paused until I looked at her. "Then I was right."

With a huff, I folded my arms over my chest and faced my meddling little sister.

"I shouldn't," I growled. "Just to prove you wrong and make it clear you can't go around renting out other people's property to further your schemes."

"Now, just hold on there a minute." She stuck her finger up in the air, and like a targeted missile, I knew it was headed straight for the center of my chest any second. "It was only you I would consider doing that to." She paused. "Okay, well, maybe Kit if I wasn't so sure he'd throw any unwelcome guest right into the ocean."

She shook her head, the tail of the lobster swaying with the movement.

"Anyway, it was the jelly gods that told me to."

"*Christ,*" I swore. "I'm going to take those damn labels away from Gigi—"

"Yeah, good luck with that, buddy." Frankie snorted. "Then the only thing you'll be carving is Gigi's cane out of your ass."

I didn't want to laugh, but I couldn't stop the brief chuckle that escaped. *Yeah, there was no way I was prying that task away from Gigi.*

"Seriously, though, Frankie," I sighed. "Just because I'm... falling... for Violet doesn't mean what you did is okay. It doesn't matter if I don't date. It's not okay to go to these lengths."

I broke off when her small, insistent hands gripped the outer edges of my jacket sleeves and she held me fast.

I questioned my phrase and my tone when the rock-solid determination on my sister's face cracked and wells of tears seeped out into the corners of her eyes.

"It does matter." Her lip trembled before the truth exploded from it. "Because it's my fault... our fault..."

I drew back. "What? What are you talking about?"

"I know about Eleanor," she blurted out.

Shit.

My mouth thinned. "What do you mean?" I asked, adding, "she's not a secret. Just an ex-girlfriend."

My sister shook her head vigorously. "Then why have you never mentioned her?"

It was less of a question and more of an accusation. And I walked right into it.

"Because you were a kid when it ended, Frankie. Christ, it was over a decade ago. Why the hell would *that* make you think I needed a dating intervention?"

Her small fist pounded on my chest. "Because you wanted to marry her, but instead you broke up with her and she moved away," Frankie pressed on with a strangled cry. "And it was all because of us..."

And whatever reassuring lies I'd been telling myself for years and was about to share with her vanished from my lips.

"Because you had to help raise us..." she finished with a soft sadness.

The air in my lungs escaped in a long, steady stream of warm, white fog into the cold night air.

"Oh, Frankie..." I grumbled, but there was no point in keeping it from her now; she deserved the whole truth, "That wasn't why we broke up. But it was part of it."

Eleanor was very ambitious, and while it was tempered living in Friendship, I knew by moving out west, she'd easily become one of those people who'd sacrifice anything and anyone to get ahead. And that wasn't the woman I saw when I pictured my forever.

My little sister shook her head sadly, quickly swiping her tears on her jacket sleeve. "I'm sorry, Jamie, but I couldn't do it anymore. I couldn't let you forget about the parts of your life meant to be lived for yourself."

For all her exuberance. For all her good intentioned and equally harebrained schemes. It was her soul-seeing perception that always caught me off guard the most.

Not because she had it but because I was conditioned to be the one looking out for her. It would always come as a surprise to hear how she'd been trying to look out for me.

"How did you know?" I wondered.

Frankie let her hands and her eyes fall. "I was visiting Lou at The Maine Squeeze a few weeks ago, and we overheard some of the girls talking about you because word has gotten around about Violet. They were saying how you never date, and they mentioned Eleanor. So, naturally, I asked."

"I see."

"Didn't take much to realize that when you broke up and she left was around the time Stonebar was really picking up when Lou and I were about to start high school." She shrugged. "Plus, I know you. I know how much you care... about the people you love. And I know, if you cared about her, there was only one reason you'd let her leave... because there were people you loved more who needed you to stay."

"I don't regret it, Frankie," I clarified. "Eleanor wasn't the one." I sighed. "Look, I can't tell you that you guys weren't part of my reason for ending it with her, but the truth is, Eleanor saw that Stonebar was going places and she wanted to use me to cash in on that."

My mouth thinned, watching my sister's eyes go wide.

"And when I told her I had no plans to let my carpentry business die in favor of taking 'my share' of Stonebar Farms, she..." I trailed off, thinking for a moment and deciding that Eleanor wasn't worth any more time in this discussion. "It doesn't matter. She wasn't the one, and it wasn't your fault; I don't regret her leaving for a second."

Truthfully, I'd rarely thought about her until recently—until what I felt for Violet dwarfed whatever it was I'd felt for Eleanor.

"But you'll regret this, Jamie," she cried, meeting my gaze once more, hers swimming with unshed tears that shimmered as they reflected the twinkling Christmas lights. "You'll regret letting Violet leave."

My jaw tightened. "I don't have a cho—"

"Yes, you do!" And there it was, the missile detonating on my chest as she poked me to emphasize each word.

"You don't have to stay for us, Jamie. We're adults—*I have my own business.* Lou is working. Stonebar is thriving. And Kit?" She hesitated. "Kit has taken care of himself in ways no one should ever have to, and now, he has all of Friendship here to help him."

My eyes swung away from her, and the truth I didn't want to hear. For a second, it locked on the lighthouse in the far distance, the light at the top of the tower the only sign of its inhabitants though my brother was certainly inside.

He didn't do crowds.

Not anymore.

"So, what you're saying is that you don't need me anymore?" I grunted, dragging a hand through my hair.

Rationally, I knew they didn't *need* me—not like they had when they were younger. But it was a fact I didn't know—didn't accept into my soul until right now.

Frankie smacked my arm. "Of course, we need you, Jamie. You're our brother," she said with a strained voice. "But we need you in the bigger ways now, not the smaller ones."

"I don't understand."

Her lip quivered, and it felt like a punch to the gut.

"You raised us to put family first because you always put us first," her voice cracked as she spoke. "You've always encouraged us to go after what we loved, and you've always supported us for it even if you didn't wholeheartedly agree."

I knew she was talking about when Kit decided he wanted to

join the Army. I didn't want him to go, but there was some part of him that needed to.

"What kind of family would we be if we didn't encourage you to do the same? Or worse, if we were what was stopping you?" she murmured. "Don't do that to us, Jamie. You've always been the hero in our story. Don't make us the unintended villain in yours."

"Frankie—"

Her small, powerful form crashed into my chest as she hugged me. I let out an unsteady sigh as I pulled my sister in tight.

"Love you, Frankie," I said softly, patting her back like I had since she was a little girl.

"I love you, too." Her voice was watery and I knew my jacket was absorbing her tears. "Which is why I'm not sorry about renting out your cottage."

Of course not. Because if she was, she wouldn't be Frankie.

"We all agree it's about time you put yourself first," she said, her voice muffled against my chest.

I cleared my throat once more, the emotion collecting in it making it tight and raw.

"All of you?" I rasped, fairly certain Frankie probably hadn't consulted the rest of our siblings about this.

"You know I speak for all of them," she grumbled. "And if they have a problem with it, they can take it up with me. And Gigi."

I groaned. "Just how much of a role did Gigi play in all of this?"

"You don't want to know."

I let out a brief laugh and shook my head. "No, I probably don't."

Her head tipped up as she pulled back from our embrace. "You can't live your whole life only for us, Jamie."

Her soft words struck a chord and brought me right back to our mom's living room the other night, standing in front of the tree when I'd said something similar to Violet, not realizing I hadn't been heeding my own advice.

You can't always live your life for someone else.

"I know, I just—" I broke off and released her, planting my hands on my hips.

"You just don't know how to not be Mr. Responsible For Us All?"

My eyes narrowed on her. "Something like that."

She smiled. "Well, you've never not figured out an answer for every dilemma I've come to you with. I'm sure this will be no different."

Her faith in me was both endearing and frightening.

"C'mon," she urged, linking her arm through mine. "We should probably catch up to Violet before Gigi starts planning your wedding."

My eyes snaked through the mulling crowd in the street and locked onto my woman, who was listening intently to my very insistent and slightly insane green-haired grandmother.

CHAPTER NINETEEN
VIOLET

CHRISTMAS EVE IN FRIENDSHIP WAS, by all reported temperatures, a *very* cold night, but I would dare anyone in the crush of small-town locals ambling down Maine Street to truthfully admit to being cold.

The street was closed to cars for the holiday, so the only tracks in the snow were footsteps that tattooed nostalgic paths down its length.

Snow from the storm and subsequent showers dusted over houses, cars, and signs, covering all of Friendship in a cold, cotton-white blanket.

The bright white was broken up with thousands of multicolored twinkle lights which fought to surpass the snow in the covered surface area. Streaming from every A-frame roof, wrapping every porch banister and lamppost, and framing every window, they lit the street in a friendly, festive glow.

The holiday spirit filled the street just as palpably as any string of traffic would normally. The smiles and laughter from every person we passed felt as though they made the lights twinkle and the snow glisten.

Hugging my mug of spiked hot chocolate tightly to my chest, I drifted away from Lou and the girls from the Squeeze, drawn to the old inn that sat on its untrodden path. It was lit with skeleton string lights and hauntingly dark inside.

"Know any good innkeepers?" Jamie's mom appeared at my shoulder.

I smiled. "I might."

Her Christmas knit scarf rose and fell with her sigh. "I wish I had more time for her, I really do. But with the farms, I just can't spare any more..."

I stayed silent, knowing with the whisky and whimsy of the night, the next thing out of my mouth would be to offer myself.

I'll do it.

I'll run it, as long as I can stay here.

With him...

"Isn't that what you do?" Lou asked, as though she'd heard my thoughts.

She might be the quieter of the twins, but I had a feeling Elouise Kinkade had ideas just as indomitable as her sister, she just went about executing them with greater stealth.

Gigi grinned widely. "Maybe you should stay and take it over, Violet," she said with an innocence so feigned it was impossible not to cough to cover up my laugh.

Carson City, Nevada.

Deep breath.

My blush deepened though, realizing she expected me to respond with all sincerity. I buried my chin deeper in my scarf and took another sip of my hot chocolate.

"I can't," I offered weakly, even though I wasn't quite sure why I couldn't.

It wasn't that there weren't a million reasons. It was just that none of them seemed all that important when I was standing here with them, in front of the kind of opportunity that tugged at the fringes of dreams I'd put on hold.

"Oh, sure you can," Gigi scoffed. "Dreams are like balloons, Violet. Easy to let soar once the ties holding you down are gone."

I gave her a small smile. "I don't have anything holding me down."

The elderly woman with her sparkling green hair stepped in front of me, squinting and staring me down with the perceptiveness of an X-ray machine that could see right into my heart.

"Well, that's one thing you have in common," she grumbled.

"Excuse me?"

"You and my grandson. If nothing else, you both share a loyalty to family to the point of fault."

"I don't—" I broke off, snapping my mouth shut when her eyebrow shot up like a bullet from a gun.

She wasn't wrong.

My eyes drifted shut for a quick moment, swallowing down the turmoil of emotions I felt regarding my family and my loyalty to them—*and their subsequent betrayal.*

Concord, New Hampshire.

"I remember when this inn was up and running in the good old days." She smiled nostalgically. "People would travel from all around for their cocktails and lobster. Oh, and their seafood soup." She sighed. "I used to flirt with so many of those French Canadians who came down here," she whispered with a devious chuckle, tacking on at the end. "Before I met Ronald, of course. They held so many parties for the whole town. Such good times..."

I smiled, grateful for her abrupt change in topic, and the alcohol running through my blood allowed the inn to come back to life for a brief few seconds as she described it. Fresh paint and candles in the windows. Guests bustling through the courtyard.

"Does it frighten you, having something with so much potential sitting right in front of you? Does it frighten you to think about how much you might have to risk to make it work?"

"Oh, no," I replied without a second thought. "That's the best thing about finding these hidden gems," I told her. "It's like the second I look at it, I can see the way it's meant to be. Like how some people can look at two puzzle pieces and see they're made to fit each other."

As soon as I finished, I turned to see she'd been staring at me this whole time.

And I realized our topic of conversation hadn't changed at all.

She wasn't asking about the inn.

She was asking if I was frightened about what Jamie and I had.

She was asking if I was afraid to risk it all for love.

I turned away, unwilling to admit that my answer remained unchanged.

"I wouldn't even know where to start," I replied, taking the conversation in a hypothetical direction since I couldn't lie to Gigi, but I also wasn't ready to admit the truth.

"I have a bunch of ideas," Lou chimed in eagerly.

"I'd love to hear them," I pressed, noticing how this was one of the few topics that Elouise seemed eager to discuss rather than fade into the silent background of observation rather than participation.

"Don't let her fool you!" Frankie exclaimed, sidling up beside me with Jamie not too far behind. "It's haunted. Lou doesn't want to be anywhere near it."

"*Francesca,*" Ailene scolded.

"That's not true," Lou protested at the same time.

"It's not haunted," Jamie promised me. "Frankie's had one too many of Ginny's spiked hot chocolates."

"It's haunted," Gigi peered around Ailene and loudly whispered.

"See!" she exclaimed. "I have *not* had too many of these." She smacked his arm. "What time is it? I need to top up my cup before the lighting."

Jamie looked at his watch. "Ten minutes."

As she disappeared, I looked to Jamie and asked, "What does she mean by 'the lighting'? I thought the tree was already lit."

At eight, about an hour after we got here, they lit the

Christmas tree in the center square, all the kids rushing forward to find their gifts. It was a Friendship tradition that in the two weeks leading up to Christmas Eve, they would place a box with their name on it under the tree. Cut into the top was a little slot where family and friends could drop in little notes of all the good things they'd done throughout the year. And tonight, they were able to take their box home and open it up to see what everyone had written about them.

Because Christmas wasn't just about presents, it was about doing good.

"Come with me." Jamie grinned playfully, his face transforming to that of someone much younger. Someone who hadn't had to grow up too quickly to be the man his family needed.

I'd have to ask him later what Frankie was talking to him about, I thought as I followed his footsteps in the snow.

Maine Street sat maybe three blocks from the coast—less in a few spots. Filing in between the Squeeze and the local ice cream shop, The Inside Scoop, we trailed along with the meandering crowd made of mostly adults, but some kids who were old enough to stay up, and filtered down along a wood-railed path toward the frozen waters.

Away from the street illuminated with Christmas lights, the darkness of the night crept in quickly. By the time the path curved several yards from the shore, the only light to be seen was in the distance at the turn of the beacon in the lighthouse.

Jamie squeezed my hand reassuringly.

A few more seconds and our progress came to a halt, packing us like coat-covered, chocolate-drinking cattle against the wooden railing.

I was right at the edge, so I turned to stare at the ocean. Completely dark, it looked like an ocean of oil moving with the tide as its inky black swells moved gently against the sand.

My attention moved to the lighthouse, wondering if Kit was home. I'd only seen him at the very beginning of the night—

presumably as he made his necessary appearance to appease Ailene and, more importantly, Gigi.

"You cold?" Jamie's voice rumbled next to me as his arm wrapped around my shoulder, pulling me closer to him.

"No," I murmured, pressing myself tighter to him as I tipped my face up to his. "What are we waiting for?"

He grinned. "The lighting."

As though that explained everything.

His head dipped down to mine, and I felt his lips caress the shell of my ear. "Sometimes, it's better to not know, Vi."

I shivered. "I don't know about that."

I felt his hand brushing along my cheek as his lips dropped gently to mine in a kiss that was both sweeter and more intoxicating than the alcoholic hot chocolate in my hand.

His fingers captured my chin and began to turn my face back out toward the sea.

"If you saw it coming, then it wouldn't be magic."

As he finished, from somewhere in the front of the crowd, someone began to sing "O Holy Night." Like moths to a flame, more and more voices joined in the carol.

My mother had always insisted that we were the people that carolers came and sang to. But, even though I'd never sung it before, I found I still knew the words and began to sing them as Jamie's rich baritone rang out from behind me, his chest vibrating each note against my back.

Warmth settled over the crowd like a blanket.

Of community.

Of friendship.

Of family.

And when we reached the portion in the song where "*O, night divine*" rang out loud and clear, my voice turned into a drawn gasp as twinkle lights began to light in a circular stream up and around the lighthouse.

Green and white spiraled up as though the lights were dusted on by magic until it reached the very top where the light sat and the entire upper observatory burst on with pale-yellow light.

Tears spilled from my eyes as the song continued while little spots of red and blue peeked out from around the conical base in subtle decoration.

It was a Christmas tree.

They'd lit the lighthouse into a giant Christmas tree.

Jamie's arms around me tightened as though he knew how overcome I'd become. And when the song finished and everyone erupted into cheers, he spun me to face him.

"I don't think I've ever seen anything so magical," I confessed breathlessly.

His eyes never left mine, holding them hostage and stealing the rest of my breath as he replied, "Me neither."

And then his lips claimed mine in another soul-searing kiss.

CHAPTER TWENTY
JAMIE

"SO THIS IS what you look like in love."

My gaze whipped to my brother and the smile that had been glued to my face the entire day wavered and disappeared.

We'd finished up our Christmas feast a little bit ago, everyone stuffed to the brim with lobster and seafood chowder, along with some other holiday favorites, to keep us full for a week.

With that done, Max strummed some Christmas tunes on his guitar with Harper singing over the crowd. Mom, Gigi, and Uncle George were in the kitchen, leaving Kit and me standing in the small hall watching while Lou and Frankie gave Violet their Christmas present—a customized "*Jamie's* Maine Squeeze" mug.

I half-heartedly rolled my eyes when they told me what they'd done, but now my whole body lit on fire seeing the way Violet smiled and blushed, her eyes slipping to mine as she bit her lip.

I grunted. We'd been in public too long. I needed to get *my* main squeeze back to my cottage. Back to privacy. And back to being naked.

"Not sure if that's a compliment or an insult," I drawled lightly and looked back at him.

This was the first Christmas I'd wanted to stay at my cottage almost as much as I'd wanted to come here and join my family.

I'd wanted to stay in bed with her all day. Waking up Violet with an orgasm was rapidly becoming my favorite way to watch her eyes open—full of lust and warmth and me.

Grunting, I shifted my seat and focused on my woman.

She adjusted the holly headpiece Lou had made for the three of them. The little red berries matched the long red sweater she wore over her black leggings that hugged her ass in the way that made my hands itch to do the same.

"What does it feel like?"

He wasn't judging. His gaze was open and wondering, even if it was layered with hopelessness. But he wondered in the same way a blind person would ask someone with twenty-twenty vision what it was like to see—the way you want to know about something you'll never be able to experience.

"Like my heart won't beat without her."

I took another sip of my whisky, watching as the three of them flipped through old family photos.

She just belonged. Here. With them. *With me.*

Fuck, she belonged with me.

My family was good at making guests feel at home, there was no doubt about that. But this... dinner... it was something else. It was as though she was one more piece in our family we didn't know was missing.

"Even though it will continue to beat," he replied matter-of-factly.

My eyes flicked to Buzzkill Kit. Whatever happened to him left nothing but statistics and an analytical mind except in his art. But his emotions... I saw how he struggled to understand what I'd said.

"And knowing the sun will continue to rise every morning doesn't mean much unless you open the windows and let in the light or step outside and feel the warmth."

His mouth thinned. He was thinking about what I said—thinking about a response. But when he couldn't find one to further his point, his head fell and he turned toward me.

"So, what are you going to do? Move back to New York?" he asked.

He didn't mean to be harsh. My artistic dreamer of a younger brother now only saw in operations and strategies, targets and casualties. There was no variation. No detour. Or if there was, it was locked away in his lighthouse that sat on the edge of the world.

Because that was where he lived: on the edge of our world.

"I don't know," I said honestly. *If that's what it takes.*

"Well, you need to," he told me. "You need to know exactly what you are willing to risk—*willing to lose*—before you commit. Otherwise, you'll lose more than you can survive."

I stared at him, hearing the *"trust me, I've learned from experience"* in his tone, if not in his words.

"You'll never lose us," he echoed the gist of my conversation with Frankie last night.

My jaw tightened and my eyes locked on Violet. And then my sisters. And my mom and Gigi.

I wanted all of this right here. But if I had to choose... I think it was past time to follow my own heart rather than continue to look out for everyone else's.

Before I could say anything else, Kit added quietly, "Of all people, Jamie, you deserve it." And then he walked away.

I downed the rest of my drink and let the thoughts come. The ones that told me my family was strong. That they'd be okay if I moved to New York to be with Violet. That my well-intentioned responsibility for them was met and surpassed long ago.

"You're going to ask her to stay."

My head tipped toward my mother's voice.

"How?" I croaked.

It had been a long time since I asked her for advice like this. In fact, I wasn't sure I'd ever asked her for advice when it came to women. Whether it was innate or out of necessity, I always had the confidence to make decisions without question that what I was doing was for the best. But now... with this...

I didn't want to lose her.

"How do I ask her to stay here? To leave everything for me?" I murmured with a tight voice, turning my head to her.

"Do you not think you're worth it?" Her eyes flicked to Violet. "Do you not think that girl would stay in a heartbeat if you asked?"

"I don't—"

"Have you listened at all to what she's told you about her family and the life that brought her up here?"

"*Mom*," I warned.

She sighed and wrapped her arm around me, pulling me close. "You know I'm just trying to get a point through that thick, handsome skull of yours."

I groaned.

"And that point is, you have to ask, Jamie. You always have to ask or you'll never know." She shrugged. "And sure, maybe I'm wrong." She paused long enough for me to get the hint that she didn't think she was. "But the way I see it, that girl fell for you just as hard and fast as you fell for her."

"Oh, yeah?" I winced. "And what if it's fleeting? We hardly know..."

I couldn't bring myself to say the words because I didn't feel them. I didn't feel like I didn't know Violet.

I knew about her life, her family, how she was raised. I knew she was afraid of the dark and recited state capitals to try to keep her anxiety at bay. I knew she liked her coffee black with one sugar and preferred the strawberry jam over blueberry. She liked meeting new people and making them feel at home in her hotels, and I knew the reason she wanted to give her guests something she never had... the feeling of coming home.

I knew she preferred flannel shirts over silk pajamas. Colorful underwear, even though she blushed every time I saw them. I knew the spots on her body that made her shiver and the ones that made her quake.

I knew everything I needed, but was it enough?

"You know how you would help Frankie with her home-work?" I nodded. "Remember how upset she'd get because all Lou had to do was read the chapter once, and she could remember it all?"

I laughed. "Yeah."

Even though they were twins, Lou got the lucky end of the stick when it came to school and studies. I would swear the girl had a photographic memory or the closest thing you could get to one.

"Well, that's kind of like love. Some people, they need time with a person, months and months to know everything about them in order for their heart to know how it feels. And that's okay. And then there are some who only need a short time, who meet someone and pick up that connection faster." She took a sip of her eggnog. "Neither is wrong, Jamie."

I knew that.

I knew what I felt for Violet wasn't wrong. *Wasn't lust or infatuation.*

I wanted her in my life. Forever. Period. *But what if she didn't want the same?*

"You think she'll want to stay?" I asked. "This isn't New York."

"And thank goodness for that." Mom laughed. A few moments later, she answered me more seriously, "I think Violet wants to stay, but I don't think that's the question you really want the answer to."

I jerked back, startled.

"The question you need to answer is what *you* want."

Kit's words echoed in my mind. *What I was willing to risk...*

"I want to be with her." It was that simple. "So, if she can't stay, then I'm going to go," I breathed out, a weight pulling off my chest. "If she has to go back, then I'm going with her."

Assuming that was what Violet wanted.

"Good." Her arm reached around me, pulling me close to her side. "All I want is for you to be happy, Jamie. We'll be fine."

I didn't ask for her assurance, but a little more weight was released from my shoulders when she gave it.

"Love you, Mom." I pulled her to me and dropped a kiss on top of her head.

"Hey, Jamie!" I looked over to Max, calling my name with a devious grin on his face. "All lips are fair game when they're standing underneath the mistletoe."

My attention snapped to Violet. Sure enough, my sisters had pulled her underneath the sprig of holly hanging from the light in the center of the ceiling.

Max pretended to jump up from his seat by the fireplace and it sent me lunging—to everyone's amusement—to Violet's side, yanking her into my arms.

"Jamie, what—"

Her sweet lavender and whisky lips crumbled under mine as I dipped her low and kissed her deep.

Whether here or in New York, the only place I cared about making sure Violet stayed was in my arms.

VIOLET

"I have something for you."

I turned, eyes wide, to stare at Jamie as he kicked off his shoes and shut the cottage door behind us.

The exhaustion I'd felt on the drive back disappeared with a rush of goose bumps, knowing I was alone with him again.

Today was the kind of Christmas I'd always dreamed of. Family. Friends. Food. Laughter.

There was no fancy dress. No show to put on for the guests or members of my mother's social circle.

Instead, I'd woken up in Jamie's arms.

Well, actually... I rubbed my thighs together, remembering I'd woken up with his head between my legs, his tongue working its own set of miracles between my thighs.

Home-cooked breakfast that we ate in bed. *More*

Christmas sex. And then left for his mother's house, which had been an evening of preserve premonitions from Gigi, raucous and inappropriate Christmas carols from Max and Nox, disappearing with Frankie and Lou to do our hair into crowns made of fake holly, and delicious food made by Ailene and George.

And Jamie...

His tender yet possessive touches throughout the night reminded me he was always there if I needed him, yet giving me enough room to make my own place.

"What?" I swallowed hard as he approached me. "Jamie, you didn't—"

"I wanted to," he cut me off and planted another kiss on my lips.

"Why?"

He pulled back, surprised.

"Why would you get me a Christmas present, Jamie?" I asked again, guilt spinning in my stomach for having nothing for him. "We haven't..."

Known each other that long?

Given an official name to whatever this is?

Decided whether or not it merits a future, let alone Christmas presents?

I gulped as the room began to fade and anxiety took over.

The thought of leaving—of leaving him—was the darkest cloud on the looming horizon.

Trenton, New Jersey.

Deep breath.

Santa Fe, New Mexico.

"Violet."

My eyes slammed open just as his mouth claimed mine, a physical barrier to the panic that began to set in.

"You're okay," he said as his tongue slid along the seam of my lips. "You're mine."

With a soft cry, I melted into him, opening my mouth so his

tongue could find mine and stoke the fire burning through my veins and burn away the darkness.

"*Jesus, Violet,*" he groaned as my hips rolled against his.

Strong fingers curled into my hips and pushed me back several safe inches.

"I didn't get you a Christmas present, sweetheart," he rasped. "I made you one."

This time, the blood rushing to my head had nothing to do with anxiety or fear and everything to do with a much more potent emotion.

"You... made me..." I choked out the words as he begrudgingly went to the bag he'd brought back from his mom's house, now sitting on the dining table waiting to be unpacked.

I thought it was filled with enough leftovers of the most amazing seafood chowder I'd ever had and enough blueberry jam to feed a small army. *I guess there was another passenger inside it that I missed.*

He pulled out a small package wrapped with layers of tan packing paper.

"Bedroom."

I gaped and complied at the one-word command, my body heating as the sight of the rumpled bed came into view.

"Jamie—"

"Sit."

I shivered, his one-word instructions making desire pool between my thighs and stripping my focus away from the package he palmed with one hand.

"Has anyone ever made you a gift before?" he asked, but the way he looked at me told me he already knew the answer.

"No," I told him, watching his arms pull and flex as he began to stoke the fire in the room, a blanket of heat flooding through the space. "I learned quickly that any handmade gifts would end up in the trash... one more thing that never seemed right about how my family celebrated Christmas."

Even the ornaments my brother and I made in school were

tossed in the trash as soon as we got home; they didn't match the musical-theme decor that my mother had picked out for the tree.

"I made you a Christmas present because you, Violet Royale, are far too special for me to just get you a gift," he told me, crouching in front of where I sat on the bed and extending his hand so I could take the present.

I bit my lip as emotion swelled inside me. My fingers brushed against his while grabbing the paper, and the electricity in the brief contact brought my nerves to life.

But he didn't let go right away.

"This place... the people... they've always been my home, and growing up here, this was just how things were," he began. "But then you showed up, and even though I know Friendship, Maine, is nothing compared to New York City, the way you looked at everything... the things you said... made me realize all the things you were missing, all the things you deserve."

He let go so I could pull the package into my lap, carefully beginning to unfurl the wrapping, the crunching noise seeming to add to the preciousness of the contents inside.

"So, I made you this because..." I looked up when he broke off to clear his throat. "Because I want you to remember everything you deserve."

"And what's that?" I asked as I pulled back the last layer.

"Magic."

The paper fell away and I lost my breath at the snow globe sitting in my lap.

But it wasn't just any snow globe.

It was his cottage.

I cupped my hand over my mouth, blinking rapidly to keep my tears at bay as I carefully—*reverently*—picked up the glass orb that sat on a base of carved and painted pine trees.

Nestled in the center was an exact replica of Jamie's cottage, surrounded by snow-covered trees. The exquisiteness of the ornate carvings was matched by the detail of the paint that brought it to life. The rich-red shutters. The warm light in the windows. Even the iron lamppost stood proudly lit outside.

"Did you..." I swallowed, unable to even form a complete sentence as I tipped the beautiful gift and let the fake snow swirl around the very cottage I was sitting in.

"I carved it all and had Kit paint it for me," he answered what he knew I wanted to know.

"Jamie... this is incredible," I gushed.

It was magic.

"You didn't have to do this." Tears slipped from my eyes, but I didn't bawl. My heart hammered and my head felt light, but I didn't panic.

"I did," he swore. "I did because I didn't want you to ever forget..."

We both froze as he trailed off.

Forget this place? Forget him? Forget what we had?

One small phrase was all it took to understand that he thought I could still leave after this.

Of all the things I'd been afraid of in my life, realizing that I'd fallen in love with Jamie Kinkade wasn't one of them.

Rising, I set the snow globe on the mantel of the fireplace. Before Jamie could stand, I reached down, spearing my hands through his hair and slanting my mouth over his.

I kissed him like it was the only gift I had to give—and because I kissed him with all my heart, it was.

"What do you want for Christmas, Jamie?" I whispered against his lips.

He growled, pushing me back onto the bed. "You, Violet." His teeth nipped at my lower lip and then soothed the tender flesh. "All I want is you."

I sighed blissfully as he stripped my clothes and then his own away. The crackling heat of the fire was a familiar track as he set to worship my body.

My body arched in demanding waves as his mouth teased and tortured my nipples. My fingers lost themselves in his auburn curls, pulling him tight as his tongue flicked and sucked on me until desire drenched my core.

"*Jamie,*" I gasped his name as his fingers delved into my pussy, sliding through the slickness pooled there and pushing inside me.

"I want you, Violet," he confessed with a violence that only comes from the deepest recesses of your heart. "You're the first thing I've ever wanted for myself. Your strength. Your touch. Your—" His low growl tore away the word I knew was coming.

Love.

The word never came, but I tasted it on his tongue as his mouth returned to mine and his hips wedged between my thighs.

With a needy moan, I felt his blunt head probe at my entrance just before he sank inside. I sucked in a breath, my hips arching up for more.

Pulling back and thrusting hard, he rubbed right against that spot inside me that brought the stars down to earth and sent me soaring toward heaven.

"Jamie..." I begged, wrapping my legs around his waist.

"I've got you, sweetheart," he rasped, shoving himself deeper and deeper inside my body—*and my heart.* "*You're mine.*"

Oh god.

Pleasure pulled in painful spirals through my body as his words sent me soaring toward my climax.

You're mine.

I screamed as my body shattered around his, clamping and jerking against him.

Jamie slammed into me with a hoarse shout, his release burying itself inside me.

The moment was so intimate and delicate, both us so fragile from our orgasms, I tried to get ahold of my harsh breaths, afraid one of them might shatter it. As my heartbeat slowed, I felt the words bubble up from inside me.

I don't want to leave, Jamie.

I've fallen in love with you.

But they couldn't break through the barrier in my chest—the

one that swelled with how perfect this day had been and how perfect this moment was. I felt the words, the way my chest thumped against his, the way the dark pools of his eyes found mine, and the way he pressed one more long, lingering kiss to my lips.

Those words fell short for this moment.

Either that, or I was too afraid they'd ruin this by going too far.

So, I swallowed them down and drifted deeper into the magic in his arms. This had been a perfect Christmas; we could talk about what the future held for us in the morning.

I took one long look at the snow globe on the mantel, the dancing fire just barely glinting off the flecks of snow inside the glass, and I made my very first Christmas wish.

Please, God, don't let this end.

CHAPTER TWENTY-ONE
VIOLET

IT HAPPENED IN EVERY STORY.

Dorothy went home to Kansas from Oz.

Wendy returned to the world from Neverland.

And I, Violet Royale, was going to have to leave my own version of a magical world here in Friendship for the cold-shouldered reality of New York City.

But I hadn't expected it to happen like this—with a phone call. *The day after Christmas.*

"Who is it?" Jamie asked. He sat at the other end of the couch, rubbing my feet in the most delicious way as the fire crackled low in the background, his fingers halting as he regarded me with concern.

"My father," I murmured, staring blankly at the screen on my phone.

Albany, New York.

It wasn't that my dad never called me. It was just that he hadn't reached out at all since I emailed, saying that I was taking a vacation.

My jaunt to the hospital had solidified in his mind that he'd made the right choice, deciding to leave the business to Gerald rather than me. They'd checked in once while I was there, asking if I was okay and when I would be discharged—the sooner the better was my impression, probably before word got out among my mother's social crowd that their daughter had a *flaw*.

Deep breaths. Raleigh, North Carolina.

"Hello?" I answered hesitantly.

There were only two reasons for him to reach out. Either something catastrophic had happened to one of my family members, or he needed answers to business questions that only I, the one ousted from the company, would know.

"Violet." His clear, crisp voice cut through the line. "When will you be home?"

My mouth opened, but no answer came out.

Bismarck, North Dakota.

Given Jamie's expression, he definitely heard what my father said. We hadn't talked about it—about my leaving. *Or staying.* We'd enjoyed the holiday together as though there was no end in sight, but now that the magical bubble of Christmas was over, I knew it was something that needed to be said.

"What's going on? Is everyone okay?" I opted for instead.

"You need to come back immediately." He cleared his throat. "The company needs you."

I felt the blood begin to drain from my face.

Oh god.

This couldn't be happening.

My eyes squeezed shut.

Columbus, Ohio. Oklahoma City, Oklahoma.

"What do you mean? I thought... I thought Gerald was going to be in charge. Shouldn't you be calling him?" As much as I tried to hide it, there was a slight bite to my tone.

"I thought giving your brother the opportunity to step up would be good for him. I was wrong. He was supposed to set up a Christmas dinner with several potential partners—people you reached out to acquire their hotels—and he botched the whole damn thing."

I could hear the loathing laced in his voice.

"There's more, but I don't have time. We need you. Royale Hotels needs you to come back."

I believed it was less shocking to see Jamie barging through the door that first night than it was to hear my father admit that he— that the business needed me.

Salem, Oregon.

I felt my mouth drying out the way it dropped. I stared at Jamie, but I wasn't seeing him. I was lost, trying to process what I'd just heard.

"Violet? You still there?" my father's voice clipped a few long seconds later, assuming the call had dropped from my silence.

"Yes. Sorry." I sat up straight, pulling my feet from Jamie's lap and tucking them underneath me. Too late, I realized what even that slight gesture seemed to symbolize. "The service isn't the best here—"

"I said the company needs you to come back, Violet. I put your brother in charge of all the acquisitions you had lined up, and they've begun dropping like flies. You need to come back. You need to fix what he's done," my father went on until he ran out of breath.

I paused.

Not because I didn't think—*didn't know*—I could do it. I paused because I'd been wanting this moment for so long, and now that it was here, I felt nothing of the things I thought I would.

"Okay."

I looked at Jamie as I said it, needing to see... something... in his eyes. This was what I wanted all along, right? This was what I'd been waiting for from them, from my family?

"I've booked you on a flight home this afternoon. I'll have Jill send over your ticket," he informed me with a huge sigh of relief.

"Okay."

That was it. No "thank you," no "how are you feeling?" But who was I kidding? The Royale family would never be like the

Kinkades, it just wasn't who they were. Apples and oranges and all that.

It would be a lie to say this call wasn't a huge step for my father—calling for help, admitting to needing me. *But it would also be a lie to say I hadn't wanted more.*

"They need you?" Jamie was the first to speak after the call ended.

Each minute that passed in his presence made me all the more grateful for it. His comfort. His steadiness and strength. But right now, I was just grateful someone else had heard what happened because, aside from the call log on my phone, I was liable to wonder if it had really happened.

Harrisburg, Pennsylvania.

I nodded, swallowing over the lump in my throat as I tried to find a way to meet his eyes.

"My brother... he's messing a lot of things up for the company. Important things my father hoped to leave him in charge of." *Important opportunities that I'd been solely responsible for creating.*

Jamie bent forward, resting his elbows on his knees as he stared into the fire.

"He wants me to go back," I answered his question, even though it felt as though I had to break my heart open a little to get the words out. "My family needs me."

"I understand."

And of all the people in this world who could ever understand putting aside personal desires for their family, Jamie could. *Jamie did.*

My phone buzzed. The notification showing my airline ticket out of Maine this afternoon meant I had less than two hours to pack my things and get to the airport.

Standing, I stepped closer to him. "Jamie..."

Tears threatened to escape my eyes.

Providence, Rhode Island.

I don't want to leave. I want to stay with you. I've fallen in love with you.

But what's the point in admitting the truth when there was nothing to be done about it?

This was my family. For better or for worse. My family that hadn't appreciated what I'd done for them, no matter how hard I tried, until now. *Now, they needed me.*

Jamie looked up at me. The warmth in his rich-brown eyes was gone. Left was a barren plane of unwelcome understanding. In that gaze, I knew even if I tried to turn down my family to stay with him, he wouldn't let me.

"I'm sorry," I murmured as he rose in front of me. "I didn't mean for this to happen."

There were many things that were pointless to admit to right now. But there was one thing I needed to say. One thing I needed him to know before I left.

"Jamie, I never expected to find you," I confessed, my voice barely above a whisper. "I never expected—"

His lips sealed over mine, tasting, swallowing the admission before it could be spoken.

I never expected to fall in love with you.

My mouth opened under his. His tongue licked and stroked a confession of equal measure against my own. The kiss morphed into all the things we couldn't say, and all the things we were leaving behind, and from there, it grew without restraint. It grew into everything I was choosing to walk away from.

For my family.

"Jamie..." I breathed his name as he pulled back.

The feel of him against me, his heart beating against mine. The way everything seemed right here, and I seemed to fit right into it. It was too much.

It wasn't real.

His thumb brushed over my cheek so softly as though anything more might shatter me.

"I'm proud of you, Violet," he said in a low voice. "You're going to go back and kick some ass."

My eyes widened. With a flush, I replied, "Thank you. I mean, hopefully, there's no kicking involved..."

Neither of us even smiled. Any attempt at lightheartedness was like using a bucket to bail water out of a ship that had been torpedoed.

"Just in case you ever doubt yourself in the future or all the things you've accomplished," he rasped, his gaze searching mine for a little piece of me to keep.

"And you deserve your own happiness," I returned.

Having my family's respect, their admiration, was something I'd wanted my whole life.

I had to believe this was a new start. I had to believe going back would be a new beginning, otherwise I'd never be able to walk away.

"I should pack," I said with a wavering voice. *Before I started crying and questioning everything.* "My flight home leaves in two and a half hours."

I couldn't stop the way I winced at the word home. It felt wrong. It felt like a misnomer for the city I'd left behind.

It felt like a lie for any place other than here. With him.

His head dipped down, and I felt the soft press of his lips on my forehead in the most heartbreaking kiss.

"I'll go get my truck and take you," he offered, and before I could thank him or reply, he was gone.

Before I could ask him why he hadn't asked me to stay.

Through the shock of it all, that small notion tore a small opening in my heart and let out all the hope—*all the love*—I'd found here over the last few weeks. Like a balloon with a pinhole, all the confidence I'd felt about Jamie wanting me—*loving me*—deflated.

Maybe I was wrong.

Maybe I was just something temporary for him, too, and that was why he hadn't asked me to stay.

Numbly, I walked back into the bedroom, doing my best not to look at the bed and see the memories we'd made in it as I packed up my things. And I definitely didn't look at the snow globe perched on the mantel. It was too thoughtful, too sweet... and far too heartbreaking to think about bringing with me, even though it was my gift.

It didn't feel real, and that was one of the reasons I clung to, for why I couldn't stay.

You don't go on vacation and decide to stay forever.

You don't go on vacation and fall in love with a handsome woodsman.

I couldn't stay here. This was a reprieve—a respite from my life.

It couldn't *be* my life.

By the time I had all my things packed, I'd reached the point in rationalizing where I was sure this was the best way for things to have ended. Without giving me much time to question and second-guess. Without any promises or declarations of love to have been spilled and then acted upon.

Without the spoken evidence that getting on the plane to New York this afternoon was going to break my heart.

JAMIE

The snowmobile barely came to a stop before I jumped off and pulled the ignition key with me.

"*Fuck,*" I swore and threw my helmet in the snow next to it and ran a hand through my hair.

This wasn't supposed to happen.

It wasn't supposed to go like this.

I took the stairs into my mom's house two at a time, having left the keys to my truck here just in case she needed to move it.

She wasn't supposed to leave.

The last time I'd felt this helpless was the day Frankie and Lou's dad walked out and left my mom on her own.

At least then I could step up.

Even if I couldn't—*and had no desire to stop him*—at least then I could do something. I could help. I could help my mom, and I could help raise them.

This time, I could do nothing. And for me, to do nothing was the worst goddamn thing in the world.

"Jamie?"

I bit into my lip, curling my fingers around my truck keys on the kitchen counter.

"Just grabbing my keys, Mom," I said gruffly, turning to her slowly.

"What's going on?" Her arms folded over her chest. Point-zero-zero-two seconds for her to realize something was wrong. Standard response time for CI-Ailene. As usual, she was clad in her fluffy slippers and her apron was folded over her arm.

"I'm going to take Violet to the airport."

Her mouth dropped. "What?" she gasped. "Why?"

"She needs to go home."

"This is her home," she retorted with a scoff.

"Mom..." I warned, my barely restrained anger inching closer to release.

"Don't 'Mom' me." She pointed a finger at me. "What are you talking about? Why is she leaving? What happened? What did you—"

"Nothing," I bit out. "I didn't do anything." I pinched the bridge of my nose. "Her family called. They need her back home... they need her back at their hotels."

"Horseshit," my mother spat.

Both my eyebrows shot up. I expected that kind of response from Gigi, but rarely from my mother.

"James Kinkade, you know damn well they may need her back, but they don't want her. They don't appreciate her. They want her back just to use her."

"Of course I do!" I roared, the anger inside me spilling open from the break in my heart. "Of course, I know that. But what am

I supposed to say? 'Don't go home, your family sucks and they don't care about you'?"

"Well, it would be a start," she huffed. "What did you say?"

"What do you think? I told her I'd give her a ride to the airport." My lower back sagged against the counter as my shoulders dropped.

"Mom?"

"Shit," I said under my breath.

Frankie flew around the corner, her eyes bulging when she saw me. "Jamie? I thought I heard you. What are you doing here?" Lou appeared behind her a second later.

Fan-fucking-tastic.

"Violet is leaving, and your brother is here to get his truck to take her to the airport."

"Thanks, Mom," I ground out just as Frankie cried out.

"What! What is wrong with you?"

I swore and ducked as a towel narrowly flew past my head.

"I told you to ask her to stay!"

"Jamie, you can't let her—"

"Stop!" I roared, holding my hands up as my chest rose and fell with harsh breaths. "Look, Violet is leaving," I repeated, making sure I met each and every one of their eyes. "Her family needs her—they called her, and she is going back to help them. Think you can understand that?"

My question was met with stubborn silence and identical looks of disapproval on all of their faces.

"It's her family," I continued, looking specifically at my mother. "It's her choice. I can't ask her to stay, no matter how much I want to... no matter how much I need her to."

My breath grew ragged. Violet was the first thing in my life I'd wanted for myself. Aside from my business—and even that, I'd partly grown it so I could take care of my family if needed, if something ever happened.

"But did you even ask her to stay?" Frankie asked softly.

My silence was enough of an answer.

"Does she know that you need her too?"

No. My jaw tightened.

"Oh, Jamie..." My mother stepped toward me, partially blocking the tortured look on my face from my siblings. "You say she chose her family... but what other option did you give her?"

I jerked back.

"What?"

"If you didn't ask her to stay, what other option did you give her?" she repeated softly, reaching up and placing her hand on my arm.

My blood turned to ice, remembering those torturous few moments when she'd been on the phone, hearing just what was happening.

But then I thought about after...

I hadn't said anything. I didn't tell her how I felt about her. I didn't tell her I wanted her to stay.

Was it because I really thought she wanted to go back to her family? To the people who'd passed her over even after all she'd done for them?

Violet knew what she was worth; did I really think she believed she deserved to go back to that?

"If you didn't tell her how you feel," she went on, "what else could she assume except that you wanted her to go?"

I tried to swallow over the lump in my throat but failed. "But it's her family."

She nodded. "I know, baby. I know." She squeezed my arm again. "But by not telling her, instead of giving her another possibility, you took away her choice."

Fuck.

My knees went weak, realizing she was right.

I hadn't given Violet a choice. I'd assumed. Her family needed her, and I'd gone and assumed they were the choice she would make even though I knew they didn't deserve her.

"I made a mistake," I choked out, my eyes rising to meet hers.

"No shit, Sherlock," Frankie chimed in from the back. "How are you going to fix it?"

I slammed my truck keys on the counter. "I'm going to tell her I love her and that she can make her own decision, but I'd really fucking love it if she decided to stay."

Frankie and Lou cheered and jumped on me as I walked by them, my mom patting my back in a silent send-off.

"C'mon, Lou!"

I whipped around. "Where do you think you're going?"

My sister met my stare, stubborn for stubborn. "We're coming behind you."

"Frank—"

"I was responsible for the start of this, I deserve to see its ending," she insisted. "Plus, Violet should know that she has family here now, too."

I was tense and ready to hold my ground, but when her lip quivered, my resolve broke. It always had. *It always would.*

"Fine." But that didn't mean I had to wait for them.

"We'll be right behind you!" She grinned at me, but I didn't have time to wonder why she looked like she had this all under control.

I turned and stalked from the house back toward my snowmobile. It was the fastest way back to the cottage in the fresh covering of snow.

It was the fastest way back to her.

Chapter Twenty-Two
Jamie

"Shit!" I cursed and jumped off the still-slowing snowmobile, snow kicking up on my heels as I ran toward the front door of my cottage. "No, no, no."

No.

I threw the door open, crashing into the reality of what I'd expected.

Violet was gone.

All of her things were cleared out. Suitcases gone. Bed made. *My goddamn shirt folded on top.*

She'd left.

I spun and pounded my fist into the nearest wall.

I was a fucking idiot.

I hadn't given her the choice to stay, so why the hell would she wait around and wallow in that all the way to the airport?

"Fuck." I stalked back outside, hearing the rumble of more snowmobiles pulling up by mine.

"Jamie!" Frankie pulled her helmet off as Lou pulled up next to her. "Where is she?"

"Gone." I planted my hands on my hips. "Fuck."

"What do you mean? You were going to take her." My sister

barged by me as though I was incapable of assessing the emptiness of my own home.

"I was." I looked in the snow, finding the small footprints made by her boots, followed by the tracks from her suitcase. "But it looks like the damn woman didn't want to inconvenience me anymore, so she called her own car."

I let out a low growl, rubbing my hands over my mouth. I couldn't think straight. I'd always been the one in control, the responsible one, and now all rational thought had deserted me.

The woman I loved was gone.

"I'll have to go back for my truck," I began to ramble, trying to think through the process of chasing someone down at the airport and trying to stop them from boarding a flight.

"Rudolph, this is Santa, do you copy?"

My gaze whipped up to Frankie, calling through her walkie-talkie.

"What the—"

"Dammit, Frankie, I told you, my code name isn't Rud—"

"Max, shut up! It's an emergency!" she cut him off.

"What? What's going on?"

"The Present has left the North Pole. She's headed for the airport. At least a twenty-minute head start. Check the traffic conditions on Route 1—"

"Frankie, what the fuck are you—"

"Calling in the cavalry," she broke off to answer me and then held her hand up as though to stop me from protesting any further.

Meanwhile, Lou stormed up to me. "Violet is the Present, and the North Pole is your cottage," she informed me. "Just wait, she has a plan."

"Jesus Christ..." I shook my head, slamming my helmet back on.

Of course, Frankie had a plan. Half the time, her plans were the whole damn problem.

I didn't have time for this. I needed to get to Violet before she got on that plane.

I froze when little Lou planted her palms firmly on my chest, the fire in her eyes burning just as brightly as her twin's.

"It's a good plan," she insisted softly. My little rational sister. "Please, Jamie."

And for her, I hesitated. Because if Lou thought it was a good plan, then maybe it wasn't so crazy after all.

"Jamie, wait!" Frankie yelled as soon as I climbed on my bike, running up to me. "You'll never make it if you go back for the truck. The roads are too snowy. You won't catch her."

"Frankie, what other choice do I—"

"We have to take the snowmobiles," she blurted out. "It's the only way we're going to catch up and check each car."

My mouth thinned.

Using snowmobiles on the road wasn't exactly legal except in emergencies.

But fuck it, this was an emergency.

"Fine."

Her face lit up with relief. "Okay, which airport is she headed to?"

"Augusta."

"Okay, well, they're probably out of Friendship and on Route 1 by now. Our best bet is to cut through the woods and meet up with the highway where it hits Jefferson Street."

At that moment, my cousin's voice came back through the radio. "*The highway is moving like a snail.*"

"Perfect."

"You copy that, Santa?"

I arched an eyebrow at my sister as if to say, "*Really? Santa?*"

And there it was—that same determined, know-it-all smirk she'd had when she walked in on Violet and me the first time.

"*Copy that, Rudolph,*" she told him, her smile broadening.

What had I just agreed to?

I shook my head.

Whatever the hell Frankie had planned, she was right on one account; the only way I was going to catch Violet now was by snowmobile.

I flipped down my visor and revved my bike, hearing her final instructions to Max over the radio just before I flew off into the snow.

"Grab the sleigh. Meet you at Jefferson. Operation Save Christmas is a go. Over."

VIOLET

Columbia, South Carolina.

Traffic was crawling.

I hadn't even realized how much snow had fallen overnight until I stepped outside with all my things, once again having to trek through several wet inches to get to my Uber.

At least it hadn't been a Prius.

Then again, the decade-old Element that pulled up wasn't much of a step up.

I stared out the window at the whitewashed landscape, feeling as though it were a mirror that reflected how cold and bleak I felt inside.

It had taken all of three minutes before the thought of Jamie driving me to the airport opened the tap to my stream of anxiety.

I wouldn't be able to do it. I wouldn't be able to go that whole time and not embarrass myself by asking to stay.

And I wouldn't let begging be an option.

It hadn't been one when my father ousted me from our company, and it wouldn't be one when Jamie ousted me from his heart.

Maybe it was my own fault. Maybe I shouldn't have agreed with my father on the phone. But what else was I supposed to say?

"Let me think about it for a few minutes because I've kind of fallen in love with a man who saw my worth from the start, but he doesn't know that yet, so let me tell him and get back to you."

I groaned.

I should've stalled. I should've pretended to lose service and hung up on him. I should've done something. But my brain was fried from working under pressure, under the weight of expectations I'd never be recognized for exceeding for so long, that all I could do was agree and hope Jamie would give me a reason to call my father back.

To tell him no.

To tell him it was too late and he'd already lost me.

But instead, ever-chivalrous Jamie had ceded the fight.

Pierre, South Dakota.

I winced, the thought making me nauseous. Maybe I would just be perpetually the worst at reading exactly what people wanted from me... *perpetually giving more of myself to people who didn't want it.*

I let out a small yelp when my phone began to ring, earning me a glare from the older male driver.

"Sorry," I mumbled as I swiped to answer Leslie's call.

"H—"

"Tell me you didn't do it," she said immediately without greeting.

"Do what?"

"*Tell me* you didn't agree to come back and work for that asswipe, Vi."

I sighed back into the seat.

"Les, I don't have a—"

"Bullshit. You do have a choice. And you one thousand percent made the wrong one."

"Thanks for the vote of confidence," I grumbled.

"What happened?" she demanded. "What happened with your Mainelander?"

My heart squeezed at her nickname for Jamie. When I told her he was a modern-day American James Fraser, her reply had been,

'So, you're falling in love with a Mainelander instead of an Outlander?'

"Nothing happened. My dad called and said he needed me and I couldn't—"

"Liar. You could have and should have said no."

"Les, stop!" I yelled, ignoring the second angry glare from my driver. "He didn't ask me to stay, okay? My dad called and I said I'd come back and Jamie offered me a ride to the airport. No questions. No fight. No... nothing."

Silence.

So much silence I pulled my phone away to see if I'd lost service.

"I'm sorry, Vi," she spoke again with a much more subdued voice. Hearing my heartbreak completely changed her tone. "But do you really want to come back? Do you really want to work with your family again? I need you to tell me the truth—and don't sugarcoat it."

No.

The thought was instantaneous.

"No." The word slipped from my mouth far more easily than I'd expected. "But I can't stay here."

"Then I have to be honest with you, Vi, because you're my best friend and I love you." I braced myself. "If you don't want to come back, you shouldn't."

"I can't just stay with a man who doesn't want—"

"Forget him for right now," she cut in. "I don't care where you stay or where you go, but if you don't want to come back here —don't. You don't owe your family a single goddamn thing. In fact, after everything you've done, they owe you, and they will never repay it; they'll only continue to take."

"Maybe not," I began, trying to sound more hopeful than I felt. "My dad said—"

"I don't know what he said, Vi. I don't know if he lied or if you just heard what you wanted, but I'm going to tell you the truth," she broke in firmly. "Yes, your father called to ask you to come back, but Marcie told me yesterday that she sat in on the board meeting and that he has no intention of giving you any part of the business."

My heart slowed as bile rose in my throat.

Nashville, Tennessee. Austin, Texas.

Marcie was my father's secretary. She had been with him for almost two decades and took notes on all of his meetings.

"He's not taking anything away from Gerald. He's asking you back to continue to do what you do and he's going to let your brother take the credit and claim the face of the company and its success."

I couldn't speak.

They always talk about things that move faster than the speed of sound. Well, it seemed like a heart breaking moved slower. Too slow to be picked up. Too slow to ever be heard. Too painful to make a noise.

Once again, my selflessness had caused my own casualty. Once again, I'd staked my hopes on this one last thing to change how my parents saw me—*they'd asked for my help, they must realize that I'm good at this, that I'm the one meant for this job.*

But no.

They didn't need me *enough* and Jamie didn't want me *enough.*

I drew a shuddered breath. *Salt Lake City, Utah.*

My heart breaking caused the world to still. And this was the second time I'd felt it today.

The first, after Jamie left the cottage. I'd started to pack my things and came to the snow globe—his gift to me.

I'd lost myself in the way the small flakes fell around the carved cottage in the center.

I'd been trapped in that magical wonderland until this morning when the proverbial globe had broken and all the magic washed away.

It was that moment when I called an Uber.

I had so many magical moments to remember in Friendship

and at the cottage. I refused to let any more of them be drowned out by sad ones.

"Vi?"

I blinked, coming out of my heartbroken reverie. "Yeah, I'm here."

"Did you tell him how you felt?"

My brow furrowed. "My father?"

She huffed. "Your Jamie."

I swallowed over the guilt-inflated ball in my throat. "No."

"Why not?"

I chewed on my lip nervously. "Because... I told him I was going back to New York and he didn't say anything."

I could practically hear the blaring of her disapproving stare through the phone.

"So, let me recap. Your dickhole father called and guilted you into coming home. You said yes without giving Jamie any indication of how you felt about him, and are surprised he didn't try to stop you... when you so eagerly agreed to go back to work for a man he must, by now, know never appreciated you?"

I gulped.

Well, when she put it that way...

"He could have said something."

"You're right. He could have," she agreed—and that was how I should've known I was in trouble. "But you didn't give him a chance. You just walked right back into your family's trap."

Alright, it sounded bad when she put it like that.

"But after that, he could have—"

"Could have, should have—forget it all, Vi, and just tell me one thing: Is what you are doing right now going to make you happy?" she demanded. "Because if not, you're coming back to the same exact place—the same exact *person* you were before you went to Maine."

Tears pricked in my eyes.

"Are you the same person, Vi?"

"No." There was no hesitation.

I wasn't perfect. I wasn't healed. *But I definitely wasn't the same.*

"Crap..." I breathed. "I'm such an idiot, Les. You're right. I should've said something. I should've taken a chance—"

"It's not too late."

"I'm already in the car on the way to the airport. Jamie will have realized I left—"

"Are you still breathing?"

I started, thrown off by her question.

"Yes..." I drawled slowly. "Why?"

"If you're still breathing, then it's not too late to stand up for yourself," she advised me. "Now, you're a smart girl, Violet Royale. I'm sure you'll figure out a way back to your Mainelander."

"Les—"

There was a click as the line went dead. The momentary bristle of my nerves faded when I realized I didn't need her anymore. I knew what I had to do.

Tapping on my phone, I put it back up to my ear, the fire in my heart about to burn down the last of this toxic bridge.

"Are you on your way to the airport, Violet?" my father answered immediately.

"No. Not anymore."

I could practically see his face turning red with blustery confusion. "What do you mean 'not anymore'? Violet, you can't—"

"Actually, yes, I can. This is my life, and you've already taken too much of it—too much of me."

"Violet, I offered you a position back at the company. I thought that was worth everything—"

"No, Dad," I informed him. "I made a mistake telling you yes. The truth is, there is nothing you can offer me that is worth more than my dignity and respect. There is nothing you could offer me that will make up for the damage you've done."

"Violet—"

"It's not all your fault," I told him. "I know part of this rests on my shoulders for not standing up for myself sooner, but this is my breaking point. And I'm done breaking for you."

I heard his enraged guffaw just before I hung up the phone.

"Stop the car."

My driver glared at me. "Miss, I can't stop the car while we're on the highway."

I looked out the window. We couldn't have been going more than five miles per hour.

"We're hardly moving," I blurted out.

"That doesn't just mean I can stop and let you out of the car," he exclaimed. "Plus, where are you goin' to go? You can't just walk—"

"Sir," I cut him off firmly, gathering my things in my arms. "I'm from New York. Not only will I jump from a moving car, but walking in some snow is nothing compared to dodging taxis."

And with that, I flipped the old-school lock on the door and pulled the handle, smirking when I heard him curse and slam on his brakes. Thankfully, we were going slow enough he didn't slide anywhere.

"You can't just—"

I finished pulling my suitcase off the seat and slammed the door shut on him.

When I turned back along the car-covered stretch of highway, I briefly reconsidered my choice.

Had we really gotten that far?

My hand stiffened on my suitcase, and I began the trek back toward Friendship. I wasn't completely insane; I knew I couldn't walk the whole way back.

Crossing over the median, I began to walk along the string of cars heading in the direction I wanted to go. If I could make it to the next exit, I could call for another car to take me back to the cottage.

I wasn't cold as my boots sloshed through the snow. I was doing this. *I needed to do this.* I needed to tell Jamie how I felt and if he didn't want me to stay, then so be it, but at least I wouldn't leave wondering.

At least I wouldn't leave without having fought for what I wanted.

For my heart.

CHAPTER TWENTY-THREE
JAMIE

I DROVE SLOWLY next to the line of cars.

This was a bad fucking plan.

I was moving too slowly. I had no idea what kind of car she was in. And what if her car was in the left passing lane?

My frustration only grew with each unfamiliar face I found staring back at me as I passed. And it wasn't a good sign since I hadn't gotten very far.

I'd lost my sisters a little ways back. My head start, combined with my speed, set me a decent distance in advance of them, but I had a feeling Frankie would stop to wait for Max before getting on the highway.

I peered in the back seat of a Jetta, greeted with the cheerful wave of a child.

I waved back even though I didn't feel like it.

Shit.

Shit. Shit. Sh—

My hand let off the gas, hearing something behind me.

Standing on my bike as it slowed, I turned around to see what the noise was. It had almost sounded like—

Jesus Christ.

My bike almost completely stopped as I stared in shock.

Frankie and Lou were blazing down the side of the highway to catch up to me. Frankie with a damn Santa hat strapped to her helmet.

Flanking her were Max and Nox on either side. Max, with a red ball taped to his helmet and pulling behind him the sled I'd build, lit and decorated with bells.

And the sound I'd heard...

Jingle Bells.

He was blasting *Jingle Bells* from a speaker on the back.

"Violet!"

My attention whipped back to Frankie's bike. Lou sat behind her, facing backward with an elf hat on, yelling Violet's name through Max's megaphone.

I waited as Frankie pulled up to me with a shit-eating grin on her face.

I flipped up my visor and yelled to her, "I can't believe you."

"Well, you better, big brother." She laughed and revved her engine. "Because believing is what Christmas is all about."

And then she floored it, and for a second, I thought she was going to lose her twin off the back, but Lou held on with a quiet, determined strength—like she did with all Frankie's plans.

I hit the gas and followed her, blowing by Nox as he began stopping every few cars and knocking on windows.

I wanted to keep up with Frankie, but after a minute, I couldn't resist slowing to see what Nox was up to.

My heart rammed up into my throat when I saw him coming up behind me—and the crowd of people now standing outside their stopped cars.

Killing my engine for a second, I heard them all.

"Violet!"

They were all helping us find her.

Damn Frankie and all her insane plans.

Kicking back into gear, I took only a few minutes before I

caught up to my sisters and passed them. My head whipped to the side with each passing car, searching for her face in every window.

Still. No. Violet.

After almost ten minutes, I let my bike slow. All the hope that bloomed in my chest seeing my sister and her crazy plan began to melt away.

What if she wasn't here?

What if they'd taken a different road? What if she'd picked a different airport? What if they'd gotten off an exit?

I ripped off my helmet, feeling the hot air of frustration inside begin to suffocate me.

I heard the second bike pull up and cut off.

"Why'd you stop?"

"She's not here, Frankie," I bit out.

"Of course she is. We just haven't found her yet."

"Frankie, please," I ground out, letting my head drop into my hands, my elbows resting on the handlebars. "She's not. I should've just gone to the airport. I should've—"

"Jamie, she's—"

"—not here!"

Everything fell into silence. Cold, desolate, empty silence. It echoed like all the caverns of my heart.

This was all my fault. Not Frankie's. Not Violet's. *Mine.*

Someone had walked into my life who'd made me want to live for myself, and I'd let her walk out of it.

"I'm sorry, Frankie," I said hoarsely. "But she's not here. Maybe her tickets were for a different airport." My chest felt as though it were bubbling over with lava, my heart melting under the burn of loss in my chest.

When I looked up, I saw Frankie checking a message on her phone and I wondered for a split second before she said solemnly, "Then I guess we should head back."

My mouth firmed, and I nodded.

"I have her number, Jamie. You can try to call her or try to make it to one of the airports..." She trailed off. "I'm sorry, I thought we would catch her."

"Don't be sorry, Frankie," I told her. "Not your fault."

And before she could say anything else, I turned my bike back on and pulled a U-turn back toward Friendship and my cottage.

A place that had once been a haven for me.

But without her there, I had a feeling all that it was going to be was hell.

Violet

After about the first half mile, I'd really begun to question my decision and my sanity.

The snow was deeper than I anticipated, and while the exertion kept me warm, I wasn't sure how long that was going to last —and at this rate, the next exit might as well be in Canada for how fast I was going to walk to it.

What if this was a giant mistake?

Groaning, I yanked on my suitcase again as though it were responsible for my hesitation.

It wasn't a mistake—because it wasn't all about Jamie or what he said.

It was about me.

It was about Violet Royale going after what she wanted to make herself happy and not anyone else.

I ignored the confused and concerned stares from the other drivers stopped on the road, giving them small smiles as I passed by.

With a huff, I stopped for a second and pulled out my phone, expecting it to be *another* call from my father coming through the line.

My steps faltered.

It wasn't my father. It was a message from VRBO from the owner of my rental—*the owner of the cottage.*

My frozen fingers moved too slowly for my liking as I tapped to open it. Inside the message was a short message: *If you've decided to follow your heart, call me.* Following it was a Maine cell phone number.

Was it Jamie's?

Without stopping to talk myself out of it, I tapped to call.

"Violet? Is that you?" the dramatic, elderly voice on the other end of the line answered immediately.

"*Gigi?*" I gasped.

I'd expected Jamie. Maybe Frankie. Possibly Ailene. *But not Gigi.*

"Well, of course it's Gigi!" she scoffed at me, like it could be anywhere else. "Where are you?"

My mouth parted as I scanned the snow-ridden highway. "I'm walking on 1 North back toward Maine Street." I paused. "I was going to call a car to bring me back to Jamie's cottage."

If Frankie had sent me Gigi's number, there was no point in assuming anything else except that the entire Kinkade family knew what had happened.

"Of course you were, dear," she said to me and then I heard her tell Ailene, "See, I told you she was going to come back. Violet has a good head on her shoulders. There was no way she was walking away from Jamie, not the way she looked at him... ooooh no."

There was no one to see, but I still blushed and laughed.

"Violet."

"Yes, Gigi."

"We're on our way to get you. Just hang tight. We'll be there in a jiffy." And then the line went dead.

What?

Was I supposed to just stand here?

I waited a few seconds and then I saw it. Barreling up the side of the highway was Uncle George's red truck. Normally, those stuck in traffic wouldn't take too kindly to someone using the shoulder as a third lane, but sure enough, Gigi's faux-fur-covered arm was stuck out the passenger window holding a small, red flashing emergency light on the roof of the cabin.

Oh my god. My chest felt about to burst, wanting to laugh and cry at exactly the same time.

I stepped back as the truck approached.

"Are you lookin' for a ride home, sweetie?" Gigi yelled out the window with a giant smile.

Home.

I nodded. "Yes, actually, I think I am."

"Well, would you look at that." She thumbed me to the back door. "Home just happens to be where we're going."

Blinking away my happy tears, I hauled my stuff into the back of the truck's cab, sitting next to Ailene.

"You alright, dear?" she asked as soon as I was settled and George was off again.

I swallowed over the lump in my throat. "I think so."

"Gigi, give me my phone. I've got to message Frankie that we have her."

My brow furrowed.

"Frankie?"

Gigi clapped her hands together after handing Ailene the cell.

"Oh, Jamie is going to be so surprised."

I looked between them. "I'm confused."

"Jamie, Frankie, Lou, and the boys have been snowmobiling through the countryside trying to catch up to you, dear," she explained. "But they've been looking on the other side of the highway."

"He…" I choked up. "Jamie came after me?"

"Of course he did, dear," Gigi responded. "I think that boy has finally learned it's high time he's loyal to his heart." She cupped a hand over her mouth and whispered, "That means to you, Violet."

I nodded in thanks, not needing but still appreciating the clarification.

"They're still out here," Ailene said. "We'll probably pass by them in a minute."

"So, you're going to tell them to stop looking?" I still felt like I was missing something.

Both mother and daughter looked at me blankly and then drew the same smile—*a smile I'd seen on Frankie's face one too many times.*

"Not yet," Ailene told me calmly. "We're going to let Jamie stew just a little bit longer."

"What?" I gasped. "W-Why? Why make him—"

Ailene reached out and grabbed my hand. "Violet, Jamie's a smart man, but he did a very dumb thing letting you walk out of his life today. He could stand to wait just a bit more before getting you back."

I'd also been part of that decision too, I wanted to argue but kept silent as she continued.

"We aren't going to make him wait too long, don't worry." She patted my hand. "Frankie's just going to delay him for a few more minutes, so we can get you back to the cottage."

"How did you know?" I wondered, tipping my head to the side.

"What do you mean?"

"How did you know I was going to change my mind?"

Ailene's gaze shifted to Gigi, whose head bobbed to the soft Christmas carols playing over the radio and nodded.

"You told me, you goose," Gigi chortled from her seat, bright-green eyes turning to meet mine. "Christmas Eve. You told me you wouldn't be afraid to risk it all for love."

My mouth dried up.

She wasn't right... but she wasn't wrong.

Sure enough, a few seconds later, Ailene tapped on the window, and I saw the crew of snowmobiles tearing up the other side of the highway in the opposite direction and my heart lurched.

Warm fingers squeezed my hand once more.

"So, you're taking me back to the cottage?" I clarified.

A devious glint appeared in Ailene's eyes as she grinned. "Of course," she told me. "According to your reservation, it's still yours for the next two days."

I let out a small laugh as we pulled off the highway.

"But I have a feeling that two is going to turn into forever."

Chapter Twenty-Four
Jamie

When the bike cut off, I sat there for several long minutes in the cold silence outside my front door.

Bile rose in my throat when I pulled my helmet off and looked at my home.

The stone was a dull gray under the overcast sky. The windows still flickered with light, but it was only a facade; there was no longer any warmth. Now, when I looked at my cottage, I saw the lonely respite of a man who'd always put family first, no matter what it cost him.

I'd never regret any choice in my life made for the sake of my family.

But today... this...

If I didn't get Violet back, I knew I would regret it.

I wasn't giving up, but for some reason, I'd blindly believed that Frankie's plan would work—because things like that usually happened with her shenanigans. And if my sister's mischievous magic wasn't enough to stop Violet... the possibility of failure rolled in my stomach like a violent storm.

Dragging a hand through my well-tossed hair, I reached for plan *B*.

Whichever airport she'd gone to, she was probably on the

flight by now. And when she got off that plane, she was going to have a voice mail from me. *And then she was going to have me.*

As soon as I turned back along the highway, I knew I was going to be heading to New York. I'd never been to the city; cities weren't really my thing. But Violet... Violet Royale was my fucking thing and if I had to cut through the concrete jungle to find her and get her back, I would.

Frankie was right—a fact I cringed to admit.

It wasn't wrong to put my family first, to be there for them like I had, or to make the choices I'd made. But it was wrong to continue to forsake my own happiness when theirs was already secure.

Covering up my bike, I opened Frankie's message that had Violet's number inside and stared at the numbers on the screen, losing hope in the words I had that they wouldn't be enough to tell her how fucking sorry and stupid I was.

But they were all I had.

The call rang with each step toward my cottage, her voice mail finally picking up when I reached the door.

"Violet," I began my message, letting myself inside. "I was wrong, sweetheart. I was wrong to let you go." I closed the door and kicked off my shoes. "An idiot, really." I looked up, prepared for the rip in my chest to deepen. "I don't care if your family needs you, I need—"

My jaw dropped and the rest of my words fell from it as my phone slid down my cheek and then fell to my side.

"Violet?"

I blinked twice, positive that the woman standing in front of me, the woman I'd been in the middle of leaving a voice mail for, *the woman wearing my flannel shirt,* was a figment of my imagination.

I staggered toward her, drinking in the sight of her standing before me, afraid any moment she was going to disappear again.

"Hi, Jamie." Her voice sent my voice tumbling with a thud to the floor.

She was here.

She was real.

With a low growl, I ate up the distance between us and, cupping her pink-tinted cheeks, crushed my lips to hers.

With a soft mewl, she opened underneath me. I delved my tongue inside the magic of her mouth, forcing her to step back until she was pinned between me and the bedroom door. *Until she was wedged so tight to me, there was no chance of escape.*

And when her arms wound around my neck, I knew leaving was the last thing on her mind.

I groaned as my tongue made itself at home alongside hers. She was warm and sweet, but above all else, she was mine. And as I stroked every corner of her hot little mouth, that was the mark left in my wake.

Mine.

VIOLET

I melted into his kiss.

Reassuring myself with each swipe of his tongue along mine that this was real—and it was all for me.

I'd heard his snowmobile pull up outside and cut off, but he made no move to come in. I almost broke then and there, rushing out to tell him he wasn't too late. But then I heard the crunch of snow and saw my phone light up with a Maine phone number I didn't recognize.

Frankie told me he'd be calling.

I stood frozen in the doorframe, wearing only his shirt. It was almost the exact same spot as the night we'd met, only I'd left the poker behind this time; I figured he'd suffered enough.

But when I saw him, looking so lost as he walked inside his own home, my heart broke and tears pooled in the corners of my eyes.

Even though it hurt, I was glad we were here. I was glad this was happening in the cottage and not on the side of some traffic-clogged highway.

And the look on his face when he saw me... God, I'd never forget that look as long as I lived.

Shock and disbelief warred with unfettered hope.

I sagged deeper into the kiss. It was possessive. *It was promising.*

And I could taste the magic that was Jamie Kinkade returning to my life, lighting up all the parts of me which had already begun to dim at the thought of returning to New York.

"Violet," he murmured and nuzzled against me, our breaths panting in the small space between our mouths. "You're here," he added as though he still couldn't believe it.

"I'm here," I repeated with a small smile. "I have a few days left on my rental, and I was told I wouldn't get my money back for leaving early."

"Forget your money, Vi. I'm not giving *you* back," he growled. "I'm not giving you back because you're mine."

I whimpered, and my body shuddered against him.

"I don't want you to... because you're mine, too."

He kissed me again, long and slow this time, savoring the taste of those words on my tongue.

"Why'd you leave?" he rasped, his lips caressing mine again as he spoke.

"Why did you let me?"

His harsh breath rushed against my skin. "Because I'm an idiot. Because I heard your family needed you and I thought, like a moron, that was most important. So, I swallowed down how much I wanted you to stay, and thought it was more chivalrous to help you go."

I didn't realize I was about to cry until I laughed and it bubbled out with tears.

"But it wasn't. And the truth is, I don't care if they say they need you," he continued. "Maybe I should... because I know how

important family is.... But I don't because I know how important
you are, Violet... and how important you are to me."

"Jamie..."

"Stay here. With me. Not because your family doesn't value
you, but because I'm in love with you."

I whimpered, shaking my head because he didn't need to say
all this.

He didn't need to because he had me at "Stay."

"I love you, too," I cried, letting the tears spill down my
cheeks, burying my head in his neck.

His hands rubbed soothingly along my sides before sliding
around me and pulling me to him.

"I can't believe you're here," he murmured. "I can't believe
you came back."

I shuddered and tipped my face up to his.

"I was calling you when I walked in to let you know I'd be on
the next flight down to New York."

My eyes widened. "Y-You were going to come to New York to
find me?"

"Violet, I'd dig a hole to China if that's what it took to be
with you."

My forehead dropped to his shoulder as my shoulders shook
with silent, happy sobs.

"But you came back..." He trailed off thickly. "Why?"

I let out a watery chuckle. "Because I'm in love with you.
Because I should've been the one to say 'no' to my father on the
phone in the first place. Because the world he offered me is no
longer the world I want. I just want you."

His face hardened. "This is a whole new world up here, Violet,
and I can't promise you it's going to be anything like New York. I
can't promise you I'll be able to give you the life you were used to,"
he told me raggedly. "But I can promise you that no one—" he broke
off and pushed his fingers under my chin and make sure he had my
attention. "I can promise you that no one will love you like I will."

His lips seared over mine, and he held me tightly just as every part of me went weak.

We kissed for several long minutes until I felt the soft cool sheets underneath my legs and realized Jamie must have moved us into the bedroom.

"What are you going to tell your father?" he asked.

I laughed and shook my head. His face, normally so strong and put together for everyone else, was so adorably attractive when it was wrought with concern and desperate need it made my stomach flip.

"I already called and told him this was it—that I was done." My head ducked slightly. "Turns out, he wasn't offering me a spot back in the business—not a real one. He wanted me back to run everything behind the scenes, giving my brother all the credit."

Rage flared in his gaze, almost as bright as the red of his hair.

"So, I called him back and told him this was it for me, though I'm sure it will need to be a longer discussion at some point for them, but it won't change anything." I shivered. "For so long, the thought of disappointing them drove me to panic. But that phone call... making that choice for myself... I was finally... free." I breathed the word like it was a miracle—one I created for myself.

"You are so strong, Vi. So incredible."

"It's easy to be strong when you know what you're fighting for."

"And you're sure this is what you want?" His thumb stroked over my cheek.

"Yes, Jamie." I cupped his cheeks. "I want you. And everything that comes along with it. Your family. This town. All the magic."

He gave me a crooked smile that sent another rush of heat between my legs.

"So, you told him you weren't coming... and then had the car turn around?"

Biting my lip, I winced. "Not quite. The driver... well... I think I've learned my lesson with Uber drivers up here." I laughed nervously. "I may have gotten out of the car because he refused to turn around until we reached another exit, and I wasn't waiting for that."

"You got out of the car... on the side of the highway?"

His hands tightened on me.

"And then Frankie sent me your mom's cell number. At first, I thought it was yours, but then Gigi answered."

"Oh, God," he groaned.

"They were already on their way to find me... to bring me back."

"They knew where you were?"

"Well, I told them which exit I was walking toward," I explained. "So, it only took a few minutes before your uncle's truck, lights flashing, came driving down the shoulder for me."

"Jesus," he swore, shaking his head with a laugh before leveling me with a stare. "Still not thrilled you were planning on walking along the side of the highway to get here."

"Well, not the whole way." I shrugged. "Just until I got to the next exit to call another car."

His eyes bored into mine, love making them shine like whisky diamonds with a million glittering facets.

He grunted. "I can't believe you came back." His lips drifted toward mine once more.

"I was on my way back whether you wanted or not. I told you, this cottage and the handsome woodsman that came with it are technically still mine for a few more days," I teased with a thick, sultry voice.

His eyes darkened and danced with laughter as his head dipped back down to mine. "Hate to break it to you, sweetheart, but technically, this cottage is going to be yours for a few more forevers."

My eyes drifted shut as his lips slanted back over mine, and I fell back into the mattress, sinking back into Jamie's embrace and letting the magic envelop me once more.

EPILOGUE
VIOLET

ONE YEAR later

"Jamie!" I giggled, struggling but not really fighting, as he hoisted me over his shoulder and carted me back into the bedroom. "We're going to be late for Christmas dinner!"

My woodsman didn't care.

"They can wait," he said gruffly before I found myself tossed back onto our bed.

The bed I'd woken up in every day for the last year, next to the man I hoped to wake up next to for the following forever.

One year had changed so much.

One year had changed everything.

Though my anxiety was always with me, the shadow cast on my life had become much, much smaller.

One week after I climbed out of that Uber, Jamie went with me back into the city. We'd stayed for a few days because New York had been a home to me for most of my life and Jamie wanted to see the parts of it that meant the most.

I'd introduced him to Leslie, who'd immediately begun asking about his brother and any other available men in his family.

And then there was a very awkward lunch with my parents.

I didn't speak to them much after turning down my dad's offer, but I made the attempts. *They were my parents, after all.* I wanted them to meet the man I'd be spending the rest of my life with, though I was a little surprised when my mother agreed to the meeting; I'd fully prepared to weather whatever excuse she concocted. It was awkward but pleasant, the looks on my parents' faces a mix of regret and happiness.

Regret that things had ended the way they had, but the pieces of humanity left in them, not clouded by business and social climbing, flickered with happiness to see me happy.

And that was more than I could've asked for.

"But Gigi—" I was cut off by his lips over mine, my argument quickly abating into his demanding kiss.

Gigi was still kicking, and her Premonition Preserves were all the more famous because of it.

For the first few months, I'd adjusted to my new life helping Jamie with his business and organization. I'd acquired contracts for him with several hotels—*not owned by my family*—in the state who purchased custom pieces of his. I would sit and watch him work for hours, learning the ins and outs of his craft and spending the time getting to know the man my heart claimed as home.

I also spent time with Ailene, George and Gigi, doing what I could to help with Stonebar's expansion, though, with Lou's help, they seemed to have it under control.

It took about three months before Ailene sat me down at her dining table, the whole family present, and asked if I had any interest or desire in resurrecting the Lamplight Inn.

There wasn't any hesitation before I said yes.

But there was a panic attack once Jamie got me home that night.

I knew how to run a hotel on a macro level. I knew how to manage. I knew how to find all the pieces and coordinate all the parts from a distance. But I'd never been the only person in charge.

"I won't lie to you, Violet," Ailene told me with a half smile. "I bought the inn to save it from being sold and likely demolished, but I have no interest—no desire really to be the one personally responsible for bringing it back to life. I think that's why it's been put off for so long. Stonebar is my passion... and I believe the reason I ended up with the inn was because it was for you."

It was exciting and overwhelming: the perfect recipe for a panic attack.

But even when the darkness closed in, Jamie held me in his arms, my head and my fearful tears buried in his chest while he told me that it was all going to be okay. *That I was strong enough to do this.*

And I was.

Strong doesn't mean you lack moments of weakness. Strong means you don't let them define you.

I moaned as Jamie slid his lips from mine, their firm warmth finding a path down along the pulse in my neck. Arching against him, I reveled in the way his strength commanded my desire.

But then all that possessive warmth disappeared, along with his weight, from on top of me.

"Jamie?" I gasped, pushing up onto my elbows as he stepped away from the bed. "What's wrong?"

Rich-brown eyes melted over me like the finest chocolate and my mouth went dry.

"I have something for you," he said with a low, hoarse voice.

My eyes widened. "What?" I shook my head. "You can't do this again, James Kinkade," I exclaimed. "We already exchanged gifts!"

I whimpered in distress.

I'd bought him a new circular saw for his shop, knowing he'd been eyeing one for some time and with all the new business he had coming in, it would be a huge help.

And Jamie... well, I *thought* the brand-new sleigh bed he'd made for us and surprised me with last night was my Christmas gift. *We'd certainly spent the night using it like it was.*

It looked like I was wrong.

"Jamie..." I whispered with excitement and warning, sitting up and scooting to the edge of the bed.

"I wanted to get you something for Christmas," he told me with a quirked smile, enjoying how the suspense made me squirm.

"You already got—"

"No, I already made you something," he corrected.

He reached out and grabbed the snow globe he'd given me last Christmas—the one that reminded me each morning that I lived inside the beautiful wonderland captured inside it. Shaking it quickly, he watched the snow as it started to settle before handing it to me.

With a querying eyebrow raised, I took the precious gift from his hands and examined it again like it was new, having the sense that I was missing something.

"What is it?" I asked.

His voice deepened. "Open it."

Gaping at him, I traced along the ornate wood carved around the base, feeling along the dips and rises of the tree line he'd sculpted into its surface. Making my way back around to the front, my fingers ran over the name again: *Kinkade*.

My fingers caught along the frame around the name, and with slight pressure from my nail, it moved.

My eyes shot to his.

It moved.

This whole time, the front piece of the globe opened.

Wedging my finger deeper, I tried to pull it out, but it wouldn't budge any farther.

"Try the *A*," Jamie hinted, his eagerness outweighing his plan to let me figure it out all on my own.

Feeling on the *A*, I flinched when the center pushed in like a latch and the frame around "Kinkade" popped out, revealing a small drawer.

My heart began to race, pressure building inside my chest as I pulled it open to see a piece of paper folded inside.

"Read it."

He didn't have to ask me twice. I opened it up, wondering what could be so serious.

My eyes flitted over the page, and my head shook in confusion. "I don't understand." I looked to him and then back to the paper before meeting his eyes once more. "This is my rental agreement."

"It is," he confirmed. "But I wondered if you read the fine print at the bottom when you signed it."

Instantly, my eyes shot to the miniature font squeezed at the bottom, completely at a loss for what was going on.

But as I began to read, I realized this wasn't the exact contract I'd signed.

This one had clauses about a handsome woodsman. Clauses that talked about flannel shirts and homemade breakfasts, delicious coffee and a crazy, loving family, and clauses that made my cheeks hot the way they talked about orgasms and snowmobile sex (a favorite of mine).

I sucked in a breath when I got to the last sentence.

The renter agrees after one year of occupancy to marry the homeowner, previously referred to as "The Woodsman" forthwith.

"J-Jamie," I garbled.

But when I looked up to Jamie, he wasn't standing in front of me any longer. *He was kneeling.*

The paper fell out of my hands as he held up a diamond ring between his fingers.

My breath lodged in my chest, knowing what was happening but still struggling to believe it. The larger center stone was flanked by six smaller stones around the outside, making it look like a glittering flower. *Or a sparkling snowflake.*

"Violet Royale," he said hoarsely. "I knew I'd be asking you this question at some point or another when I made you that globe. And I wasn't sure I'd be able to wait long enough to do it now."

Tears slid down my cheeks, leaving hot and happy trails behind them.

"But the truth is, I'd wait forever, I'd move anywhere, I'd do anything to be with you."

"Jamie..." I gulped as he reached for my hand, holding it with his.

"So, will you make me the happiest woodsman in the world? Will you marry me, Violet?"

I nodded, unable to speak, hardly able to see.

"Yes," I managed to choke out as the cool metal of the ring began to slide onto my finger. "Yes. Yes. Yes."

It wasn't even on the whole way before I lunged at him, crashing my lips against his.

After several long minutes of kissing, I pulled back and we both gasped for air.

"You didn't have to put it in the contract, you know," I teased lightly.

He grinned. "Well, I just like to cover all my bases."

My mouth drifted back to his, stopping abruptly when I heard the rumble of engines outside.

"What's going on?" My brow crinkled.

"Time to celebrate." Jamie smiled and winked at me, and I had to wonder if my new ring should've come with a new set of panties along with it.

"Here?" I squeaked.

His smile grew. "Well, we did decorate and cut our own tree."

My mouth dropped.

Jamie had never decorated his cottage for Christmas. He said he'd never had a reason until he asked me to stay, that the cottage was his house but never his home until I trespassed into it.

So, this year, the Kinkade family had cut down *two* trees, our two lobster ornaments now gracing our own evergreen. Twinkle lights made the cottage shine bright in the middle of the woods, making it appear even more magical on approach.

"But your family..."

"Is all for making new traditions, sweetheart." He dropped a kiss on my forehead and grabbed my hand, tugging me toward the living room just as a loud knock sounded on the front door.

I stood by the edge of the couch as Jamie opened the door and his family flooded inside. Greeting them with a "*she said yes,*" they quickly dumped their armfuls of food and presents onto the nearest flat surface to congratulate us.

"I'd say welcome to the family, but you've been a part of the family for some time now," Ailene said, wiping tears from her eyes as she pulled me in tight.

"Thanks, Mom," I replied.

It had taken all of three weeks after permanently moving here before Ailene asked if I would just start calling her "mom" already.

"Jamie finally snagged his Purple Princess," Gigi beamed as she wrapped her surprisingly strong, delicate arms around me.

"Yes, he did." I laughed, remembering the phrase she'd written for Jamie right after he'd brought me to the house.

All of us turned to see Frankie squeal and throw herself around Jamie, laughing.

For a few minutes, everyone crowded around me, oohing and ahhing over the ring before dispersing to get Christmas dinner started.

"Alright, alright," Frankie began once her feet were back on solid ground. "Where's my present?"

"Your Christmas present?"

"No." She waved him off. "My master matchmaker present."

Jamie groaned and the rest of us broke into stitches. Frankie was always quick to remind us all that she was the one responsible for this fairy tale.

Jamie and I just laughed and agreed. *Because she was.*

Only later, once she was satisfied, would we share a look and sometimes a conversation that the man who tried to claim Frankie was in for one heck of a ride.

After a giant hug from both of the twins, Kit stood before me with the barest hint of a smile on his face.

It was the most happiness I'd seen from him over these many months—months that he'd grown more secluded at the lighthouse.

While I held on to Jamie in my times of darkness, Kit locked himself in with his demons.

He grunted his congratulations and squeezed my shoulder—the greatest show of affection I could expect—and moved on.

Ever-perceptive Lou murmured, "He's just upset because the school is giving him a hard time about the lighthouse."

"I heard," I confessed as I hugged her.

The University of Maine was responsible for the lighthouse and its upkeep. Apparently, they wanted to do more research from the coast, which meant an invasion of Kit's well-worked-out privacy.

As Lou joined her sister, I had to wonder if I was wrong about Frankie and if it was really Lou whose heart, so guarded and pure, that would be the hardest to claim.

Then again, with brothers like theirs, any man would have a steep mountain to climb.

"I love you."

I tipped my head up and back just as Jamie came up from behind and wrapped his arms around me.

"I love you, too." I leaned back against him, wondering if I'd ever been so happy, or felt more at home.

I was home.

With this family.

In his arms.

In my woodman's cottage.

The End

Thanks for reading Jamie and Violet's story! For details on future books for the rest of the Kinkade family, subscribe to my newsletter.

For more standalone holiday romances, check out I'll Be Your Santa Tonight and A Cowboy for Christmas.

OTHER WORKS BY DR. REBECCA SHARP

COVINGTON SECURITY

Betrayed

Bribed

Beguiled

Burned

Branded

Broken

Believed

Bargained

Braved

THE VIGILANTES

The Vendetta

REYNOLDS PROTECTIVE

Archer

Hunter

Gunner

Ranger

Carmel Cove

Beholden

Bespoken

Besotted

Befallen

Beloved

Betrothed

The Kinkades

The Woodsman

The Odyssey Duet

The Fall of Troy

The Judgment of Paris

The Sacred Duet

The Gargoyle and the Gypsy

The Heartbreak of Notre Dame (TBA)

Country Love Collection

Tequila

Ready to Run

Fastest Girl in Town

Last Name

I'll Be Your Santa Tonight

Michigan for the Winter

Remember Arizona

Ex To See

A Cowboy for Christmas

Meant to Be

THE WINTER GAMES

Up in the Air

On the Edge

Enjoy the Ride

In Too Deep

Over the Top

THE GENTLEMEN'S GUILD

The Artist's Touch

The Sculptor's Seduction

The Painter's Passion

PASSION & PERSEVERANCE TRILOGY

(A PRIDE AND PREJUDICE RETELLING)

First Impressions

Second Chances

Third Time is the Charm

STANDALONES

Reputation

Redemption

Revolution: A Driven World Novel

Hypothetically

Want to #staysharp with everything that's coming?

Join my newsletter!

About the Author

Rebecca Sharp is a contemporary romance author of over thirty published novels and dentist living in PA with her amazing husband, affectionately referred to as Mr. GQ.

She writes a wide variety of contemporary romance. From new adult to extreme sports romance, forbidden romance to romantic comedies, her books will always give you strong heroines, hot alphas, unique love stories, and always a happily ever after. When she's not writing or seeing patients, she loves to travel with her husband, snowboard, and cook.

She loves to hear from readers. You can find her on Facebook, Instagram, and Goodreads. And, of course, you can email her directly at author@drrebeccasharp.com.

If you want to be emailed with exclusive cover reveals, upcoming book news, etc. you can sign up for her mailing list on her website: www.drrebeccasharp.com

Happy reading!

xx

Rebecca

Made in United States
Orlando, FL
19 September 2024